Abominable Reaction

Genetic Harvesters Series

John Castillio

John Castillio

ISBN: 0990732924
ISBN-13: 978-0990732921

PROLOGUE

Ingrid could barely recall her own name as she gravitated towards awareness. Cold, vibrating metal pressed against her cheek. She knew she was lying on her stomach, but she couldn't move. She couldn't turn over. Her mind reached out for limbs and found voids where limbs should be. She couldn't feel her legs, her arms, nothing. God help her, she couldn't feel anything except the humming metal searing the skin of her left cheek. *Where am I?*

She tried uselessly to open her eyes. Somehow, she knew they were already open. But, if that were the case...*Why can't I see?* Freezing tendrils of dread wormed a possibility into her brain. *Am I blind? Was I in some kind of accident?* Perhaps, she had fallen off her horse. *Surely, it's something like that.*

She could be ill, her mind reasoned. She tried to speak, but with even less success than seeing. Her mouth was a desert and her tongue was buried under a mountain of sand. A shooting pain pierced her temple. *What is happening to me?* Her windpipes felt as though they were collapsing under the weight of her thoughts.

Focusing on the last thing she could remember, she willed herself to stay calm. *I was in the ridges.* She felt a small victory. *Bloodroot! I was gathering bloodroot.* But winter had come a bit early and so the root had been harder to find. She often sold bloodroot to the town physician. Sometimes, she could even earn a bit of extra money if she ground the roots before selling them. As scarce as it had been, she had to expand her search for the precious medicine. It was either that, or risk losing the farm. *So...I climbed higher.*

Her memory was coming back slowly and in bits. *I heard a noise...like a grunt.* But no matter how hard she tried, she could remember nothing else. That was all. *A strange noise.*

And then the black.

Ingrid steadied her nerves and listened, searching for any sounds that might help her understand what was happening to her. There was the strange hum that permeated the area, but underneath it, there was something…*else*. She strained for clarity, ordering her ears to filter the hum. *Almost…*

She held her breath. *What is that…?* Her thoughts were snaky whispers.

And then the humming stopped and a thousand icy winds raced into her core. In an instant, she knew she would never feel warm again. The noise she had so wanted to hear took center stage in her ears…a hundred or more tortured voices screamed in tandem from the blackness.

Fear choked her, strangling the wind from her lungs. A tear rolled, trailing her face. Her mind frantically searched for the words to make it all better.

The Lord is my Shepherd, I shall not want. He ma—

Her silent prayer was cut short as black instantly shifted to blinding white. The screams rose in volume. Fear settled like sticky oatmeal in the pit of her stomach as she wished for a miracle.

Moments later, a miracle did happen…

She found her voice and joined the screaming chorus.

CHAPTER ONE

"Doctor Castle," Carlos whispered dreamily as he stared out the small dorm window. Outside, the sun dried the afternoon rain into a memory as he scanned the lawn of St. James University School of Medicine for his brother, Jim. He was easy to spot under the weight of his cumbersome luggage. His dark hair waved lazily in the breeze, as he made his way around the wrought iron and wooden benches that offered the students a place to sit and ponder their lives.

Carlos and his brother shared many similar features. They both had dark hair, brown eyes, the same build, and tanned skin. But there, the similarities ended and their differences abounded.

He watched his brother climb the stairs of the housing unit until he was out of sight. Other freshmen carried their luggage, as well. Carlos could imagine the congestion in the stairwells, full of excited young men. So, when Jim had offered to fetch the trunks, he had been happy to let him. He had not relished the thought of wading through the masses of smoky suits and scotch breath, but not Jim. He could feel at home around anyone. And he had a way of making people feel at home around him. It was a gift.

Carlos shifted his thoughts back to his future.

Dr. Castle. Carlos took a deep breath and took it all in; the sprawling grounds leading to the newly constructed ledgestone buildings, each with a specific purpose of learning, the perfectly tended greens, and the poplars standing at relaxed attention, leading the way. It felt grand, yet oddly welcoming. He was an eagle perched atop a world that belonged to him.

And he had earned it.

His mother would be proud. He could almost see her smiling, her eyes lighting up as he earned his future degree. *If only she were here.* Carlos vainly tried to push the thought away. *That wound may never heal.*

His mother had died of consumption, just wasted away. He cringed remembering how desperate her lungs were to find air…and how helpless he had felt when she died. That was why he had wanted to become a doctor in the first place. *I'll never be that helpless again. I'll nev—*

"That's the last of it," Jim said as he heaved the heavy trunk onto the bed, shaking Carlos from the past. "It's a madhouse out there," Jim said smiling. "Can you believe we were both accepted?"

Jim wagged his head in disbelief. "Doctors."

"Yeah, that's if you can keep your act together," Carlos teased his brother.

"Me?" Jim looked indignant at the thought. Then a slow smile played across his lips. "I'll do my best."

Carlos laughed. It was an empty promise. Jim didn't know how to stay out of trouble.

"Classes start tomorrow, we sh—"

"No class today, though, Carlos," Jim said, cutting him off. "We should explore the grounds. Come on," he begged. "We can unpack later." Jim's voice held the excitement of a child and it was infectious.

"For a bit. Then we need to finish unpacking."

St. James was one of the few universities that believed in co-education, and even though the student class was primarily made up of the male persuasion, there was still the odd female carrying books and study material around campus. They looked like rare flowers dotting an otherwise barren landscape.

"At least the scenery is nice," Jim said as they walked the grounds that afternoon. Carlos followed his brother's look and at the end of it, found a particularly rare bloom in a blue cotton dress. Her hair was golden in the sun, and even at a hundred paces away, her eyes sparkled like bits of emerald.

She was sitting on a bench with a sketchbook in her lap. Artistic strokes moved the black chalk across the paper with one hand, while the other kept the edges from lifting in the breeze.

Carlos sighed, slowing his pace. "Yes, I would have to agree."

A hearty slap on his back and Jim was trotting off towards the young woman. Carlos watched as his brother plucked a purple tulip from the stretch of them that lined the walkway. With the tulip in hand and a wink at his brother, Jim sauntered across the lawn. Carlos stopped where he was and watched.

It always amazed him at how fearless Jim was. Carlos could never just approach the girl. Sometimes he wished he could be more like Jim, easy going. He could do the same, surely. *Just pick a girl, pick a flower, and go for it.* But then, he would hear his mother in the back of his mind, *"Listen to me, Carlos,"* She had rasped from her deathbed. *"You must be certain in your path. Your brother is a free spirit. He will need you to guide him, when I'm gone. Promise me."*

He had promised her. And then, two days later, she had died.

That was why, when he went to stoop, it wasn't to pick a tulip. Carlos fumbled at the laces of his boot while he watched Jim bow gallantly at the beautiful artist's feet and present his flower.

The girl shielded her eyes from the sun and said something that Carlos wished he could hear. And then he watched his brother stand up from his bow, rejected flower still in hand. Jim laughed hard, clearly amused, and started looking around. Carlos realized too late that he was searching for him. Spotted, Carlos could do nothing but come, when Jim waved him over.

"Damn it," he swore softly to himself as he stood up and jogged towards them.

"Carlos," Jim began when he came to a stop at his side. "This is my brother Carlos, by the way," Jim said to the lovely young woman.

Carlos could see that with surety, now. Soft pink lips produced a smile so warm it could melt the iciest of hearts. Carlos returned her smile, though he was certain that his own paled in comparison.

"Carlos, this is…eh…" he looked at her hopefully.

What is he doing? Carlos could feel the heat rising in his cheeks.

"Anna." Her voice was music. "It's a pleasure to meet you, Carlos."

He did not miss the stress she placed on the word *you*, however slight. Neither did Jim.

"Ahh, you hear that Carlos, she wounds me." Jim playfully grabbed at his heart.

Anna laughed.

Carlos couldn't help but smile. His brother had a way of doing that. *A real charmer…*at least that was what his mother had called it.

"She rejects my flower…and me."

"You know, if he's bothering you, I can—," Carlos began, teasing.

"Et tu, Brute?" Jim cut in and grabbed at his heart with both hands, clearly to illustrate Carlos' betrayal.

Anna looked at Carlos, laughing. "That won't be necessary. I have brothers; I know how to handle him." She said with a toss of her head at Jim. Then she lifted the hem of her skirt and silver flashed in the sunlight.

That surprised Carlos.

It delighted Jim. "So she bites, as well." Jim laughed. "You have to be mine, now," he begged.

"Yours?" Anna laughed, incredulously. "You can't just command something like that." Then her voice dropped seductively lower, "You have to earn it."

"I'll do anything," Jim feigned desperation.

Anna looked at Carlos, questioning.

"He's right. I've known him my whole life and nothing is out of the question." He only said it to hear her laugh again. It was like honey. And he was the bee.

"You must be certain in your path." His mother's voice was never far. *This one is trouble.*

The sky overhead was fiery orange. In a few minutes, the world would turn gray around them. "It's getting late," Carlos said. "We should finish unpacking." He nudged his brother in the arm.

Anna stood, holding her sketchbook close, and the early evening breeze carried her scent, rushing the smell of roses to his nose. It was intoxicating. "I should be going, too. I'm losing the light, anyways. It was nice to meet you, both of you." She smiled at Jim, and then took the flower.

Carlos felt a twinge of...*something*. He didn't know.

"You go ahead, Carlos." Jim said, smiling. "I'll make sure she gets back safely to the women's housing."

What could he say? "Sure, but don't take too long. I'm not unpacking for you." A wave and a smile and they were gone, leaving him alone on the campus lawn. "Yeah," he whispered to himself. "She's trouble."

**

Jim intentionally took the long route back to the women's housing unit. Anna seemed prettier with each step. Her eyes seemed to come alive with green fire as the orange deepened overhead. She kept her sketchbook close.

"Can I see?" he asked, hoping she would show him what had captured her attention that day.

"Maybe someday." She left him with hope.

"You will be mine, Anna," Jim said with all the confidence in the world. *She's so pretty. And smart. I bet she's talented, too.* He wanted to see her sketching, but he knew better than to press his luck.

"Who are you trying to convince with that?" she asked, smiling, as they walked. "Me...or you?"

"Whoever needs convincing," he teased.

He really liked her and he was pretty sure that the feeling, at least, could be mutual. He had never been one to hold things back. His mother had made sure of that. Even on her deathbed, she had made him promise. *"You should always follow your heart, Jim,"* she had managed through her coughing. *"Your brother is often too serious. He will need you to lighten his burden, when I am gone. Promise me."*

Death came for her soon after.

"We don't even know each other," Anna offered her excuse.

"Well that's remedied easily enough. My name is James Castle. Jim is what everyone calls me, though. I am here to be a doctor and—"

"Everyone is here to be a doctor, Jim." She said, shortening his speech. "Tell me something I don't know."

"I'd rather be a journalist," he said, surprising himself with the admission.

This must have surprised her, as well, because she suddenly stopped short. Deep green pools met his eyes. "I never told anyone that, before." He smiled, awkwardly.

"Then why aren't you studying to be a journalist?" She asked with sincere curiosity.

They continued walking.

"My brother wants to be a doctor…and he needs me. I'll be a journalist one day…just not today."

A strange expression crossed her face and then she smiled. "I have a class in the morning at eight. If you meet me here a half an hour till, I'll let you walk me."

Jim was afraid that if he smiled any bigger, his jaw would break. She was just so damn easy to talk to…and he really, really liked her. She wasn't like any other woman he had known. It wasn't just that she was pretty, but that she had a head on her shoulders, as well. *And a quick wit with a sharp tongue.*

"Oh, I'll be here. With time to spare." He watched her twirl the tulip in her hand, much like she was twirling his heart. "Rest well, pretty Anna," he told her as he deposited her safely at the steps of the women's housing.

He watched her until she was tucked away inside, then he took the route back to his own dormitory. He felt like whistling, so he did. There were only a few students in the hallways when he climbed the dormitory stairs up to his room. Most people were inside, candles burning, looking over their schedules, or getting a head start on their reading, hoping to impress the professor.

Carlos is probably doing just that. Jim still had to unpack, so he picked up his pace. Doing a bit of reading didn't sound like such a bad idea. It had taken several late nights and hundreds of candles to pass the entrance exam. For Carlos, school was easy, but for Jim, it had always been more of a challenge…unless it was some form of writing. Then Jim always seemed to shine.

But Carlos needed him. And he had promised his mother; therefore failure had been out of the question. So, he had buried himself in his studies and he had passed the entrance exam… by two points.

"I went ahead and unpacked for you," Carlos said as Jim walked in the door. He was seated, going over his schedule, just as Jim had figured.

The room was small, but adequate, featuring two narrow half beds, two bare desks, and two tiny closets. The mostly clean fireplace would keep them warm in the winter and the small window would bring in the summer breeze. Jim plopped himself on his bed by the wall, arms outstretched to prop himself up. Carlos' bed was by the window, undisturbed. The shutters were drawn and there were two small candles lit, burning away the shadows.

"She's beautiful, isn't she, Carlos?" Jim asked, his mind on Anna.

Carlos tilted his head and gave him a serious sideways stare. "She's a distraction." Then he smiled. "Yes, she's beautiful. But, she did not seem to return your admiration." Carlos laughed, teasing him.

"That's where you're wrong. I'm walking her to class in the morning."

Jim kicked off his boots. They landed with a thud, softened by the wool rug that decorated the ash wood flooring.

An expression fleeted across Carlos' face, but it could have been shadows, so quickly was it gone. Jim dismissed it.

"Have you looked at your schedule?" Carlos asked as he laid his own schedule on the desk. "You may not make it." Carlos said seriously.

Jim stood up and retrieved the class schedule from his bag. He hadn't looked at it since it was handed to him earlier that day by the welcoming committee. He had to admit that that morning, he had still been reeling from his actual acceptance, and the schedule had been nothing more than something to occupy his hand.

There it was in black and white.

Orientation: 7:30 am.

"Damn it," he whispered softly. *Well, there's the stone in the shoe.*

"You have a conflict in your schedule?" Carlos teased.

"It's just orientation…" he paused, thoughtfully, "…you could fill me in," Jim nearly begged. " I wouldn't ask, except that I promised her."

Carlos sighed heavily and said nothing for a long minute. Jim knew better than to persist while Carlos was in thought. "Fine," he said, finally. "But don't continue to make promises you aren't certain you can keep. I might not be able to bail you out."

Jim smiled and clapped his brother heartily on the back. "I won't, brother. Thank you."

And just to show Carlos how serious he was, he hit the books, brushing up on some anatomy. Truthfully, it was Anna's anatomy that most interested him, her perfectly round cheeks, her soft moist lips, and a shape hinting at so much more waiting beneath the folds of her skirt. *Stop it Jim and focus!* He admonished his lack of willpower more than once before he finally reassumed the task and managed to spend some time furthering his knowledge.

The halls were quiet when he finally blew out the candles and settled in his bed.

CHAPTER TWO

Carlos woke the next morning with a burst of nervous energy. The first day of class was bringing about an excitement that he hadn't felt in a long, long time. Everything he had ever done, every book he had ever checked out from the library, every lecture he had ever snuck into, every test he had ever studied for, all of it had culminated to this point in his life. And it was just day one.

Jim was up at dawn, too, but somehow Carlos knew that it wasn't excitement over the first day of class that had his brother in an exceptionally good mood. That responsibility lay solely at the feet of a beautiful young woman. *Anna.* Carlos smiled. Jim was already straightening his tie, anxious to get out the door.

"Thanks again, Carlos," Jim said for the hundredth time that morning as he turned to go.

"Just make it to the lecture hall on time," Carlos said, also for the hundredth time.

"Sure thing," Jim said. Then he left.

Carlos splashed some water on his face from the small wash basin and looked himself in the mirror. A shave and a few strokes of the brush later, and his appearance was in order. He slipped on his shirt and secured the buttons.

Outside, the day was shaping up nicely. The sun was peeking out, drying up the dew. Carlos opted to carry his jacket, instead of wearing it that morning. He would have it…if he needed it. He spotted Jim's jacket adorning the back of his chair and shook his head.

Grabbing his bag of books and his own jacket in one hand, he used his other to snatch his brother's coat as he left their shared dorm room. He would see Jim at the eight o'clock lecture and give it to him then…*if he makes it on time.*

The smoke from last night's celebratory cigars still lingered in the air as he made his way up the hallway and down the stairs. Orientation was to be held on the front lawn, and upon exiting the building, Carlos could spot a building sea of early freshmen, anxious to tidal wave headlong into their future.

He wondered how many would actually finish. St James was well known for placing high expectations on its student body. Plus, there was the nature of the program itself. Sickness was often an ugly sight. Not many would be able to handle the gory parts of it. Washing out because he couldn't stomach the sight of blood or the smell of vomit, didn't concern him in the least. *I've seen sickness. I've seen too mu—*

"If everyone will gather around," interrupted a young man, standing on a bench a few feet from where Carlos had come to join his fellow student class. "We can get the orientation started." The man waited a few moments while everyone began to gather close. "That's it." He said, urging the crowd. "Can everyone hear me?" The crowd was affirmative. "Great. My name is Adam Little. I'm a senior here at St. James and I would like to welcome all of you to your first day of class." He then retrieved a piece of paper from a small briefcase that was lying open on the bench beside him.

Carlos and his fellow students waited patiently for Adam Little to continue. He held the paper up. "I know you have a busy day ahead, so let's get on with it. Each of you will be assigned to a student advisor. Your student advisor will help you become oriented to life at St. James. To find out who your advisor is, you will need to reference this list, which I will be posting, here, shortly. Any questions?" he asked. No one voiced any concerns.

"Great," he continued as a few students came to stand in a line beside the bench where Adam Little stood. He acknowledged them with a wave of his hand, "Here are your student advisors. If you have any questions about rules or codes, or if you need help finding something, just talk to your advisor. Thanks and have a great first day." The man then climbed down from the bench he used as his podium and walked to the nearest tree. He fished a tack from his pocket and secured the list to the tree.

Carlos waited a few minutes for the crowd to thin around the tree before he approached the advisor list. He needed to search for his brother, too and he didn't want to hold anyone else up, while searching out both his and his brother's advisors. But that proved an unnecessary curtesy as it appeared as if each advisor was assigned a student housing hall, which meant that they, too, shared an advisor.

"George Kinley." Carlos read the name aloud.

"Hi, I'm George Kinley," A short, chubby, baby-faced kid in specs with a few hairs out of place announced at his side. "I'm a sophomore and part of the orientation process. I'll be your advisor." The man's pudgy hand was extended in welcome, so Carlos extended his own in the customary measure.

"Hi George, I'm Carlos Castle. I guess I'm your advisee, per se." Carlos said, releasing the man's hand. George's smile was friendly.

"Nice to meet you, Carlos. Do you have your schedule with you?" George asked eagerly.

"Yeah, I do," Carlos fished his schedule from his bag of books and handed it over.

George quickly looked it over, "Lecture Hall this morning, first thing. Professor Smith. You'll either love him or hate him. He can be very blunt and polarizing. He's crazy brilliant, though. So listen to him. Do you know where the Lecture Hall is?" he asked, shifting streams.

"Er...yeah. I was able to walk the grounds with my brother yesterday and we found most of the buildings." Carlos answered truthfully, and George's face betrayed a slight disappointment that he could not be more helpful. He handed back the schedule and Carlos placed it back in his bag. "But thanks so much for the advice about Professor Smith. I am sure that will come in very handy." George beamed. "I've got to get going," Carlos said, before turning on his heel.

"Just let me know if you need anything," George called after him.

"Will do." Carlos waved, jogging away towards the Lecture Hall.

When he got there, there was still ten minutes to spare. So after scanning the hall and finding no sign of Jim, Carlos located two seats, side by side. He took one, and set his bag, along with Jim's coat, in the other. After that, it was a constant headshake, back and forth, between the door and the clock. *Damn it, Jim.* He shouldn't have promised the girl. He should have been at orientation. *Period.*

**

"Fine," Anna said, relenting, to Jim's merriment. "I'll meet you on the campus lawn this evening and I'll show you my sketches. Now go! You already skipped your orientation, *which* I knew about, even if you didn't. You don't want to be late. Go." She shooed at him from two steps up to the main building, which housed a majority of the classrooms.

Of course, she knew about the early morning orientation. He was the new face. She was in her second year at the university. "So, did you expect me to show?" he asked, his curiosity rising levels in a moment.

"I honestly didn't know what to expect," she said and then lifted her lavender skirt and ran up the stairs to class.

Jim watched her until she disappeared inside the building, then he took the shortest route possible to the Lecture Hall. Although his mind should have been focused on getting to the lecture on time, his thoughts were drowning, weighed down by a spirited blond artist. She had agreed to see him again, this evening, and that was all that mattered, at the moment.

He made it to the Lecture Hall with two minutes to spare. He found Carlos after a quick scan of the large room and trotted towards him.

"What took you so long? You were nearly late." Carlos asked with a clear edge to his voice.

"I'm sorry," Jim told him, "but nothing to worry about. I made it." Jim said, just as the double doors were closed, barring entrance to those who were unfortunate enough to be late. Carlos grabbed his bag and placed it on the floor, giving him the seat his brother had obviously saved for him. Jim took his coat and slipped it on.

As he sat down, the wiry, older man took the podium. *Guess he's the professor.* The man's hair was mostly gray, though Jim could tell that it was once a deep black. His eyes were a lively bright blue peeking out from under thick graying brows. His suit was brown and a bit crumpled. He almost looked as though he were recovering from a night spent drinking one too many.

The professor cleared his throat several times while a couple of students set up a table. On top of the table, the students lay what looked like bone fragments. To his left, Carlos straightened in his seat, obviously interested.

Jim relaxed, obviously not.

For the next hour, Jim was only half-interested as the professor gave his lecture, his mind kept wandering to Anna. Carlos was right. *Anna is a distraction…of the healthiest sort, though.* A nudge from Carlos every once in a while helped him to, at least, get the most of what the lecture had been about.

The last five minutes of the lecture seemed the longest for Jim. His next class was at half past nine and when the lecture carried over for an extra five minutes, Jim thought he would die from boredom right in his seat.

"Guess the evolution of human anatomy just isn't for me," Jim yawned to Carlos when the lecture had ended. All around him, the Lecture Hall bustled to life with students preparing to leave for their next class. Jim stretched, stood up, and gathered his things.

"I thought it was fascinating," Carlos said, sincerely.

"I have no doubts that you did," Jim said. "I'm meeting Anna this evening. She's going to show her sketches to me."

"Just leave some room for your studies…" Carlos told him. "That's all I can hope."

"Of course. Haven't let you down so far, have I?" Jim asked.

"There's always a first," Carlos teased, smiling.

Jim and Carlos reached their next class with plenty of time to spare, which pleased Carlos, immensely.

"After this class, we're free until after lunch," Jim said. "Why don't we go for a ride? I bet Pearl would love a good run." Pearl was their gray mare and she was spirited to say the least. She had carted them both when they had left their farm in North Dakota for the university. In truth, she belonged more to Jim than to Carlos.

"That gray beast? Ha!" Carlos said, clearly against it. "You can ride her, alone. I'd prefer to do some reading in the library. "Oh!" he said as though remembering something important, "By the way, our student advisor is a chubby fellow by the name of George Kinley. He's nice enough, though, if a bit round. And you were right. There wasn't much to the orientation."

"Good. I think I *will* take that ride into town, but I'll keep it short. I'll meet you at noon in the commons and I'll bring us some lunch, brother. Lord knows we'll need the energy for all the studying you have planned," Jim told his brother in good nature.

Carlos nodded his head affirmatively, just as General Chemistry started.

Jim settled himself for another boring class. The rigors of medical school was going to be time consuming and mind numbing, but he was willing to put forth the effort, if it meant that he would be keeping his promise to his mother.

Carlos would pass all the exams and classes, easily and with high marks. Of that, there was no doubt. But, in doing so, life would pass him by. Jim wanted to make sure that Carlos experienced life, as much as his discipline would allow. For him, that was what mattered.

As soon as class ended, Jim headed to the stables. Pearl looked irritated that he had left her stalled for so long. She whinnied as he entered her stall. "What's the matter girl?" he asked, then dodged swiftly as she tossed her head, giving him a piece of her mind. "There, there." He rubbed her neck, patting her firmly. Once she was calm, he saddled her within moments. And moments after that, he had her at a trot, heading into town.

Clinton was a growing town, full of new businesses, new people, and new ideas. There was a constant excitement in the air. Pearl could feel it, too. The mare tossed her head and seemed to dance in place as Jim brought the horse to a stop. He raised himself in the saddle, looking around for a place to get a meal for him and his brother. He settled on a small promising shop that beckoned his nose as he secured Pearl.

When he stepped into the establishment, there were several

people sitting at various tables, eating their lunches. The smell of frying chicken permeated every inch of the restaurant. The sound of utensils clinking against dinner plates, pots and pans clanking from the kitchen, and the steady hum of people in conversation clashed in his ears. He chose a small table near the kitchen and took a seat.

Within moments, a server was there. "Fried Chicken and Potatoes is our special today," she said. Her brown hair looked as though it was successfully escaping the bun on her head and her dress was stretched tight across a tired, but ample bosom. She was shifting back and forth as though she was in a hurry.

Jim decided to oblige her and make it short. "I'll take two servings and can you wrap them up for travel?" he asked. "And let me get a cup of coffee while I wait."

"I'll put in the order and be back with your coffee, shortly," she said and headed towards the kitchen. A few moments later, she returned, coffee cup in hand. She set it down in front of him, and then trotted off to take another order.

He took a sip of coffee. It was blistering hot and a bit weak, but it was better than drinking nothing while he waited for his order. He had just finished his cup of coffee, when his server deposited the two pouches on the table. The smell of the fried chicken grew strong and his mouth started to water. He paid for the food, tipped his waitress, and was back in his saddle in no time.

By the time he made it back to the commons, the lunch had gone from piping hot to lukewarm. "Very good," Carlos said. "I'm starving."

"Me too," Jim replied and took a healthy bite of fried chicken. They finished the meal in silence, both of them taking the opportunity to do some reading while they ate their lunch. The natural light in the common room made it a favorite for study groups. There were several such groups scattered with their heads together.

The rest of the day, Jim counted the minutes until he could see Anna…and each one passed agonizingly slow. By the last minute of his last class, he could barely stand it. He made Carlos take seats by the door, so that he could be the first one out. And he was the first person out of the door.

"What the hell, Jim?" Carlos called from his side, struggling to keep up. Jim scanned the lawn. There was no sign of her, yet. *It's still early.*

"She's not here, yet." Jim said.

"Oh, yeah," Carlos said, "Anna. You're supposed to meet her. I forgot. I'm going to study at the library." Carlos turned. "See you this evening. We'll do some studying when you get to the room."

"Sure, Carlos." Jim said as his brother walked away.

He scanned the area for Anna, again, but his eyes met nothing but a steady throng of students he didn't know. Just as he was about to give up, she emerged from behind some trees, sketchbook held close as she walked the grounds. Her golden hair picked up every ray the sun had to offer. Emerald eyes searched the grounds for…something…him, most likely.

He ducked behind a great oak that offered a trunk thick enough to hide him from her wandering eyes. Then he circled around behind her, careful to avoid detection. When he was close to her back, he whispered, "Sweet Anna, you came!"

She whirled around to face him. "Jim, I thought you weren't going to come. I thought yo—"

"I wouldn't miss it for the world. Did Pope Julius II miss the unveiling of the Sistine Chapel?" he asked, her eyes lighting up as he spoke.

"Well, I am hardly Michelangelo."

"I'll be the judge of that." He took her hand and led her to one of the empty benches dotting the lawn. She sat beside him with her sketchbook on her lap.

"These are not for the faint of heart, Jim," she began, fingering the corner of the book.

"I'm not worried." He smiled for reassurance. *Damn, she is beautiful Jim thought.*

"Well, you were warned." She handed him the book with a brave smile, though her eyes betrayed her. She was nervous showing him her sketches. Jim didn't care if what was contained within the book was little more than the doodles of a five year old. He would praise her as though she had a hand as skilled as the great French painter, Monet.

But when he opened the sketchbook, he wasn't greeted with fields of flowers, trees of spring, or the multicolored sky. Instead, he found himself staring at sketches of internal organs…and of the heart, in particular, and in her work was no lack of talent. Each valve and chamber looked alive as it formed the human heart upon the paper, looking every bit as though it were in between beats.

"These are wonderful," he said truthfully. There had been no need to lie to save her feelings. Anna was a talented rare artistic bird that he intended to catch.

"Really?" she asked, unsure. "You don't find them macabre?"

"Not at all." His finger traced the flow of blood through the chambers, careful to avoid smudging. There was a vibrant beauty in her work. As he flipped through the pages, his eyes picked up all manner of sketches, from lungs to kidneys to spleens and livers, each one just as meticulous in detail as the last. "They're strangely beautiful…," he said, his voice trailing as he absorbed them in his mind.

"I've always thought so," she said, pleased. "But most people don't. They find my fascination odd, to say the least."

Jim could understand that. Most people weren't interested in what was contained within the flesh. And most people weren't studying to be a doctor.

"I want to be a surgeon," Anna said.

At the same time, Jim blurted out, "You should be a surgeon."

They laughed, completely in tune with one another as the talking points wandered along with their thoughts. The sun was setting, when he finally deposited her on the steps of the women's housing unit.

Jim's heart was thumping out of his chest as he held her hands to his heart. He looked into her eyes. "Can I kiss you, Anna?"

"No, Mr. Castle," she said smiling and Jim's heart nearly stopped beating. "But, I'll kiss you." A soft, light peck on his cheek and she pulled herself from his grasp and raced up the stairs.

"Can I see you again, Anna?" he called after her.

"Tomorrow," she laughed and then disappeared inside.

CHAPTER THREE

Spring had all but gone, replaced by the melting heat of one of the hottest summers on record. Carlos was sweating bullets as he and Jim walked to their first class. While Carlos had been spending his free time in the library or working in the lab, Jim had been spending all his free time with Anna. Carlos looked at his brother.

Jim was whistling, merrily oblivious to the humidity that drenched the air. He was barely passing his classes. But at the very least, he was passing. So, Carlos could only complain, so much. If Carlos was being completely honest with himself, he was jealous. And in his heart, he knew he didn't have a right to be.

"So, what are your plans this evening, brother?" Carlos asked, forcing a smile, and pushing away any thoughts of jealousy.

"I plan to study, tonight. Anna's class has gone to a clinic in Bryson. They will be there observing over the next few days. So, I'm all yours," Jim said.

This was news to Carlos. Jealousy slipped completely away and a smile spread on his lips. "Let's skip the studying."

"What?" Jim asked, stopping short. Carlos paused a foot ahead.

"Just for tonight," Carlos told him. "Let's go into town and have a round. I'll buy."

"Sure." Jim said, beaming. They resumed their walk.

They had another lecture with Professor Smith and Carlos was excited. He had thoroughly enjoyed the one on their first day of class and he was hoping that the Professor had been able to do some of the field research he had planned. It would be interesting to see if his field team had actually found the remarkable evidence he had hoped to find.

Carlos picked up his pace.

"What's the rush?" Jim asked from his side.

"I want to make sure that we get a good angle, in case he has evidence." Carlos said.

"Evidence of what?" Jim asked. Of course, Jim hadn't paid attention to the first lecture. *He had just met Anna.*

"Man from ape evolution. I mean…" Carlos pondered. "What if he proves it? Think about the advancements in science." Carlos said, absorbed in the implications for medicine. *What if we could learn to manipulate our evolution towards immunity of dis—?*

"Think about the repercussions." Jim said, cutting into his thoughts. "Anyway, don't get your hopes up. No one has ever found actual proof…and I'm not sure that I want them to," his brother said, earnestly.

"You are probably right," Carlos said, though it didn't subdue his excitement.

They reached the lecture hall with plenty of time to spare and found good seats near the front and center of the lecture stage. As before, students set up tables, upon which they placed artifacts.

Disappointment crawled through Carlos as he realized there were no new pieces on the table, just the same ones the Professor had used in his last lecture.

It wasn't long before the wiry, graying Professor entered the hall and proceeded to the podium. Carlos pulled out paper, pens, and ink. Part of the supplies, he passed to Jim. "Take notes, this time. The man is a genius."

Beside him, Jim sighed, clearly already bored.

"The evolution of human anatomy," the Professor began, "is still a mystery. We are no closer to answering that today, than we were 40 years ago, when Darwin first dared to pose the question." Professor Smith cleared his throat. "That is why it is imperative that I expand my research team." The Professor reached into his bag and produced a signup sheet, which he placed on the table.

Carlos sat up straight in his seat and nudged Jim.

"What?" Jim whispered the question.

"Ssshhh, listen," Carlos whispered back.

"We are going to need all hands on deck. This fall, I am leading a research expedition into Deer Mountain. Some of the artifacts that you see on this table were found there, or near there. We are so close and I would like to find the missing link that will tie all of this evidence together. The locals say there is a creature on that mountain that looks like an ape and walks like a man. These artifacts say that is a possibility, as well." He paused for dramatic effect, "This fall, I will find that creature. Anyone who wants to be part of the expedition should sign up before the end of the summer. Does anyone have any questions?"

Carlos only had one. He looked at Jim, "You want to go?"

**

No.

Jim didn't want to go to Deer Mountain. The more clinics that Anna's courses had piled on her busy schedule, the less they were going to see each other already. "We'll see," Jim said, not wanting to discourage his brother completely. "There's plenty of time and besides, our schedules may not allow it. You know that testing is in the fall."

"You're right. We should wait and see." Carlos smiled. "That's very responsible of you. Sometimes, you surprise me."

"Sometimes, Carlos, I surprise myself." Jim laughed.

The Professor's lecture became more of a question and answer session after that and Jim tuned it all out. As always, his thoughts were on Anna. He wondered where Anna was and how she was doing. He wondered if she were enjoying her time away from him, or if she were like him, wishing for every minute to speed up. He wondered a great many things before the session had ended and Carlos was nudging him.

"Get up. We don't need to be late," Carlos said.

Jim got up and gathered his things, but his mind was still in Bryson with Anna.

By the time he and Carlos had finished the day's classes, Jim was ready for that drink Carlos had promised.

"How about I go and cart Pearl and you take our bags back to the room?" Jim asked Carlos as they filed out of the building with the other students.

"Sure, I'll meet you by the stables," Carlos said, taking Jim's bag.

Pearl whinnied when Jim entered the stables. "I missed you too, old girl." He rubbed her neck, patting her firmly. The horse leaned into his affection, snorting. Then she started nuzzling at the pocket of his jacket.

Jim pulled the apple he had saved for her from his pocket. "Here you go," he said, feeding her the apple. As Pearl crunched the apple, core and all, Jim readied the reigns. When he had them fastened, he led Pearl out of the barn to the cart that would carry him and his brother into town.

Carlos arrived just in time to help with the hitches. Once they had the cart secure, they both climbed into the makeshift seat and left their studies behind.

The sky was a fiery pink as they entered the edge of town. The heat of the day was slowly extinguished by the evening, leaving a comfortable breeze to enjoy as they made their way through town to one of the local drinking establishments.

"You know, this is the first break you've taken since we got here," Jim said as he brought Pearl to a stop outside *The Barley Mow*, one of Clinton's many watering holes. Piano music, hearty laughter, and the aroma of hot beer and tobacco wafted out the door to greet them.

The tables were full of customers downing mug after mug as they gambled on their poker hands. There were empty stools available, so Jim and Carlos worked their way through the bustle and up to the bar.

Within moments of sitting, the bartender had two shots of bourbon waiting in front of them. Jim was about to down his when Carlos stopped him with a hand on his arm. Carlos' glass clinked against his. "To us."

"To us," Jim said and then downed the muddy brown liquid. The warming sensation sank through his body, settling in his limbs. Beside him, Carlos coughed deeply. "Another?" Jim asked when

Carlos cleared his throat.

"Another," his brother replied, nodding.

"You guys look as though you're celebrating," said a male voice to Jim's right. "Can I ask, what is the occasion?"

"Life," Jim replied, jovially.

"Yes, life. Well put, brother." Carlos beamed. "We were about to order another round. Would you care to celebrate with us?"

Your tongue is loosened, Carlos. Jim attributed Carlos' sudden chattiness to the bourbon.

"Sure. Why not?" the man said and pulled his stool closer to Jim and his brother. "My name's Lloyd Turner, by the way," he said extending his hand.

Jim was closer, so he took the man's hand and gave it a hearty shake. "Jim Castle. This is my brother, Carlos."

Carlos waved for three drinks and the bartender added another glass to the table. "What do you do?" Carlos asked as the bartender poured another shot of bourbon.

Lloyd smiled, "I work for the Clinton Weekly. We're a small weekly paper that comes out on Sundays. What about you, gentlemen?"

"We're in our first year at St. James," Jim answered, easily. He would trade places with Lloyd in an instant, if it meant he wouldn't be abandoning his brother. "How do you like working at the paper?"

"It's a labor of love," Lloyd said as he raised his glass, "I believe we were drinking to life?"

"Yes, we were, Mr. Turner," Carlos said, raising his own glass. "To life!"

"To life," Jim said, following suit. Again, the warming sensation melted through him. He waited a moment to enjoy the intensity of the alcohol, before asking, "So, what are you working on, now, Mr. Turner?" Jim was sincerely interested.

"Well, to be honest, I am investigating a disappearance," he said, "and call me Lloyd, by the way. Every time you say, Mr. Turner, I think my father is standing behind me."

Carlos laughed.

Jim was interested. "A disappearance?"

"Oh yes. A girl. Ingrid Bledsoe. She disappeared a few weeks, ago," Lloyd said, and then his eyes shifted in mock suspicion, "Either of you wouldn't happen to know what happened to Ingrid Bledsoe, now do you?"

Carlos laughed, "No, but if we do, you'll be the first to know."

"Better me than the Sheriff. The whole lot of them, sheriff...deputies, they're all useless," Lloyd sighed. "Hey, let me buy the next round."

"Sure, but after that, we need a meal and then we need to get back to the university," Jim said.

"He's right. We may not have an early class tomorrow, but that doesn't mean we can afford to be lax," Carlos chimed in.

"Far be it for me to keep you from your studies," Lloyd smiled. "The health of the nation depends on it."

"Surely," Jim said and waved at the bartender.

Moments later, they had left the bar behind and were in search of a meal to share with their new friend, a friend who happened to be the very thing that Jim wanted to be...*a journalist*. And Lloyd was working on a story. Jim enjoyed the man's company and the opportunity to live vicariously, if only for the one night.

When the time came for them to part ways with Lloyd, Jim couldn't help but wish that he and Carlos had more time. But, that was a futile waste of thought...*nothing stops time*.

"Have a good evening, gentlemen. I wish you luck in your studies," Lloyd said, before turning on his heel.

"Good luck on your investigation, Mr. Turner," Jim called out to Lloyd, as he walked away.

Afterwards, there was nothing left to do but climb into the cart and head back to the University. In a matter of minutes, they were back at the edge of town.

There was scarcely any light to see. The moon was small and cloud covered, as Jim drove Pearl down the rutted road. "I had a good time, Carlos. Mr. Turner was a nice distraction. And what a mystery with the missing girl! I hope for her sake, he's able to find out what has become of her."

"Yes, it would be nice if there were a happy ending, but often that is not the case," Carlos said, logically. A moment passed in silence and then, "There's Deer Mountain," his brother said as the clouds opened, bathing the mountainside in moonlight.

"You want to go on the expedition, I know," Jim smiled. Carlos didn't often get excited about things, but the field expedition was one of those exceptions. Suddenly, he felt guilty over not agreeing to go on the expedition right away. And then he was mad at himself for letting his selfishness, about his time with Anna, keep him from being honest.

This is a vicious cycle. He was going rounds on the inside.

"What was that?" Carlos asked, jarring Jim from his thoughts.

"What?" Jim pulled back on the reigns, bringing Pearl to a stop.

"That," Carlos said, suddenly pointing towards the mountain. Jim stared at the mountainside, allowing his eyes to adjust to the shadowy outline. "Just wait," Carlos said, lowering his voice to a whisper.

Jim felt a chill crawl down his spine. Without the creaking of the buggy, the silence was an eerie...*nothing.*

For a minute or two, they stared at the mountainside and nothing strange at all happened. Jim was about to chalk the whole experience up to tricky moonlight and bourbon, when a sudden flash, emanating from near the top, bathed the trees in an intense blue light. Then as suddenly as it appeared, it was gone.

"What the hell?" Jim asked, stunned at being able to find his voice.

"You saw it, too. Thank God," Carlos said, relieved. "I thought I was seeing things."

No, brother. I saw it, too. But for some reason, Jim couldn't bring himself to say it aloud. So, he loosened his grip on the reigns and let

Pearl carry them back to St. James.

Later, as they neared the University, Jim still wondered if their imagination, along with the bourbon, might have played a part. The creepiness had diminished with each bump and rut in the road. And by the time, they had stabled Pearl for the evening, the feeling of uneasiness had vanished completely...*like it never happened at all.*

CHAPTER FOUR

The days went by fast, after that, for Carlos. With Anna gone away for clinic observations, he and Jim had the whole of Clinton, the university, and everything in between at their feet. They had been swimming at the river. They had been dancing at a local music hall. They had even had their portrait made on the steps of the main university building, a gift, which they had sent to their father.

Nearly every night, they spent their evening meal at a different establishment where they enjoyed spirited drinks and conversation. They even managed to maintain their grades, still finding time enough to study. *But, it's getting harder...*

Carlos woke with his mouth full of mud. All he could taste was the bourbon from the night before. His head hurt, but not as bad as he would have thought. He slowly sat up in bed and looked across the room. Jim was still asleep.

I'll fix that. Carlos' pillow sailed through the air, landing right on Jim's face. "Get up," Carlos said and rubbed the sleep from his eyes.

"That's not funny." The muffled reply originated from underneath Carlos' pillow. He wasn't moving. "I don't think I should have had that last round."

"Or the two drinks after?" Carlos asked.

"Or that."

"I told you to have a cup of coffee, instead."

"'I told you so' is a pointless statement, Carlos." Jim threw the pillow half-heartedly, ending short of his directed target.

Carlos laughed. "Come on, we've nearly slept the morning away." Carlos got up and drew back the curtains. Sunlight flooded the room.

"Oh, for the love of God!" Jim yelled. His eyes were squinted shut.

Carlos grabbed the pitcher from the small vessel sink. "Go get some water. We can't go to class without a shave and a good wash." He tossed the pitcher at Jim, who barely managed to sit up in time to catch it.

"You're wrong, Carlos."

"Just go…and hurry." Carlos sent his brother out the door. *The fresh air will do him some good.* While he waited for Jim, he laid out his clothes for the day, all the time wondering what they could do that evening. Carlos could easily admit that he had enjoyed his time with his brother while Anna had been gone. But, it was a relief that she was gone, as well. She stirred feelings inside him that he knew were wrong. His heart beat faster whenever she was around. His palms sweated, and not just because of the heat. His tongue would often betray him by tying itself in knots. *Why can't I be more like Jim?*

"Because, you're not Jim." He could hear his mother inside his head. Thinking of her was painful, even though he sometimes felt she was with him. And he didn't want to be in pain. He had been enjoying himself too much, lately. So, he pushed thoughts of Anna from his mind and focused on his present dilemma. What could he and Jim do that evening?

We could go back to the music hall. It was always good for entertainment. *Or, we could try our hands at the card tables. That would be a cha—*

"She's back, Carlos!" Jim said in excitement as he rushed back into the room with the full pitcher. Drops of water hit the hardwood. Carlos didn't have to ask. *Anna.* Anna was back.

"Did you see her?" Carlos asked.

"No," Jim said, out of breath, "but I saw a girl who's in her class, so I'm assuming."

"Well, I guess you're in a hurry, now." Carlos could feel his mood changing as the full realization of Anna's return sunk in. Jim would be spending the evening with Anna. It was a fact that Carlos was helpless to change.

"You bet I am. I'm going to try to catch her before her next class. She must have returned last night while we were in town," Jim said as he poured water into the sink. After lathering up, his hands were steady as he shaved with the straight razor.

"You could be a surgeon," Carlos told him.

"Hardly," Jim said, and then pulled the blade across his chin with a sure hand. Moments later, he was washing the lather from his face. After he toweled dry, he carried the sink to the window, where he slung the soapy water to the grounds below.

Carlos poured his own water as Jim quickly dressed behind him. Shaved and dressed, Jim looked a much better sight than earlier. "How do I look, Carlos?"

Carlos looked away from the mirror, "Like you had best not be late to class," he said. When he couldn't shake the smile from Jim's face, he relented, offering one of his own, "Go on. Give Anna my best."

"Of course. See you in class." And then he was gone.

With an hour left before class, Carlos decided to take a walk. So when he was ready, he made his way out of the dormitory and onto the campus lawn. It wasn't long before his shirt was soaked through and he was looking for a place to retreat inside. The lecture hall was a welcome reprieve from the beating sun as Carlos ducked inside.

"Yes," Carlos heard the familiar voice. "Finally. It has arrived. Hertz has made the most wonderful advancement. Imagine a signal that can travel up to a mile and a half without interference. Astonishing!" *Professor Smith!* Carlos whipped his head around to find the wiry little man stooped over a long wooden crate. "Of course, we will never get that distance, even with the new alkaline battery system that we are testing. But we could possibly achieve a signal of up to a half mile in the mountainous terrain."

Carlos didn't want to interrupt but he didn't want to leave, either. So, he slipped into a seat and kept to himself while the Professor and his team began wiring strange metal boxes to even smaller, stranger metal boxes.

It was fascinating, even if he didn't understand exactly what was going on. After they had wired the first set of boxes together, the professor pulled out a concave glass with a handle attached to wires coming out of…yet another black box. After some adjustment, the faintest of chirps seemed to emanate from the device. Once, twice, three times, it chirped before the Professor declared, "It works! Continue to wire the rest of the devices." Then the professor looked around and his eyes fell on Carlos, "You there, care to help?"

Carlos swallowed, nervous. "Sure, as long as it won't take too long. I have a class in a few minutes."

"I need to see what kind of range we have. Can you carry this out past the entrance to the school?" Professor Smith asked, his eyes sparkling with hope. The Professor's enthusiasm was infectious, which was why Carlos found himself sweating through his shirt as he carried the two connected boxes outside the campus grounds.

The professor had given him explicit instructions, "Keep a solid pace until you are off campus, then find a place to stop and stay where you are and I will find you." That sounded like it could take more than a few minutes to Carlos, but he had already agreed. Moreover, it didn't hurt that his curiosity about the whole thing was driving him forward. *It's exciting!*

But his excitement was diminishing when it became clear that the professor might not be finding him any time soon. Long minutes passed by with no sign of the Professor or the strange device that made the noises. With each passing moment, Carlos became more certain that he was going to be late for class. He debated about leaving, but there was still a nagging bit of curiosity keeping him rooted to his spot.

As he waited in a pool of his own sweat, his mind began ambling. He wondered if Jim had found Anna before her next class. *Probably.* Carlos wiped the sweat from his brow. *And I bet he didn't need all these damn black boxes to d—*

"Hello there!" He heard the Professor call to his right. "I found you. Brilliant. Absolutely brilliant." Carlos didn't wait for the Professor to come all the way to him. He knew he was already late. He wondered what Jim must be thinking about his absence.

**

Where the hell is Carlos? After his brother's warning about tardiness, Jim was extremely shocked when class was five minutes

34

into session and Carlos was still a no show. It was so unlike Carlos, that Jim was simply mystified by the whole event. *He could be sick…or injured. But…how? And when? I just saw him an hour ago.*

All sorts of possibilities for Carlos' absence ran through Jim's mind before the class door finally crept open and Carlos ducked inside, finding his seat beside Jim. Had he fallen asleep studying? Been detained by school officials? Or simply lost track of the time?

None of the above. The answer was much stranger than that. Jim couldn't believe the tale that Carlos told him as they walked to their next class. Boxes wired together emitting invisible signals that travelled through the air. Devices detecting these boxes from far away. It sounded like some of the writings by Jules Verne. Ideas so farfetched…*they must be fiction.*

"But they aren't," Carlos said, his eyes betraying his excitement. "They're real. If I hadn't seen it with my own eyes, I wouldn't believe it either. I wish you had been there," Carlos said. "Oh," Carlos added as though remembering something important, "Did you find Anna?"

"I did. She's great. She had a good time at the clinic in Bryson, but I could tell she missed me." Jim said, remembering how she threw herself into his arms when she spotted him hanging around waiting for her as her class had ended.

"Good," Carlos said, smiling. "I know you're glad she's back."

A long moment passed in silence.

"I think I might love her, Carlos." There, he had said it. The truth was, Jim needed some advice, and he was hoping Carlos would have some that was helpful.

Carlos cleared his throat and didn't speak for a minute or two. Jim waited patiently. Carlos often thought well before he spoke. "Have you told her?" he finally asked as they crossed the campus lawn to their next class.

"No," Jim answered. "That's the problem. I want to, but…"

"It's hard."

"Yes," Jim said. Somehow, he knew Carlos would understand.

"You see a future with her? A family?" Carlos asked, in all

seriousness.

Jim hadn't thought quite that far ahead. But when the question was posed, he could honestly say that he could. He had fallen head over heels for Anna from the moment he had met her. "Yes," he said, surprising himself.

But where do I go from here? Do I tell her? And if so, how do I tell her? In times like these, Jim missed his mother the most. She had always known just what to say to make things clearer…easier somehow.

"Then you have no choice," Carlos said, softly. "You have to tell her."

"But how?" Jim asked. He knew he sounded pathetic. *Damnit!* It was making him crazy. "I'll die where I stand if she doesn't feel the same, Carlos," he offered as his pitiful excuse.

The building and the next class were just steps away and Jim was just as confused now as he had been before telling Carlos.

"She is crazy about you, Jim. You worry for nothing, I promise." Carlos smiled. "We best get inside. Dr. Gray likes to start early."

Carlos was right about Dr. Gray. But he wasn't so sure that Carlos' conviction about Anna's feelings were based on any type of fact. How could anyone know the workings of the female mind? *At best, Carlos is guessing.* He wished more than ever that his mother were still alive.

The classes seemed to drag by and Jim was counting the minutes when he could catch up to Anna. When he was with her, everything was better. When he was away from her, his doubts were fast growing weeds filling the cracks of his mind.

When the last class of the day was finally over, Jim quickly gathered his things, urging Carlos to hurry. "Come on, let's get out of here."

Carlos matched Jim's quick pace as they exited the building. Jim scanned the campus lawn, his eyes falling on the bench where he first met Anna. There she was with her sketchbook. *God, she's lovely.* The sunlight magnified the gold of her hair.

Jim was just about to break into a jog, when Carlos nudged his shoulder, "Look!"

Jim turned to see where Carlos was pointing. Dotting the trees, were flyers, advertising a summer break festival for the students of St. James. Upon closer inspection, Jim could see that the event was being held at the music hall in Clinton.

"We should go! We won't have classes. It'll be fun!" Jim said. "Me, you and Anna could have a great time." And this might be the right time to tell her how he felt.

"Sure," Carlos said, smiling. "I'm game, since we'll be on break."

"Great," Jim said. "Let's go see if Anna wants to go."

"Of course, I'll attend the festival with you, Jim Castle." Anna said, green eyes dancing in the sunlight. "I can't wait. I'm gonna make you dance with me until you can't dance anymore, then I'll let your brother give you a break. I could really use some time away from my studies. This is exciting!"

"It's official, then, Carlos," Jim said, smiling at his brother, "You have to learn how to dance, now."

Carlos laughed, punching him in the arm. "Thanks, brother. I know I have two left feet, but she could have figured that out on her own without you telling her."

Counting the days to the festival was excruciating for Jim, mainly because he had decided that the festival would be the perfect backdrop for telling Anna that he was in love with her. *Oh God, please feel the same way.* His doubts were still there, but they had become increasingly manageable, the more time he spent in her company.

She was just so easy to talk to, which was one of the main reasons he had fallen in love with her.

"So, we'll meet at the stables after class, right?" Anna asked on the morning of their last day of classes before the summer break.

"Yes," Jim said, bringing her hand to his lips. "Carlos is supposed to hitch the cart to Pearl and saddle your horse, while I take our bags back to the room. We'll be in Clinton before the festival begins." He kissed the soft hand again, before releasing it back to its owner.

Jim knew it would be a long day as he attended classes without Anna. Time seemed to slow down when he was away from her. He had come to expect it.

What seemed like an eternity later, the campus grounds filled with students, each anxious to get on with summer break. Jim dodged through the crowd on his way to stow his and Carlos' bags in the dorm room.

His stomach was filled with flutters, knowing that tonight, he would tell Anna exactly how he felt about her. He knew he loved her beyond any doubt and Carlos had been right. He needed to tell her. But knowing what to do and actually doing it were two entirely separate things.

His stomach turned a flip as he climbed the stairs to the dorm room. *How?* He was elbow to elbow with other aspiring doctors as he made his way to the room he shared with his brother. When he opened the door, his stomach felt like a nervous pit of vipers, writhing over one another.

He threw the bags on the floor and spun his head, just in time to lose his lunch in the sink. The taste of partially digested cheese and bits of apple that had been his lunch, left a bitter taste in his mouth

Must be the nerves. Jim rinsed his mouth, gargling, and washed his face, feeling a little better. He looked at himself in the mirror. His color was a shade paler than normal, but otherwise, he looked healthy. *I just got myself too worked up, that's all.*

He was back out into the crowded hallway within moments. And a couple of minutes after, he was nearing the stables.

True to his word, Carlos had hitched Pearl and he was stroking Anna's horse, Jolly, as Anna pulled herself into the saddle. He had never seen her in riding pants and Jim loved the way the pants curved over her frame.

She swung into the saddle, easily. She had often said how much she loved to ride. Carlos spotted Jim, first, "Hey Jim. You made it."

"Yeah, I could barely get down the hallway for all the foot traffic." Jim said.

"Hello, Jim!" Anna said, smiling from atop her horse. "I'm so excited."

"Me too," Jim said and his stomach took another turn. "We

should go and beat the crowd." He fought through the queasiness, but only for long enough to get into the cart. His head was soon hanging over the side.

His embarrassment only doubled when Anna's concern for him drove her to get down from her saddle. "Jim? Are you all right?"

"Yeah, yeah," he said, but he wasn't sure. He had thought his condition could be chalked up to nerves, but now he knew that wasn't the case. The snakes in his stomach refused to be still.

"You don't look so good, Jim," Carlos said, concern filling his brother's voice.

"Truthfully, I don't feel so good, either." He hated what he was about to say, but he couldn't see any help for it. He was obviously sick. "I think I need to go back to the room and get some rest," he said, hating every word. "Probably just something I ate," Jim said to calm their fears.

"Well, you should probably go on back to the room. I'll unhitch Pearl and be back be—"

"No. Just because I'm sick doesn't mean that you and Anna can't have a good time. All you're going to do if you *don't* go is watch me rest. I'll be fine. It's not like I'm a complete invalid. And look around," Jim said, growing weaker the longer he sat there, "there's no place better to be when you're sick than surrounded by a bunch of doctors."

Anna felt his forehead, "He's not feverish. It probably is a slight case of food poisoning. It happens." Then she looked Jim in the eyes, "Are you sure you'll be okay?"

"Yeah," Jim said as he climbed down from the cart. "Don't worry about me. You guys can tell me all about it, tomorrow. Have fun."

Anna kissed his cheek, and then regained her seat in the saddle. Carlos waved one last time before turning Pearl onto the rutted road. Within moments, they were gone and Jim felt a sudden loneliness settle into him as he weakly made his way back to the dorm.

CHAPTER FIVE

Carlos was worried for Jim, but he knew Anna was right. Without the presence of a fever, the possibility of Jim's sudden sickness being truly serious was slim. So, he and Anna decided to do as Jim had asked, and enjoy the festival.

Anna had Jolly at a trot beside the cart as they made their way to Clinton. "I haven't been dancing in so long," Anna said, wistfully, as they entered the edge of town. "I've heard that there will be drinks and food, as well. I have to admit that I skipped lunch and now I'm paying for it."

Carlos felt strange around her without Jim. But, it had been a while since lunch, so he could relate. "I'm pretty hungry myself. Why don't we get a bite to eat first, and then you can watch me make a fool of myself on the dance floor."

"Deal," Anna said, laughing. He had forgotten how musical her laughter could be.

Suddenly, he felt a lot more at ease and talking to her began to come naturally. He could see why Jim had fallen for her. She was smart and fun. She had a quick tongue. But she was kind and genuine. In short, Anna wasn't like any girl he had ever known.

By the time they had reached the festival and tended to their horses, they were laughing and talking freely, as if they had known each other their whole lives.

"When I was a child, Father took my brothers and me to a fair in the capitol. There were more people there, than here, but the atmosphere was the same. You can feel it, can't you, Carlos?" Anna was standing beside him outside the music hall. The music was a muffled sound, standing on the walkway. The sound of laughter and celebration penetrated the air around them, reaching farther than the music.

Yes. He could feel it. "It's like the excitement is a living breathing entity."

"Exactly," she whispered. She grabbed him by the hand and pulled him in through the double doors. The music was loud as they followed the smell of food. A banquet had been set up on one end of the room. On the other end was a bar, serving up various sorts of alcoholic beverages to the students who had gathered there. Between, was a stage where musicians were playing old favorites and new, along with a dance floor.

"I'm going to have one of everything!" She exclaimed when they had reached the banquet table. "Well. Maybe not one of *everything.*"

Carlos laughed. But on the inside, there was a building turmoil. *Why does she have to be so smart? So funny? So damn beautiful?* But, worse than that, why did she have to be Jim's? For the thousandth time, he wished he could find someone like Anna, someone who made him feel...*like Anna makes me feel.*

They piled a variety of food on their plates, but Carlos had simply been filling his plate to fill it. In truth, he didn't really care about the food. He was much more interested in his company. "Come on," she said smiling up at him. "Let's find a place to sit."

A table in the corner was vacated soon after their search began. Carlos pulled out Anna's chair. At least the manners his mother had instilled in him, early on, still served him well.

"Thank you," she said as she settled in the chair.

"I'll go get us some drinks. What would you like?" Carlos asked.

"You know when I was gone for observations in Bryson, some of my class fell in love with this new drink from California called a Gibson. I want one of those, please," she said, her green eyes seeming to see right through him.

"Two Gibsons coming up," Carlos said, and then headed for the bar. Within a few minutes, he had returned with their drinks. If he had to dance with Anna, he thought he would need the extra courage.

"I need to change into my skirt. Could you be a gentleman?" she asked. "*Being a gentleman*" meant going back to the cart, holding up a blanket, and providing privacy for Anna as she changed from her riding pants into her skirt.

Carlos felt an odd warming sensation crawl his skin. *Does she know how uncomfortable she's making me?* Staring down, while holding the blanket, he saw the snug fitting riding pants fall to the ground. A rustle of her hoop skirt and within moments, she was done. Carlos was thankful and in need of another drink.

So, once they were back inside, he bought another round, building up his courage before they went to the dance floor.

"I feel the need to warn you, again," Carlos said, "I am n—"

"I know, you aren't a good dancer," she said, pulling him through the other people showing their skill on the dance floor. When she found a spot with enough room to allow a dance between two individuals, she pulled him to her, placing her arms on his shoulder and allowing him to take lead.

Carlos did his best to remember all the steps. Polkas were the most popular of the evening and somehow Carlos managed to keep his feet on his side of the dance steps. Before long, he was comfortable enough that he was even enjoying himself.

When the third polka had ended, Anna led them off the dance floor to catch their breath. "I am having such a good time," she said, smiling.

"Me too," he replied. And he meant it. He was having a great time. She was just so damned easy to be around, and talking with her was as easy as breathing. He wanted to kiss her, but the thought was so wrong, it was like sandpaper against his brain. *Stop it!*

He ordered two more Gibsons, thankful for the opportunity to do or think anything else. Each time he had to touch her, his skin felt like the air after a bolt of lightning…*electrified.*

"You dance better, the more you do it, Carlos. You'll be a professional by the end of the night," Anna said, smiling as she nursed her drink and swung her small frame freely on the barstool, facing him.

"I highly doubt that, but I appreciate the vote of confidence." Maybe his problem with dancing had always stemmed from not having the right partner. But Anna wasn't the right partner. He knew that. Anna was Jim's partner. *And I am nothing more than a substitution.*

Soft pink lips pressed against the rim of the glass and Carlos squeezed his hands together so tightly that he lost feeling in them. He was thankful when she had finished her drink and set it down, saying, "Ohh, I love this music. Break time is over!" She grabbed his hand, dragging him back out to the dance floor.

He was as obedient as ever, allowing himself to be led back into the fray of laughing students and loud music. And he suddenly knew that pleasing her would never be a chore. It was something he wanted to do.

One polka later and the music switched tempos, slowing down for a much more intimate dance. He was about to pull away, when she placed her arms around his neck and stepped a foot closer. "You didn't think you were going to get off that easy, did you Carlos?" Anna asked, smiling. Sparkling emeralds stared up at him. "I came here to dance."

He could feel himself being ripped apart as his mind warred with his heart, pitting logic against irrational bliss. He placed his hands on her waist and somehow concentrated on his steps. But, *one, two, three…one, two three, pivot, turn…,* soon became, *I wonder if her lips are as sweet as they look?* Yet somehow, he managed to control it all as he made it through the dance.

Two lively dances later and they were back at the bar for one last drink before calling it an evening. "These are such good drinks…these…what are they called again?" Anna laughed.

"Gibsons."

"Gibsons, right." She laughed again, "I forgot. I also think I may have had enough."

"I quite agree," he said, smiling. "It is not the smoothest of rides between here and St. James."

"I have had the most wonderful time tonight, Carlos. Thank you," she said and before he knew it, she had kissed his cheek. The warmth from that small innocent kiss spread faster than any bourbon or gin he had ever consumed.

He walked on weak knees, alongside Anna and when they reached the horses, he was thankful to stand still a moment.

Anna dug into the back of the cart and produced her riding pants and blanket. She tossed the blanket to Carlos. "Do you mind?" she asked.

He spread the blanket open and looked away, just as a gentleman should...but it was hard. Her hoop skirt hit the pebbled ground with a soft rustle. And then, he could hear her squirming as she pulled up the riding pants. "Done," she said and took the blanket from Carlos.

"Are you sure you'll be okay to ride?" he asked her, suddenly worried that she may have had too much to drink.

"That is so sweet of you to worry about me, Carlos," she said. "But I'm fine." She leaned into him and hugged him. He held her and then instinctively hugged her close. The scent of her was intoxicating. The feel of her in his arms was like nothing he had ever experienced. It was as if God had molded his arms for the shape of Anna.

And he knew that she could feel it, too.

When her eyes looked up into his, they burned with a longing green fire and set his soul ablaze. He was no longer in control of himself. Leaning down to kiss her lips wasn't something he thought about. It was just something he did.

The passion she returned was completely unexpected and stole the breath from his lungs. She tasted like alcohol and ginger with a hint of honey. Her breasts were buried in his chest and her golden hair tickled his wrist as it hung about her waist. She was firm where she needed to be and soft where she didn't. She was perfect. Everything was perfect.

And then it wasn't.

His mind jumped to Jim and he stiffened. At the same time, she broke away and took a step back, pulling herself from his grasp. She might as well have ripped the heart from his chest, when he saw her face. She was stricken with shame. "Oh no. Oh my God." she managed to say. "I love Jim. Oh my god, what have I done?"

As Anna was saying these things, they echoed, bouncing around in Carlos' mind. *What is wrong with me? How can Jim ever forgive me? Oh my god, what have I done?*

"I'm sorry," Carlos said. It was the only thing he could think of to say, and he knew it wasn't enough.

Anna began crying, "I love Jim. I didn't mean to." Then, she went to Jolly and pulled the reigns from the post.

"Wait, Anna!" Carlos called to her as she mounted her saddle.

He grabbed at the horses reigns, but Anna veered the horse away, "I need to think, just leave me alone, Carlos."

He tried for the reigns again. He knew she wasn't thinking clearly. "Anna, please," he begged as she kicked her heels into Jolly's side. The horse whinnied and was gone, taking Anna away.

"Dammit!" Carlos yelled as he climbed into the cart and drove Pearl as hard as he dared.

With the moon under cloud cover, Anna was out of sight in no time. After a few minutes of chase, Carlos finally slowed Pearl down to a trot. Trying to catch up to Anna was useless, especially in the dark.

She's probably back at the university by now. She's probably telling Jim. He's going to hate me. How could I do this? Carlos' emotions were like a tightly coiled spring, ready to explode. He loathed himself with each passing moment. He had failed. He had failed himself. He had failed his brother. He had failed his father. But worse, he had failed his mother and the promise he had made. The wedge that this was likely to drive between him and his brother would see to that.

When Carlos passed through the best part of the road to view Deer Mountain, he didn't even look up like he usually did. His thoughts were with Jim and Anna, and not on the field expedition.

After stabling Pearl, Carlos went to face the music. His relief at finding Jim asleep and not waiting for him with accusations was a shameful cross to bear as he climbed into his bed. *And where is Anna?* Jolly wasn't in the stables.

If she had wanted to see him, she would have been in the stables, waiting. *Right?* She had had plenty of time. *She probably doubled back to the festival, avoiding me.* Carlos wished that he could avoid himself. He was in for a fit of a night. It was a good thing that there were no classes the next day, because he was almost positive that he wouldn't be getting any sleep.

**

When Jim woke up the next morning, he was feeling much better. "Guess it wasn't anything serious, Carlos," he said. "I'm feeling much better. Maybe a bit weak, but much better." Jim stretched in his bed and then sat up.

He looked over at Carlos' bed. The covers were pulled back and the pillow bore an indentation, but the bed was empty. Carlos was gone. *Probably already enjoying the day.*

They didn't get much time off from their studies and so far Jim had wasted part of it being sick. He couldn't wait to see Carlos and Anna and find out what the festival had been like. He hated missing it. He had been going to tell Anna that he loved her there, but...

That didn't matter. He'd tell her today.

Jim washed and dressed quickly. Before he knew it, he was already descending the stairs of the housing unit. It was dry and hot when he stepped out into the sunlight. He waited a moment for his eyes to adjust and then he did a quick scan of the grounds.

There were students enjoying their time off. A couple of people were flying kites, while others tossed balls around. Still others were enjoying the fresh air, sitting down with books and picnics. It was a lovely day, and he was exited to share it with Anna.

Where is she? His search of the campus grounds had produced neither Anna nor Carlos. He decided to try the library. Both Anna and Carlos enjoyed reading in their idle time. *Probably got their noses stuck in books.* Jim couldn't believe they weren't enjoying the sunshine.

When he got to the library, he was as confused as ever. While there were a few students taking advantage of the vast amount of books, Carlos and Anna weren't among them. So, he tried the classrooms, the lab and the lecture hall, all without any success.

Where the hell are they?

After one more look around the campus grounds, Jim decided to check the stables. Maybe they had gone for a ride. It was the perfect day for it. He was kicking himself for having slept too long. When he got to the stables, he knew that he had missed them. Neither Pearl, nor Anna's horse was stalled. He was about to turn around and go back to the dorm, when he heard a rider in the distance.

While looking towards the sound of hooves on the hard, dry ground, it soon became clear to Carlos that he was seeing Pearl. And on her back…*Carlos*. Jim felt a wave of relief. He might have missed the ride, but there were other things they could do on their day off. His brother waved. Jim waved back. Carlos never stopped waving. In fact, he was waving frantically and calling out, "Jim!"

The desperation in Carlos' voice made the hairs on Jim's neck stand. *Something's wrong!* Jim scanned the horizon for another rider as Carlos drove Pearl hard and cried out to him. *Where is Anna? Shouldn't she be with Carlos?*

"Jim!" Carlos called again, bringing Pearl to a stop. The dust flew at Jim from Pearl's abrupt stop, filling his nose and eyes.

"What's wrong, Carlos? Where's Anna?" Jim cried, staring through watery eyes. Carlos looked haggard, as if he hadn't had a wink of sleep in days.

"I don't know…never came back…festival…back and forth looking for signs, but…so many tracks…everyone at the university…road," Carlos spewed. It was too much information, all at once. "Need to get you a horse…find her, Jim. I'm afraid…happened," his brother continued.

"Stop it!" Jim said, "Slow down!"

"She's missing!" Carlos told him and gave him a moment to process the information.

Anna's missing? "How? When?" It was all that Jim could manage.

"I don't know how. But she never came back last night."

"You didn't come back together?"

Carlos shook his head. "I've been looking for her all morning. Jim, we need to get another horse. We'll cover more ground."

"Give me, Pearl." Jim told Carlos. He was numb.

Carlos didn't move from the saddle. "You're not thinking clearly, Jim."

"Get down, Carlos," Jim said. He wouldn't tell him again. After the briefest of hesitations, Carlos climbed down from the saddle. Jim took the reins, looped them back over the pommel, mounted Pearl and was gone.

At a trot, he scanned the road, looking for anything that might tell him something about Anna's whereabouts. But Carlos had been right, there had been too much traffic to tell anything. And yet, he pressed on all the way into Clinton.

Once the town was in sight, his worries slowly migrated away as his mind began to rationalize the probabilities. *She was probably tired from the festival and rented a room.* And to test the theory, he proceeded into town, where he began to seek out any place that rented lodgings.

After tending to Pearl, he walked into the Sleepy Inn. On one side, a sweaty bald man greeted him from behind the front desk. On the other side, a tall broad lumberjack tended the bar.

He chose the front desk. "Can I help you, sir?" The man's jowl wiggled as he talked.

"I'm looking for a girl," Jim said. "A pretty blonde girl with green eyes."

"Let me guess," the clerk said. "Her name is Anna?"

"Yes, yes." Jim felt relief wash over him and then confusion followed. "How did you know?"

"There was a guy in here a couple of hours ago, asking about the same girl." The man wiped his brow with his kerchief. *Carlos.* Of course, his brother would have already thought of this as a possibility. Jim left without another word and walked to the next establishment that rented rooms and it was the same story the first clerk had told...*just out of a different mouth.*

With each new establishment he visited, his heart climbed higher into his throat. Anna was actually missing. Suddenly, the strange disappearance of the girl, Ingrid Bledsoe, told to him by the journalist so many nights ago, paraded into the forefront of his mind. He pushed it away, mounting Pearl.

Carlos had been right, as usual. And had Jim listened, he wouldn't have wasted precious time confirming what Carlos already knew. *Anna is gone...*

CHAPTER SIX

Carlos had done nothing, except relive the events from the previous night.

When he had returned to St. James, he hadn't been able to sleep and the longer he had been left alone with his thoughts, the sorrier he had felt for what had happened. He had felt a burning need to tell Anna that he was sorry, to try and mend the damage that he had done when he had kissed her.

So he had waited for her in the stables. And then it had become apparent that she wasn't coming back to the university. He had watched the sun come up as he was entering Clinton. He had checked the hotels, the music hall, and any kitchen that served hot meals. If she or Jolly had been in Clinton, he would have found them.

On his way back and with better light, he had studied the road, looking for any sign of Anna. But the road had been so riddled with tracks, that he had to give up, knowing he would need help. *At least one more horse and rider to expand the search area.* Which was why he hadn't lingered at the stables when Jim had ridden off half-cocked with Pearl.

He scanned the campus lawn, looking for a familiar face. Then he spotted one. George Kinley. "George!" he called out waving. George looked up and waved back, then he began closing the gap between them, moving his chubby frame at a brisk pace.

Carlos was nearly out of breath, when George reached out to shake his hand. "Carlos, right?" he asked with a smile. Carlos didn't really have time for friendly greetings, but he knew better than to be dismissive of the formalities, when he so desperately needed George's help.

Carlos shook George's hand, "Yes, that's right. I am sorry to be in a hurry, but I really need your help."

George's smile was round and his eyes lit up at the prospect of being of some assistance…of actually earning his title of student advisor. "Of course. That's what I'm here for."

So he got directly to the point and told George about Anna and her sudden disappearance, stopping only to answer a question or to clarify a detail, if George asked.

"Yes, and there are too many tracks, too many disturbances. I think the search needs to be expanded. I think if we wait too long, any trail might fade away." Carlos took a deep breath. His nerves were on edge. The longer Anna went missing, the better the chances were that something terrible had happened to her. *And it's all my fault.*

Why had he kissed her? Carlos had asked himself the same question, over and over until he thought his brain might finally snap. His mother's voice remained silent, though. Her murmured advice, from beyond the grave, had not even presented itself as so much as a whisper.

And that haunted him.

Of course, he could remember her words and phrases, but the feeling of her presence was gone, leaving something much heavier behind. It weighed on him. But he was driven to find Anna, to set things right, and to mend any damage he had caused. *If that is possible.*

Pushing against the burden that threatened to crush him, Carlos nearly staggered when George's voice pierced his bubble of thoughts, "I'll organize a search party and get as many people as we can to search a wide berth between here and Clinton. Sound good, Carlos?" George asked him.

It was the best news he'd heard all day. "Yes, George. That sounds great. Thank you."

"No problem. Spread word for anyone who's interested in helping with the search, to meet at the stables in an hour. From there, we'll gather horses and split up into groups and search areas." George said, taking charge. Carlos couldn't be more thankful. He shook George's hand once more, before spreading the word about Anna.

Jim arrived back at the school as those interested in helping with the search were gathering at the stables. Holding Pearl by the reins, he walked over to where Carlos was standing.

"I thought she might have gotten a room. But you already knew that she hadn't. I'm sorry. I should have listened to you," Jim said. Pain splintered in Carlos' mind. He rubbed his temple. Jim had apologized to him. It was so wrong that Carlos' shame returned in a wave that tried to devour him. He should be the one apologizing to Jim.

"I'm sorry," Carlos said.

"It's not your fault, Carlos. You're the only one getting anything done. I've just been wasting t—"

"Can everybody hear me?" George's voice rang out in the middle of the crowd, forcing Jim into silence. Carlos didn't think he could handle any more of Jim's thankfulness or praise. It was making him sick to his stomach. "Good. Now as you all are aware. We have a missing girl. Anna is blond with green eyes of medium height and small build. I'd like to make a wide search area of about a mile on either side of the road and then carry that search to the town limits. Understand?"

Everyone nodded. "Now," George continued, "Pair off into groups of three or four. We'll meet back here in about four hours. Thanks for your help and remember to be safe out there, we don't need to create a bigger problem by getting turned around or not paying attention to the surroundings."

Saddles swung in the air onto the back of horses and before long, there was a descent sized search party about to depart with the sole purpose of locating Anna. Confidence built inside Carlos that Anna would be found. In what condition, though, he didn't know. *She was so upset.* Jim stayed atop Pearl, while Carlos found space inside a small wagon along with George.

The buggy rolled along the grooves in the dirt, as Carlos watched his brother head off with his own small search party. George decided that their best utilization of time would be to use the buggy to rest as they took turns walking the road. "I think something could get missed from horseback. It's probably best if some eyes stay closer to the ground."

Carlos agreed. "Yeah. I counted about 35 horses leaving the stables. Walking the road may give us a different perspective."

It also gave Carlos time to think, which is what he didn't want to do. He wanted something to take his mind off the night before. *And I need to tell Jim what happened.* But now wasn't the time. They needed to find Anna first and make sure that she was okay. *But as soon as she's found, I'm going to tell him...regardless of the consequences.*

The first mile went slowly. George was methodical, leaving no stone unturned. Every few minutes, he would have them stop to check out some lost artifact half buried in the dirt. So far, they had discovered two broken spurs, an odd piece of wood that looked like the leg of a table, and one fraying piece of brown fabric that no hygiene conscious female doctor would dare let touch her skin.

This is useless.

The next mile seemed to go slower than the first, and still there was absolutely no sign of Anna. "If we still haven't found anything by the time we reach Clinton, then we'll go on into town and file a report with Sheriff Ghetts," George said.

Carlos nodded in agreement. It was a solid plan.

It wasn't until he was actually walking into the Sheriff's office, that he realized, he hadn't really thought it would come to that. But as he was speaking with the tall, lanky officer it felt finalized somehow. Anna was truly missing. "Waist length blonde hair. Green eyes. About five foot six. Her name is Anna...er...I'm sorry. I don't recall her last name," Carlos said, feeling like a complete failure.

"That's okay," Sheriff Ghetts said. "I can talk to the records department at the school. Chances are, though, she'll turn up before I get that far." Carlos could only hope that would be the case.

There was not any sense in wasting more time searching the way they had been, so Carlos and George rode back to St. James, forgoing any further search. "We'll probably get back and find out she's fine," George said after a few minutes of awkward silence.

"Probably," Carlos said, but he didn't hold out any real hope.

"I think we'll make it back before sunset," George said, after another twenty minutes of silence.

Carlos was so deep in thought that he barely heard him. "That would be good," he managed to reply. He looked up at the sky. George was right. They would make it back to the school before sunset. He wondered how many search parties had returned empty handed. What if something had happened to spook Jolly and Anna had fallen from her horse. *She could be...*

Carlos couldn't finish the thought. So he kept his eye on the horizon. When St. James came into view, he was glad to be getting back. He would soon know more, even if that knowledge was nothing more than the fact that Anna was still missing.

As they neared the stables, there were several people gathered. Some horses were stabled, others were being led by their owners back to their stalls. Carlos spotted Pearl; Jim was still mounted in the saddle. He looked fearful and it tore at Carlos' heart. *This is my fault.* Each word pounded into his brain.

As George brought the wagon to a stop, Carlos jumped from his seat and jogged over to Jim. As soon as Jim saw him, he said, "Carlos! We found Jolly spooked out of her mind. Damn horse came tearing off the side of Deer Mountain running straight at us. No sign of Anna. Carlos, I'm scared. Something has happened to her. Something bad."

Deer Mountain. He hadn't even thought that would be a possibility. "We'll find her, Jim," Carlos said in an effort to calm his brother. "Pearl is lathered up and we'll never be able to find Anna in the dark. First thing in the morning, we'll head for the mountain and see what we can find, okay?"

Jim stared off. Carlos wasn't even sure that Jim had heard him.

**

Jim knew that Carlos was being logical. His brother was good at that. He also knew that his brother was right.

"It won't do Anna a bit of good, if something happens to us because we're riding around on the side of the mountain in the dark, Jim." Carlos said.

"Goddammit!" Jim hated this with every part of his being. *It feels like giving up.* After a few more moments, Jim dismounted and led Pearl to the stables in defeat. Jolly was still stirred up, but being back inside her stall, had calmed her tremendously. He stroked the horse's neck, while Carlos tended to Pearl. "It's okay. I'll take care of you until she comes back." He told the horse in a soothing voice. Jolly leaned into his touch, in need of the affection. "I wish you could talk."

"I'm glad they can't. Pearl would probably complain our ears off," Carlos said from Jim's right. "I brushed Pearl down and gave her some water and fresh hay. Jolly looks comfortable enough. Are you ready?"

With Pearl and Jolly both taken care of, there was nothing left to do but go back to the dorm room. "Yeah," Jim said.

The sky was dark gray when they entered the men's housing. With each step Jim climbed, his body felt heavier. Walking down the hallway was one of the most tiring things he had ever done, because he was fighting with every shuffle not to turn around and continue the search. When they reached the room and the door closed behind him, it became official. Anna would remain missing for yet another night.

"You need to eat something, Jim," Carlos told him softly and then proceeded to fish some jerky and leftover bread out of a bag that hung on the bedpost. The only reason that Jim ate any of it at all was because of Carlos' concern.

"Did she just ride off ahead?" Jim asked, suddenly, surprising himself.

Carlos hesitated for a minute, as though weighing the question. "Yeah, pretty much."

Jim figured it was something simple like that. Anna could be impulsive; it was the main trait that drew him to her like a moth to a flame. She thought with her heart. And he had always liked that about her. *No.* That was wrong. He didn't just like that about her. *I love that about her.*

And now he didn't know if she were dead or alive. She could be injured and bleeding. She could already be dead. He didn't know and it was eating him up on the inside, like so many other things. He hated himself for not telling her how he felt. *Now, I may never get the chance.* It would serve him right.

After a cold dinner, Jim found himself in bed. And even though he fought to stay awake with his worry, it wore him out. He finally fell asleep in the small hours of the morning and his dreams were vivid nightmares of darkness and beasts, strange lights and noises. But then they, too, faded into nothingness as his body claimed the rest it so desperately needed.

CHAPTER SEVEN

Carlos was losing sleep by the handfuls. Anna's disappearance was an anchor around his neck and he was sinking fast. For three days, he and Jim had searched for Anna at Deer Mountain, with no luck. Rumors had begun spreading at St. James that Anna was dead. And their reasoning for not being able to find a body? She was probably eaten by wolves and there's nothing left. It was a harsh reality to face, but completely plausible. That's why Carlos didn't want to believe it.

To believe that fate for Anna would be awful...*at best*. As long as she was found alive, he wasn't a murderer. Carlos wanted to crawl out of his skin and escape the shame that he felt. All he had to do was *not* kiss her, and then none of it would have happened. "Dammit!" Carlos swore under his breath as he descended the stairs of the men's dorm.

There was only two days left of the summer break. Two days left to find Anna, before he would admit that she was most likely dead. Carlos swallowed hard. The worst of it all was watching Jim decline as it became apparent that Anna may not be found alive. But what more could he do? Jim felt like it was a waste of time to visit the Sheriff's office again. And Carlos didn't want to continue to search Deer Mountain aimlessly. They were at an impasse.

Carlos looked across the campus lawn and spotted Jim at the bench where he had first met Anna. It had become a habit for Jim to visit that spot. *Almost like he expects she'll just show up, one day.* He trotted over. "Look, I've been thinking," Carlos said tactfully. "Wandering around the mountain from day to day isn't working and neither is expecting the sheriff to do his job."

"What else can we do?" Jim asked with a touch of exasperation seeping around the words.

Carlos ignored it. "Why don't we go to the paper and talk to Mr.

Turner? He has experience with cases involving disappearances and he also has experience in dealing with Sheriff Ghetts. I think he might be able to help."

Hope flashed in Jim's eyes. "You might be right. It has to be better than what we've been doing, right?"

"That was my way of thinking," Carlos told him. Jim didn't need any more convincing. He was ready to try anything else. His brother had been nothing but desperate to find Anna. *Because, he loves her…and I killed her.* He knew he should stop with the self-accusations. It was just a kiss. *That started a lethal chain reaction.* No matter how hard he tried, he still could envision nothing except the worst.

"He might even do a story in the paper."

"Possibly," Carlos said. "It's worth the effort, anyway."

Jim had taken over care of Jolly. So he was astride Anna's horse, while Carlos wrestled the reins of the temperamental Pearl, as they travelled the familiar road to Clinton. After a quick breakfast, they found the Clinton Weekly office.

The bell jingled as they opened the door and crossed the threshold. The smell of fresh ink and reams of paper permeated the office. There were two people working on the press. When they heard the ringing of the bell, they turned. Carlos was quick to spot Mr. Turner on the right. "Carlos, Jim! What a nice surprise. What brings you to the paper?" Then he turned to his coworker, "I think we're about finished up here. Let's do a test print, okay?" Then Mr. Turner pulled a kerchief from his pocket and wiped the smeared ink from his hand before he extended it in a warm greeting.

Jim was quick to shake the man's hand. Carlos worried about the transfer of any wayward ink as he gripped the newspaper man's hand, firmly. Mr. Turner invited them to take a seat in a small office located just to the right of the front entrance. Once inside, with the doors closed to the noisy press, Jim told Lloyd all he knew of Anna's disappearance and the subsequent search. Carlos kept his mouth closed. No one needed to know the part he played in Anna going missing…*at least not yet.*

"The similarities between the two cases are striking, and I suppose that's why you're here," Lloyd said.

"Yes," Jim answered. "We're hoping you might be able to help."

"This new case really opens the eyes. There's no way that Sheriff Ghetts can continue to ignore this." Lloyd wrote some things down on a piece of paper. "I'd like to come out to the school and do some investigating. Someone may know something, and while they wouldn't be willing to share the information with the sheriff, they might feel more at ease talking to me."

"Yeah, that sounds great," Jim said, appreciatively. "If you need an extra hand around here, I'd like to help out. I do some writing."

Carlos couldn't be more shocked. He didn't know any of that. "Seriously?"

Jim ignored his question.

Lloyd smiled. "I can use all the help I can get around here. It's just me and Mr. Potts. Mr. Mathews left. Went back home to Louisiana. Sold me the place for a song." Lloyd shook his head in disbelief. "I'd like to see some of your work, and if it's up to par, you're hired."

The shock crushed Carlos like a ton of bricks. "What about your studies?"

Again, Jim ignored him. Anna's disappearance was changing his brother in ways he couldn't even fathom. And he could blame no one, but himself.

"To begin with, the job will be part time," Lloyd said, "so I'm sure that you'll have time for school." But, even this statement did little to calm Carlos' internal turmoil. His mind was so busy working that he didn't even hear the rest of the conversation.

Before he knew it, Jim was standing, saying, "Thank you, Mr. Turner." Carlos stood, as well.

"What was all that about?" Carlos asked, when they were back outside and on the street.

Jim looked weary, and he seemed to be aging overnight. "I think it's a good way to stay close to the investigation. And you heard, Lloyd. It's only part time."

"Okay." It was all Carlos could say. He wouldn't press any

further, even though his mind was chewing him up on the inside. And he couldn't help but keep returning to the same thought. *This is my fault.*

**

Jim couldn't believe how easy it had been to convince Carlos of his joining the newspaper staff. He would have smiled to so easily get his way, except that he wasn't proud of the way he had done it. The other thing that had permanently removed the joy from his face was the disappearance of the woman he loved. It ripped his heart out…*a little each day.*

Why had she ridden off? Carlos was worried because she had been drinking. That worried Jim, as well. But, why did she ride up into the mountain? She should have followed the road. The terrain in the mountain was treacherous in the dark. *Everyone knows that.* And Anna was not an idiot. He had reminded himself, more than once, that she was more than capable of taking care of herself. But if that were truly the case…*where is she?*

The thoughts were wheels, turning circles in his mind. It had been this way for days, his mind on an endless loop.

"What would you like to do now, Jim?" Carlos asked when they had reached the horses.

"Go back to St. James and wait on Mr. Turner. He said he would be coming out this afternoon. Didn't you hear him, Carlos?" Jim asked his brother.

Dark circles from a lack of sleep had begun to ring Carlos' eyes, just like his own. "I guess I must have missed it."

Jim suddenly felt guilty for having pushed his brother so hard since Anna's disappearance. "We could both use some rest."

"That, we could." Carlos answered. Jim heard the doubt in his voice. He knew the feeling all too well. It was the feeling of being bone weary and knowing that there was no real rest in the future.

Jim couldn't believe how his life had turned. One day, he was thinking about a future with Anna. The next, that future was snatched away. He had always been the type of person to live for the moment and the moment he had wanted to plan for the next, it was gone. The whole thing was so unfair. *"Life is often unfair,"* his mother had told him more than once. *"That's why you need to make the most of it, Jim. Time is gone before you know it."*

Had he only heeded her advice, Anna would have at least known how he felt for her before... He couldn't finish the thought. It hurt too bad, dug too deeply.

When they made it back to St. James, it was just as Jim had suspected. There would be no rest. George was waiting for them at the stables. "A message came while you were away. It's not good," George said.

"Has someone found Anna?" Jim asked, suddenly intent on George's every word.

"I'm sorry Jim, no," George was quick to reply. "It's your father. He's sick."

Jim didn't know how much more bad news he could handle. Carlos stood stock still, beside him. "Did the message say what's wrong with him?" Carlos asked. His face was a mixture of tiredness and fear, and Jim imagined that it echoed his own.

"The message was sent by someone named Lobo Joe. He says your father has tick bite sickness," George answered, "They sent a telegram into town, this morning, so I knew it was serious." Lobo Joe was an Indian who had been a longtime family friend. Joe would often check in on their father since he and Carlos had left for school.

"Tick bite sickness," Carlos whispered. "I need to go home."

"I can't go, Carlos," Jim said, torn between wanting to see his father and abandoning the search for the woman he loved.

"There's no need," Carlos said and squeezed Jim's shoulder, understanding. "You're needed here."

Jim was relieved that Carlos did indeed understand. He needed to find Anna, and at the very least, he needed to find out what happened to her. "Make father understand."

"I will," Carlos replied.

"If you want, Carlos, I can gather some medical supplies from here at the school that may help your father, while you pack,"

George offered.

"That would be great, George. Thank you for all your help, and not just with this…with Anna, too," Jim told George.

George beamed. "It's no trouble. This is what I'm here for."

Soon after, Jim found himself inside the dorm room, helping Carlos get his things together. He heaved the heavy trunk out from under the bed. After placing it on the bed, he opened it. The trunk had been his father's and the smell of the man still lingered. *Hoyt's Nickle Cologne.* His father had worn it for years.

Carlos began filling the trunk with clothes. Jim grabbed his brother's books and shaving kit and easily found a spot for them inside the large trunk. Moments later, the trunk was closed and latched. "Are you sure that you don't want me to help you get it to the stables?" Jim asked for the second time.

"I can manage just fine. Besides," Carlos said, "I would rather that you try to get some rest before Mr. Turner arrives."

Jim nodded, reluctantly, "Okay, be careful." Carlos reached out his hand to shake and Jim grabbed his brother and pulled him to him, hugging him. "Take care of father, Carlos. I love you."

Carlos looked at him, thoughtfully, for a moment, as though he had something to tell him. Then his brother sighed, "You will find her, Jim. Just be careful in those mountains. I love you, too, brother." And then he was gone.

Jim looked around the empty room. It felt so lonely, but after a few minutes of looking at the bed, he accepted its invitation. The pillowcase was cool to the skin of his cheek as he allowed his sleep debt to take its due.

CHAPTER EIGHT

Carlos left the men's housing and was soon back at the stables in no time. Twice, he had had to keep himself from turning around and telling Jim about the kiss. He would tell him later. *Now, just isn't the right time.* After she was found, he would tell him then. He owed them both an apology and it wasn't one he wanted to repeat.

He had just finished hitching the cart to Pearl, when George arrived with a small wooden crate. "There's some Japanese knotweed and some cat's claw. Dr. Gray said these will help to kill the sickness in the body. There's also some various teas, that may help to sooth the pain."

"Thank you, George. I honestly don't know what I would have done without you," Carlos said as he put the precious medicine under the driver's seat. Then he shook George's hand, climbed into the car, and left St. James, headed for home.

The trip would take two days of hard travel, if all went well. After only a mile, he was so tired, it was hard not to stop. But, worry for his father managed to keep him in the driver's seat. His mind felt split into, half his mind was with his father, half his mind was with Jim and Anna and none of his mind was on the road in front of him.

He was startled when he looked up and spotted another rider, not more than fifty yards in front of him. As the rider drew closer, he could see that it was Mr. Turner. Carlos pulled back on the reins and Pearl came to a stop.

"Carlos, I thought I was going to meet you and Jim at the university?" Lloyd said as his horse stopped trotting.

"We've had bad news from home. Our father is ill. Jim is staying, though. He's waiting for you."

"I'm sorry to hear it. I hope your father's health returns," Mr. Turner said.

"Thank you, Lloyd. I do, too," Carlos told him. "If you'll excuse me, I need to be on my way."

"Of course, I wouldn't want to keep you. Safe travels, Mr. Castle," Lloyd said.

"To you, as well," Carlos replied. He loosened his hold on the reins and Pearl, once again, set the cart in motion.

About five miles on the other side of Clinton, he was ready to drop. So he stopped at the first inn, in the first town he came to. His meal was hot and his room was small and tidy. In fact, being away from Jim and Anna's situation, along with the knowledge that he had a plan of attack when it came to his father's illness, allowed him the best night's sleep he'd had in days.

Leaving well before sunrise, he made good time the next day and decided to press on into the evening in order to get on home. It was dark when he finally rode up to the house. Lobo Joe met him outside, carrying a lantern. His long dark hair left ghostly shadows across the old Indian's face. Carlos traded the reins to Joe in exchange for the light. "How is he?" Carlos asked, anxious, skipping the friendly greetings.

"He rests, now," Joe said. Dark eyes studied Carlos. "Go on in, but try not to wake him. We didn't expect you until tomorrow. Where's Jim?"

"I'll fill you in, inside. It's been a very long day," Carlos said. He'd been alone with his thoughts all day. He was looking forward to interactions, if only to still his overactive mind. But first, he needed to see to his father.

"There's some leftover supper on the stove, if you're hungry. I'll be there in a bit," Joe said, and then patted Pearl's neck. "I'll just see to this old girl." Carlos grabbed the box of medicine that George had gathered for him from under the driver's seat and then went inside the house from his childhood.

In the months that he and Carlos had been gone, nothing had changed in his father's house. The same green drapes hung over the window in the living room. The third floorboard from the kitchen still creaked. And the stove was still made level by a smooth piece of river rock. *Nothing has been altered, in any way.* But, he hadn't really expected it, either.

He set the box down in the kitchen, grabbed a kettle of water, and put it on the hot stove. Then he went to look for his father.

Soft snores greeted him outside his father's bedroom. Carlos twisted the knob, gently, and stole inside the room. A small lamp burned low in the corner, casting a soft yellow light. His father lay in his bed, covers up to his chin. He gently pulled back the covers. After a quick inspection, he found the common rash that normally accompanied the often-fatal illness. A light touch to the forehead told him his father also had the fever, another common symptom of tick bite sickness.

Joe was right, there was no need in waking his father, just yet. There was no doubt his father needed every bit of res t he could get. He would prepare a tea out of the herbs, first. He knew he needed to go ahead and start a treatment regimen. So he quietly left the room. When he got to the kitchen, the kettle was steaming. He'd just begun to grind the herbs, when Joe came inside. "When did he fall sick?" Carlos asked.

"He started feeling really tired about a week ago," Joe began. "A day later and his joints started hurting him so bad that the pain sent him to his bed. We thought he might just have a cold. But, when the rash came a few hours later, I knew. That's when I sent for you."

Carlos continued to grind his herbs. "These are some medicines that Doctor Gray thought would help. Has he been able to keep anything down?"

"No food. Just some drink and sometimes, it still comes up," Joe said. "Coffee?" he asked. When Carlos nodded, Joe pulled down two cups from the cupboard and filled them from the pot on the stove. Carlos ceased in his grinding just long enough to take a healthy drink of the strong brew.

Refreshed by the coffee, he had the herbs in cheesecloth, steeping in a small amount of water. It would just be a couple of sips, but there should be enough medicine to pack a punch. Carlos knew he couldn't miss but a couple of days of classes before he would risk falling too far behind. He needed his father well, *quickly*.

It was almost a relief to focus on something other than Anna's disappearance, but that relief was short-lived.

"So, you want to tell me why your brother did not come, Carlos?" Joe asked.

Carlos took another long drink of coffee. Then he told Joe everything. He told him about Anna and Jim's whirlwind romance. He told him about Jim's sickness. He told him about the festival. He even told him about the kiss. Somehow, he knew Joe would never judge him for it. And when he told him about Anna's disappearance, Joe's expression never changed.

"So Jim is searching for her. It was the right call," Joe said.

"Yes," Carlos thought... *but for whom?*

Just then, a weak call echoed through the house. "Clara..." It was his father's voice, calling his mother's name.

"He's awake. His pain must be bad if ghosts are visiting his bedside," Joe said, standing.

Carlos removed the cheesecloth of herbs from the hot concoction, quickly straining it and setting it aside for the next use. Then he scooped up the medicine and followed Joe to his father's room.

After a few minutes of trying to talk rationally with his father, Carlos gave up and had Joe hold his father as he forced the medicine down. It was torture to watch his father's mind go. He talked to Carlos, as if he and Jim were still children. He called for his dead wife, more than once, and each time he did, Carlos' heart would break. He would fight to get up from his sickbed, only to be so weak that he would fall back down into the covers. It was a gut-wrenching process for Carlos.

When the medicine finally took hold, his father fell into a deep sleep. Joe brought in blankets and pillows and made Carlos a pallet on the floor. He had told Joe that it wasn't necessary, he could doze perfectly fine in the oversized chair. But sometime before dawn, he crawled down onto the pallet and slept for hours.

When he woke, the sun was high in the sky. He rose with purpose, anxious to lay eyes on his father. He was sure that another dose of medicine was long past due. Thankfully, his father was still asleep.

Carlos slipped from the room, rubbing the sleep from his eyes. As soon as he opened the door, the smell of bacon and fresh coffee infiltrated his nose, crawling for his stomach. He realized, then, that he couldn't remember the last time he'd ate. He found Joe in the kitchen, his tall frame, bent over the stove, frying eggs and bacon for breakfast. "Sit," he said and put a cup of coffee on the table in front of him.

"But I need to give him another dose."

"I already gave it to him," Joe said. "You need to eat."

Carlos sat down and gripped the mug, allowing the heat to relax the muscles in his hand. After a moment or two, he took a long sip. Soon, Joe had a steaming plate of scrambled eggs and bacon placed at two settings. Carlos dug in, like a man half starved. When he was done, he drained his cup, washing down the saltiness of the bacon. Then he cleared their plates and set about washing them. "How was he, when you gave him the medicine?" Carlos asked, drying a plate.

"Much better than last night. He no longer sees ghosts. You had the more fitful of sleeps in your father's room. Your spirit is eaten away by your betrayal to your brother," Joe said. "And you think too little of your brother, if you think him incapable of forgiveness and understanding."

"I don't want him to forgive me. I don't deserve it," Carlos said.

"You need to forgive yourself, first, Carlos."

Joe was too smart for his own good. He'd always had a way of seeing the forest, no matter how many trees there were growing up out of the ground. Carlos did need to forgive himself. Maybe he could, if he could find the right time to apologize. "I don't know if that's possible. Can't you see that all of this is my fault, Joe?"

"The girl did not see it that way. She shared the blame or she wouldn't have acted that way," Joe replied, simply.

Carlos hadn't really thought about that. He had been so wrapped up in his shame. Anna had returned the kiss with vigor. Heat rushed over his skin as he remembered. Of course, she had felt a portion of the blame when her feelings had betrayed her. Carlos also knew the dark thoughts he had entertained, shortly after, when his shame had mingled with the alcohol, nearly overwhelming him. He had thought of leaving school, leaving Jim, leaving everything and everyone he ever knew. Could Anna have had similar thoughts...*or worse?*

He didn't know and he really didn't have time to care.

"Carlos...Joe..." His father called out, weakly. Carlos pushed the thoughts of Anna far from his mind. His father needed his undivided attention, and he would give it to him, regardless of how much Lobo Joe might nag him.

"Carlos." His father smiled, faintly. Carlos had been wrong. Something *had* changed since he had left to become a doctor. The lines in his father's face had deepened and he had aged years in a matter of months.

"Father," Carlos said as he reached the man's side.

Warn and knotty hands found his own. "It is good to see you, son."

"You, too, father. How are you feeling?" Carlos asked, concerned. His father's color was still pale and the rash was still present.

"Better, now that you're here. Where's Jim?" His eyes searched around the room.

"He stayed at school. Someone needed to hold the fort down," Carlos, said. He put a hand on his father's forehead. He was still hot, but not as hot as he'd been twelve hours earlier, when his mind was stuck in the past.

Carlos looked at Joe, "The medicine seems to be working."

Joe nodded. "Time will tell."

**

Jim felt lost without Carlos. If it hadn't been for George and Lloyd keeping him focused, Jim would have still been wandering aimlessly around the foothills of Deer Mountain. Lloyd had hired him immediately after reading his first written work. "This is really good, Jim. You are a talented writer. You have a gift for opinion pieces."

Jim had smiled for the first time since Anna's disappearance, listening to Mr. Turner's compliments about his work. "Really?" he had asked, in disbelief.

"Really. The pieces are quite interesting," Lloyd had said, smiling. "When can you start?"

"Is today too soon?" Jim asked, feeling excitement for the first time in days. The fact that he could allow himself to feel excited about something so soon after losing Anna, made him feel guilty beyond measure. And all Jim had to do to contain his excitement was let his mind wander to Anna and the fact that she was possibly dead.

The investigation had been a bust, so far. Lloyd had talked to some of her classmates and her professors, but none of them had offered any information that was particularly helpful. In fact, the only helpful advice had come directly to him from George Kinley, his student advisor.

"Professor Smith is leading that field expedition to Deer Mountain, in a couple of weeks. I've heard that they go all over the mountain on those trips. I'm not sure, but I think he's still taking volunteers. If he is, you should sign up; it will give you an opportunity to expand your search. You might even find something," George had told him. Jim was always afraid of what that something might be. He had heard the whispers. Most of the students at St. James had written off the possibility of anyone finding Anna alive.

"Thanks, George," Jim said. It was solid advice, and had he been thinking more clearly, he wouldn't have needed it. He would have signed up for the expedition days ago. But, he hadn't been thinking, at all...*it's just been too much.*

That was why he was jogging across the campus grounds to the lecture hall, at that moment. *What if they've stopped taking volunteers?* His thoughts were all doom and gloom as he walked through the doors of the lecture hall. The hall was busy with students moving black boxes and packing them inside wooden crates. Jim stopped a short, brown haired girl with a nice smile by the door on her way out, "Is Professor Smith still taking volunteers for the field expedition?" he asked.

"Yeah, there are three spots left. If you're wanting to go, you had best sign up soon. Once the classes start back, tomorrow, those spots will fill up quickly. I can't wait. Can you imagine? What if we find one of those half-evolved humans?" the girl asked, as if they were old friends.

"It would be something," Jim said, barely audible. He left the girl, standing, and went down to the tables. After a quick scan, he located the signup sheet. The girl was right. There were three empty spaces down at the bottom of the paper. He added his name to the list. And directly below his name, he added his brother's.

He mentally checked that task off his list of things to do. Next, on the list was a trip into town. He hadn't been to the Sheriff's office in a couple of days...*and it never hurts to prod a stray bull.* The sheriff had been exactly what Mr. Turner had said he was...*completely useless.* And to make it worse, the man had been stubborn in his uselessness. He had insisted that Anna would turn up the next day, for two consecutive days. And when she didn't, he didn't go search for her. He had changed his tune entirely, saying, "I'm sorry, son. The bears or the coyotes probably got to her."

It had been all that Jim could do not to buy a gun and shoot the man. But, he had never been the violent sort. And he hadn't needed any trouble. "Besides," Lloyd had reminded him, at the time, "You have the power of the press at your disposal. And he's an elected official."

Jim left the lecture hall, heading for the stables. George joined him, matching his stride. "Hi, George. Just signed up for the field expedition. I hope you're right and we find something that will tell us what happened to Anna," he told the man. Jim had grown to like George. He was smart, helpful, and a very good friend. He had been out with Jim a couple of times, searching for Anna, since Carlos had left to care for their father. He had organized the search where they had found Jolly. And it had been his idea, to sign up for the expedition.

"I do, too," George said. "What do you have planned, today?"

"I'm riding into town. Sheriff Ghetts is really starting to irritate me. After that, I have to go to the newspaper office," Jim replied.

"So, you aren't going to the mountain?" George asked

"Not today."

"Then I think I'll bow out today. I have some studying to do before classes start back tomorrow." It seemed to Jim like George felt awful for abandoning him to his own devices that day.

Jim did his best to smile at his friend. "Don't worry about it," Jim said, sincerely. "I'll catch up to you tomorrow after class and fill you in."

After a friendly pat on Jim's shoulder, George was gone, leaving Jim's mind to wander. Since he was at a standstill in his search for Anna, his thoughts roamed primarily to his father and Carlos. He was worried that he should have gone with his brother. He had found nothing that could lead him to Anna. So far, his staying had been pointless.

Jolly seemed happy to see him, when he entered the stables. Jim fished a carrot from his pocket. Jolly whinnied. "I'm glad to see you, too." He told the horse. After a few moments, Jim had the horse saddled and was gone, leaving St. James and heading towards Clinton. When he reached the fork in the road, where he normally turned the reins towards Deer Mountain, he pulled them to the right, veering toward town.

Gray clouds darkened the skies above Clinton, threatening to spill down onto the dusty streets below. The rain would be welcome, so long as it stayed more than just a few minutes. There was nothing worse in the hot summer, than a short rain driving up the humidity. *I'll take a dry heat, any day of the week.*

Jim made his way down the street to the sheriff's office, a small, one-story building with a crooked sign and fading paint. He swung open the door and stepped inside. He had made it no more than two steps, before a deputy called out to him, around a mouthful of chewing tobacco, "Sheriff Ghetts ain't here, Mr. Castle." *It's a wonder he can speak at all.*

"When do you expect him back?" Jim asked, cordially.

"Probably tomorrow. There was some trouble out at the Carlson ranch. Probably Bo and Itty up to no good, like usual." The man spit brown tobacco juice on the floor.

Jim was genuinely surprised that Sheriff Ghetts was actually out doing something along the lines of his job, because so far, he couldn't see what good the sheriff's office was up until this point. "Tell him I stopped by." Jim walked back out the door without another word.

He stepped back out onto the boardwalk, just in time to see the first few drops of rain splatter onto the dusty street. He picked up his pace, hoping to gain the newspaper office before the downpour. He barely made it inside the safety of the small building before the sky opened up, releasing a surge of water that seemed to cascade, rather than fall in tiny droplets.

The bell at the top of the door announced his arrival, but the sound of it was soon lost behind a loud clap of thunder that rattled the window panes of the Clinton Weekly. "Jim!" he heard Lloyd cry out behind him. "You just barely made it before the deluge."

Jim turned to see his friend and employer. Lloyd's hands were covered in ink, as usual. "Owning one of these things, isn't all it is cracked up to be," Lloyd said, head nodding at the old press.

"She down, again?" Jim asked, shedding his wet jacket and hanging it on a rack by the door.

"Yeah, one of the rows came loose again. Crazy thing was printing every other line. I tell you if it ain't one thing, it's another in this business. You sure you want to be a part of it?" Lloyd asked, wiping his hands on a kerchief.

Jim was absolutely certain. Being a journalist was what he had always wanted to do. "I'm positive."

"Good, I want you to write an article."

Already? Jim couldn't believe his ears. "What about?"

"Well, if you can truly be objective about it, we need to write up the story on Anna's disappearance and see if we can tie a connection to Miss. Bledsoe's case. Can you do it?" Lloyd asked.

The thought of it made him feel wonderful and terrible, all at the same time. On one hand, he was happy to be writing his first journalism article. On the other, the subject matter was a weighted noose around his neck, threatening to squeeze. *Am I too close to be objective?* It was a legitimate concern. After a moment or two of hesitation, he nodded, "I believe so." And he would do his best to keep his opinions to himself.

"Good, good. I would do it myself, but I can't. Our new advertisement section has generated quite the buzz and I simply don't have time. Besides," Lloyd said, smiling, "I have complete faith in my new journalist."

Jim smiled, hoping that he could live up to Mr. Turner's expectations.

CHAPTER NINE

Carlos looked out the window of his father's bedroom at the building turmoil in the sky. The dark clouds churned in the soupy gray sky. At odd intervals, a flash of lightning would illuminate the room, but so far, not even a drop had fallen. "It'll be coming down, soon," his father said weakly from the bed.

"Yes," Carlos said, hoping for clear skies the next day. He had stayed as long as he dared. Classes had started back that day and he really couldn't afford an even longer absence because of inclement weather.

Carlos left the window and poured a glass of water from a pitcher at the bedside table. He held the glass to cracking, dry lips and waited, patiently, for his father to drink his fill.

"Thank you, Carlos. You're a good boy," his father whispered.

Carlos felt his forehead. There was no sign of fever and the rash was fading by the hour. The medicine seemed to be doing the trick. But, tick bite sickness was a funny thing, often abating just to show back up later to finish the job. *Please, don't let that be the case, here.* "You say that now, but when we were children, you did not think so. I saw the wrong side of your belt, more than once."

His father's laugh turned into a coughing fit and the sound was a haggard rattle in the room. Carlos held a kerchief to his father's mouth until the fit had subsided. "Thank you," his father managed, weakly.

"I'll have to leave tomorrow, father. But Joe knows how to prepare your medicine and you seem to be doing better as time goes by," Carlos said. A loud drum of thunder shook the house, punctuating his sentence.

"Don't worry about me. I'll be fine. I know you need to get back to your studies, Carlos," he said, and took a long deep breath, sighing. "Your mother would be so proud of you, boys," his father whispered.

Carlos didn't say anything and within moments, his father had begun snoring softly. He had been in and out of consciousness since Carlos had arrived.

Carlos slipped from the room, looking for Joe. He found him outside, shuttering the windows before the storm. With his father asleep, Carlos had nothing better to do than to help prepare for the storm. After all the animals had been shut up in the barn and all the doors and shutters closed against the wind, they retreated into the safety of the farmhouse to weather the storm.

Within moments of Carlos and Joe stepping inside, the wind began to howl. Sheets of rain lashed at the siding and flashes of light found their way around the cracks in the shutters, illuminating the room with every loud smack of thunder. The storm was a wild thing, as though it were alive.

Carlos set a kettle of water on the stove to boil for some coffee and then found Joe in the living room, with his boots kicked off and his feet propped up. "I'm making some fresh coffee, if you want some," he said, sitting down on the sofa.

Joe grunted, affirmatively.

Beside him on the end table, Carlos lit the small oil lamp. His book on anatomy was within arm's reach, so he decided to do some studying while he waited on both the coffee and the worst of the storm. But after a few minutes of looking at the pages, Carlos gave up on studying. His mind was miles away, looking for Anna. He was also worried about Jim. He really hadn't considered Jim finding Anna while he was gone as a possibility, until that moment, as the storm raged outside. But now that he had entertained the thought, it was eating him alive. *What if Jim found Anna and she told him about the kiss?* Jim would never forgive him. Carlos had had days to tell Jim the truth...*and I didn't.*

But, the timing has never been right. It was a sorry excuse. Carlos knew it. But, it was the only one he had. Carlos found himself pacing, without even realizing he'd gotten up from his seat.

"You're too nervous," Joe said, from under his hat. "You're

making me nervous."

"Sorry," Carlos apologized. *I have a lot on my mind.*

Carlos left the room, allowing the smell of a fresh brew to lead him into the kitchen. He returned, moments later, with two cups of steaming, dark liquid. He handed one to Joe, then took his cup to the sofa. He sipped, allowing the warmth to travel to his extremities, while the storm dumped a small lake overhead.

An hour's worth of storm later and Carlos could barely hold his eyes open. The constant roar was lulling him to sleep. He curled up on the couch and let his body relax. He was asleep in minutes.

When Carlos woke, the storm was nothing but a memory. The constant roar had been replaced by the chirping of birds in the trees outside. Joe had already opened the shutters on the windows and let in the sunshine, by the time his eyes opened.

He felt stiff from his time on the couch, so he stood and stretched. Then he gathered the cup of cold coffee and carried it back into the kitchen. After checking on his father, he went outside. The wooden floorboards of the porch were sill soaked and the ground was riddled with fresh puddles that were drying up fast in the summer sun. The air smelled as though it had been washed clean. He took a long deep breath and then stepped off the porch, heading to the barn.

Once inside, he gave the horses some fresh hay and repaired a spoke on the wheel of the cart that had come loose on his way back home. He needed something to keep his mind off things he couldn't change and that was the good thing about being on a farm. *There's always work to be done.* And work was a proper distraction.

After repairing one of the stall doors in the barn, Carlos went inside to get some lunch and check on his father. A pot of stew was already boiling on the stove when Carlos entered the kitchen, and a loaf of two-day-old bread lay sliced on the counter. Joe was already at the table with a piping hot bowl in front of him.

"Jack looks much better today."

"Yeah, I'm hoping he'll be able to keep something other than medicine down, today," Carlos said as he scooped a ladleful of stew into a bowl. "I gave the horses some fresh hay and repaired the stall door in the barn."

Joe grunted his approval around a mouthful of stew.

Carlos grabbed a slice of bread and used it to sop up the savory broth. After two bowls, he'd had his fill. Grabbing a clean bowl, he skimmed some broth off the top and filled it for his father. He also placed a piece of bread on a saucer and carried it, along with the broth, to his father's room.

Carlos hated to wake his father, but he also knew that eating was the only way his father would ever regain his strength. After setting the saucer and bowl down on the table beside the bed, he opened the drapes and let the sunshine flood into the room.

Carlos had to help his father sit up in bed and that action alone, nearly wore the man out. "Thank you, Carlos." His father's voice was barely above a whisper.

"I've brought you some broth and bread. It should help you get your strength back," Carlos told him and then proceeded to feed his father by hand. After about ten spoonful's of broth and two bites of bread, his father was done, and although Carlos wished his father had eaten more, he was genuinely happy with what he *had* eaten. *It's a start, anyway.*

By that evening, his father's color was better and he was eating another bowl of broth, this time, feeding himself. It was a slow go, but it was definite progress, and Carlos' decision to leave the next day to head back to school didn't weigh on him nearly as much, because of it. As long as there was no relapse, his father's health should return over the next few days. *He'll be himself in no time.* Carlos was convinced of it.

**

Jim was about to attend his last class of the day, when he spotted a familiar form hauling a trunk across the lawn. *Carlos.* He took off towards him with mixed emotions. He couldn't help but feel anxious for news of his father, and yet, he didn't want to admit to Carlos that he hadn't found a single clue about Anna's whereabouts. The only reason he stayed was because he was convinced he would find Anna. And yet, he hadn't.

"Jim! It's good to see you," Carlos said and hugged him.

"You too, Carlos. How is father?" Jim asked him, worry creeping into his voice.

"He was doing better when I left. But I still worry for him. Tick bit sickness is known for coming back," Carlos said. Jim knew that far too often, the victims of tick bite sickness would have periods of remission. Very few actually survived and those who did, usually suffered with other ailments the rest of their lives. "He said to tell you that he loved you, he was proud of you, and you made the right decision."

"I'm not so sure about that," Jim said, getting to the point he had been dreading. "I haven't found Anna."

"I'm sorry, Jim," his brother replied, though Jim had thought he detected relief flash across Carlos' face, but it was so out of character that he shrugged it off.

It couldn't be. Why would Carlos be relieved that I haven't found Anna? It was a preposterous notion that he easily flung away from his mind. "It's not your fault, Carlos. I'm glad father is doing better. How was Joe?" Jim asked, genuinely curious about Carlos' visit home.

"As serious as ever," Carlos said, smiling. Jim laughed. He had missed his brother. "So, are you a reporter now? Did Lloyd hire you?"

"Yeah," Jim answered. "He said I was really good at it, Carlos."

Carlos opened his trunk, right there on the lawn. He pulled a bottle of bourbon from inside. "I think we should celebrate," his brother said.

Carlos was right. And if Anna were there, she would agree, as well. Jim had earned the right to be happy for a moment. His father was better. He had a new job that he loved. He had his brother to support him. There were more than enough reasons to celebrate. "Sure, I just have this last class—"

"Forget the class, Jim. Today, it isn't important. We'll worry about important things, tomorrow."

And so they spent the rest of the day, holed up in their dorm room, smoking cigars and trying to find the bottom of the bourbon bottle.

CHAPTER TEN

Carlos spent the next day catching up on his classes. He hadn't missed so much time that a few extra hours reading wouldn't fix. He hated bowing out on Jim, but it would be better if he spent the time alone.

At least that was what he kept telling himself.

The truth was that he was avoiding the issue of Anna. He couldn't do it forever, he knew. But, the longer he waited, the harder it was becoming. A small part of himself even entertained the notion of not telling Jim about the kiss, at all. *What good would it do?*

Anna would still be missing. And worse, Jim would hate him at that point.

So he found himself inside the library after his last class, while Jim rode Jolly into Clinton to turn in the article he had been working on for the paper.

Carlos was still trying to wrap his mind around the fact that Jim was working for the paper. He wondered how much he didn't really know about his brother. It bothered him. Why hadn't Jim told him about his love for writing? *Probably because it didn't fit into my plan for him…for us.*

But, what right did he have to decide Jim's future? Carlos had let no one decide his own future. He had known he would be a doctor since his mother had died. *And I'd known that Jim would be a doctor, too.*

"Oh my god," Carlos said, snapping his book shut and tossing it on the table in front of him. Why had Jim allowed himself to be pushed into something he probably didn't want to do? *Because, he didn't want to let me down.*

"I am such an idiot," Carlos whispered loudly.

"And a noisy one," a man said to his right. Carlos had been so absorbed in his thoughts that he'd forgotten where he was.

He looked over to see a fellow student leaned back on the soft leather sofa, reading a book. "Sorry," Carlos said.

Studying was useless when his mind was thick with stewing thoughts, so he grabbed his book, stuffed it into his bag, and left the library. His mind spat out accusation after accusation as he crossed the campus lawn. *What have I done to Jim?* He had forced his own ideals on his brother. And by doing that, he had, in essence, stolen Jim's future. And when that wasn't good enough, he had tried to steal his girl, too. *And what right have I ever had to feel jealous of J—*

"Mr. Castle!" Carlos' thoughts stopped dead in their tracks from the interruption coming from behind him. When he turned around, Professor Smith waved him over. Carlos held back an exasperated sigh that quickly turned into a yawn.

Putting on a smile, he trotted back the way he had come. "Professor Smith," he said throwing out his hand in greeting. The man's hands were small and the handshake was limp affair that Carlos contributed to the man's age.

"It's good to see you, again, Mr. Castle," the man said, smiling. "I noticed you signed up for the expedition and I was wondering if you'd be willing to help me run equipment tests," the professor began. When Carlos hesitated, he was quick to add, "After classes, of course."

The man's blue eyes sparkled with hope. Carlos thought for a moment, "Sure." With Jim spending most of his free time either searching for Anna or working at the paper, Carlos was glad to have something to do that would occupy his thoughts. Left alone to his own devices, he would surely go mad.

"Wonderful news," Professor Smith said. "Come with me." The man moved faster than Carlos would have expected and he had to walk quickly to keep up.

When they gained the lecture hall, Carlos realized that he was just one of several volunteers. He spotted George wearing one of the strange devices that the professor had made him wear the last time he sought Carlos' help. George noticed him too and waved. Carlos threw his hand up as he followed the professor to the long table.

"Now that we have enough hands on deck it's time to see if multiple signals can be differentiated and detected," the professor said. A student next to Carlos handed him one of the familiar wired boxes. "It will take some time for me to find you all, but once you are found, please return here and wait for me. You can hide anywhere, except the housing units. I can't be breaking the school rules by following a signal into women's housing, now can I?" The professor chuckled and continued, "If I haven't located you within two hours, you can assume that the test has failed and return here. Have fun and hide well. Make it hard for me. Now off you go!" he said shooing them all out the double doors.

Carlos had no idea where he was going, so he just kept walking. He started to head back to the library, but someone else carrying the black boxes walked up the stairs and slipped inside just as he was about to do the same.

I'll bet the professor doesn't want us to hide too close to each other. So he walked to the stables. He needed to hide and he was also curious to know if Jim had left, yet. The stables would satisfy both of those.

He felt a wave of shame at his relief to find Jolly's stall empty. Every time he was with Jim, there was a war going on in his mind. On one side was the need to tell his brother, on the other was the need to preserve their relationship. Lobo Joe had told him to trust Jim, but Carlos wasn't the trusting sort. And Jim wasn't always logical. He thought with his heart. And once his brother found out about the kiss, the next thought to cross Jim's heart would shatter it.

Carlos kicked Pearl's stall door. "Dammit!"

Pearl whinnied, clearly annoyed. Carlos felt instant remorse for letting his thoughts get away from him. He stroked Pearl's neck, calming her. Then he gave her some fresh hay and water, but the whole time, his thoughts tortured him. The whole business with Anna and Jim, along with the worry in the back of his mind over his father, was making him crazy. *I should just tell him and be done wi—*

He was jarred from his thoughts by the creaking of the stable door. "Hey Carlos," George called to him. "We found you." George swung the door wide.

Professor Smith stood there holding the same contraption he had used to find Carlos the first time he had helped to test the equipment. "Excellent!" the professor exclaimed. "So far the tests have been very successful. Please return to the lecture hall. At this rate, I'll be there shortly. You can return, as well, George. Have everyone start packing up the equipment."

"Sure thing," George said. Moments later, Carlos and George were on their way back to the lecture hall.

"These devices are amazing, aren't they?" Carlos asked, making conversation.

"They are that," George said. A moment passed and then, "How's your brother? I can't imagine what he must be going through, what with Anna and all."

"He's doing as well as can be expected, I guess." Carlos replied, though he honestly didn't know how Jim was holding it together. Telling him about kissing Anna might be the straw that breaks the camel's back.

"How's your father? Did the medicine help?" George asked with genuine concern.

"He was doing much better when I left. My hopes are high for a full recovery," Carlos answered.

"Good, that's great to hear," George told him, cordially.

Once they were back at the lecture hall, Carlos busied himself with packing the radar equipment. But, his mind wasn't fully on the task and after nearly dropping one of the expensive black boxes, he ducked out, leaving the hall behind.

**

"This is really good work, Jim," Lloyd told him for the third time. "I especially like the way that you called on law enforcement to search for more similarities between the cases. Very subtle."

"I'm glad you think so," Jim told the journalist.

"I want to get it to print for this Sunday," Lloyd said. "Give this to Mr. Potts and go ahead and get the letters set. What do you say?"

"Sure," Jim told him. He couldn't believe Lloyd was going to put his article in the paper. He felt like it was a good article, but it meant so much more to know that Mr. Turner felt the same way.

A couple of hours later and the letters were set, ready to hang the giant ream of paper. It was hard work, but Jim enjoyed every minute of it. He had especially liked it when he had set the letters for his own name. It was then that it finally hit Jim. *My name is going to be in the paper.* He smiled in spite of all the turmoil in his life. Anna still weighed heavily in his thoughts and he hadn't given up his hope of finding her, but at that moment, he was content. He had finally accomplished something, completely on his own. He was proud of himself.

"That should do it," Mr. Potts said as he inserted the paper into the rollers. "We'll give her a test print. Once Mr. Turner approves the test copy, we'll be ready get the wheels turning."

Lloyd took his sweet time, carefully reading over the test print. He marked two places to change. The first was a misspelled word. The second was letter that had been inserted backwards. "Other than that, it's perfect," Lloyd told him. Then he handed the test print to Jim. "Here. I still have the test from my first article. You should keep it, if you want."

"Yeah," Jim said, without hesitation. "You know, I think I'll send it home. I think my father would like to see it. Should I go ahead and start making copies for this week's edition?" Jim asked.

"No. Mr. Potts and I will take it from here. Besides, it's getting late and you have class tomorrow," Lloyd said. "You should go ahead and get back to St. James."

Jim decided to drop by the post office before he left town. He was anxious to send the test print home to his father. Jim could imagine his father as he read the first of many articles that Jim planned to contribute to the Clinton Weekly.

After paying for an express shipment, Jim left the post office. Mounting Jolly, he was ready to get back to St. James and tell Carlos about his article. As he closed in on the sheriff's office, he saw two natives astride two beautiful Nakotas. But, as he drew closer he could tell that one of them was a white man who had shaved his face and grown his hair. If he hadn't looked at Jim with piercing blue eyes, Jim would have bet money that the man was a full blooded Lakota Indian. The woman was definitely a true Lakota tribe member, though.

Jim found the whole scene strange enough to slow Jolly down to a walk. When he noticed the Sheriff talking to the man, his curiosity was piqued. He couldn't imagine what would bring them into town. *And why are they talking to the Sheriff?*

Jim hoped they didn't need any help, because if they did, they were talking to the wrong man. So far as Jim could tell, Sheriff Ghetts had never done one damn thing to earn his title. Jim brought Pearl to a stop in front of the Sheriff's office.

"I'm sorry about your daughter, Jake. I know you must be worried sick, but you and Chumani know those mountains better than us and you know it," Sherriff Ghetts said. Tobacco juice hit the boardwalk, landing just an inch from Jim's boot. Jim stepped over the brown spreading stain. "I don't know why you think I can help."

Jim bit his tongue so hard that he tasted blood. What he wanted to say was that they would be better off asking for help from a rock. But what he did say was, "Evening, Sheriff."

"Good evening, Mr. Castle." It was a stony reply. "I'll take a ride out that way and ask around," he told the Indians.

"Thank you," the man said. Then he exchanged a meaningful look with the woman, before turning their horses away and riding off.

"What can I do for you, Mr. Castle?" the sheriff asked.

"What was that all about?" Jim asked, ignoring the question.

"I don't see as how that is any of your business. There ain't no story here, Mr. Castle. I know you been working at the paper office," he said as though he had caught Jim in some sort of criminal activity.

"Seems to me, you spend more time worrying about where I am than where Anna or Ingrid is. Great work." Jim was tired of holding his tongue. And he felt like venting.

"Seems to me, you can't face the facts. Your girlfriend is dead. And there's nothing left of her to find," the sheriff said. Red, hot anger exploded inside Jim and he took a step forward. "It's getting late, Mr. Castle, and it's a good little ways to St. James. Best be going. Be ashamed if something happened to you, too." Brown weathered fingers touched the cold steel at Ghett's hip. *…he's an elected official.*

Lloyd's words came to him. They were calming. *And I have the power of the press.* Sunday, when the article hit the streets, it would be the first of many nails that Jim planned to hammer into the coffin of the sheriff's career.

Besides, he didn't have time to waste on Sheriff Ghetts, anyway. He wanted to catch up to the Lakotas. He felt drawn to them by his curiosity. He could smell…*a story.* He mounted Jolly and turned the horse after his next article.

He gained them just outside of Clinton. Startled eyes met his, as he brought his horse up beside them.

"Excuse me," Jim said, "My name is Jim Castle. I was wondering if I could have a word with you?"

Apprehension played across the man's face. "What do you want, Mr. Castle?"

"I noticed you talking to the Sheriff. Can I ask why?" Jim couldn't stop himself. He felt a kinship with them.

The man looked at the woman, who nodded. Then he sighed. "Our daughter was stolen from her bed five days, ago," he said wearily. "We were looking for help."

So that was the kinship that he felt towards them. He recognized the same longing and hopeless expression in his own eyes, when he looked at the man and woman. They had lost someone they loved without explanation, as well. "You won't find it with the sheriff. But, maybe we can help each other," Jim said. "I work for the Clinton Weekly…"

CHAPTER ELEVEN

"Their child was taken, Carlos. And get this. Their tribal land is just on the other side of Deer Mountain," Jim said. "And this isn't the first time. According to Lakota Legends, this has been going on for generations."

Carlos thought a moment. It was a curious thing. "Really?"

"Yeah," Jim said. "Usually it happens twenty or thirty years apart. But, this is the third child in the past two years. There are no tracks, no one ever sees anything, and all the searching has yielded nothing." Jim paused a moment, catching his breath. Then he shook his head, almost in disbelief. "She was convinced that the gods had chosen her child…that the baby was taken because it was special. But even though Jake has lived with Chumani's tribe for nearly five years, he can't accept that. He wants to find his child."

"Of course," Carlos said. Any father would want the same. "So what's your next move?" Carlos knew that expression on Jim's face. *He's digging in.*

"Well first, I need to talk to Lloyd and make sure that it's a story he would be interested in. It would be a complete waste of time if it's not something he wants to print," Jim said. "If he says yes, then I need more than just the parent's perspective. I need to talk to other members of the tribe."

That could take Jim away from his studies for days. Carlos was beginning to wonder why Jim was still attending classes, at all. Being a doctor was clearly not important to him anymore. *Has it ever been?* Carlos didn't know. And it didn't look like he was going to find out.

A sharp knock sounded on the door. Before Carlos could get to the door, there were three more knocks. His heart panicked and sunk into his stomach when he saw the look on George's face. *Someone's found her…and not alive.* In his heart, he had known it would happen this way. So when George said, "It's your father, Carlos. I'm so sorry," he couldn't speak for being completely taken off his guard.

Jim materialized behind him, "What is it?"

Carlos was still at a loss for words. "I'm sorry, Jim. Your father's sickness came back with a vengeance," George said, as he passed the telegram over. "He slipped away three days ago."

"A day after I left," Carlos whispered. "Thank you, George." Carlos softly closed the door, pressed his head against the mahogany wood, and cried like a child.

For an hour or more, neither he nor his brother spoke. So when Jim broke the silence, it startled Carlos, causing him to nearly gasp. "We should get packed. We have a long ride ahead."

Every move that Carlos made after that, felt slow and clumsy. He couldn't keep his mind on even the simplest of tasks. Fastening the trunk was an even greater chore than packing it had been. And carrying the trunk down to the stables was almost painfully slow.

George met them at the stables. Considerate as always, he had Pearl carted for them, already, saving him and Jim the hassle. After stowing the trunk and saying farewell, they were off.

"I need to stop by the newspaper and tell Lloyd," Jim said. Carlos nodded. They rode in silence the rest of the way to Clinton. And Carlos' guilt was building exponentially. Why had he left his father? He was going to be a doctor. He knew the dangers of tick bite sickness. *I was stupid. I never should have left. If only I had stayed, this might not have happened.*

Carlos pulled back on the reigns, bringing Pearl and the cart to a stop in front of the Clinton Weekly. Carlos stayed in the cart, while Jim went inside to talk to Lloyd. The sun was beating sweat into his eyes, mingling with leftover tears for his father. *Damn, this is my fault, too.* And where was his mother's voice? Surely, it would soothe him now. *I don't deserve it. I couldn't stay because I was afraid of falling behind in my studies? And because I was worried about Anna? I am a completely selfish ass.* And he was being punished. *When will it end?* Carlos knew the answer.

When he stopped lying and told the truth. His decision-making skills had proved poor since he had kissed Anna. And now, his father had suffered, as well. He wondered if he would ever be able to forgive himself. He already avoided the mirror in his room because he didn't like to see the man he was becoming. He hung his head in shame, remembering the words his father had said. *"I'm proud of you, Carlos."*

The dams broke and he wiped away tears before they could travel down his cheeks. He took a long deep breath. *Hold yourself together!* He needed to be strong for Jim. He couldn't let his brother down…*not again.* So he steeled himself and pushed his grief away, stuffing it into the corners of his mind, like bulky furnishings cleared to make a backbreaking pallet on a hardwood floor. This was the bed that he had made for himself…a cold, lonely, hard pallet on the floor of his soul. And he resigned himself to the fact that he would have to lie in it.

**

Jim walked into the newspaper office with a heavier heart. Lloyd waved to him from his office. But as soon as Jim entered the office, Lloyd held his hand up and waved for him to sit down, while keeping his eyes focused on the test print in front of him. "Just give me a moment."

Jim hadn't really planned on sitting down, but he did. After a moment or two, Lloyd looked back up. "There, that should do it," Lloyd said and then, "Jim, what are you doing back? Shouldn't you be back at St. James?" And then it was as if Lloyd were really seeing Jim for the first time since he sat down. "What's wrong?"

"I have to go back home for a few days, Lloyd. My father died." There he had said it. Jim fought back his emotions. Saying the words somehow made it fact…an irrefutable piece of information. He could no longer refer to his father in the present tense. As he had worried over everything in his current situation, his father had slipped into the past.

"I'm so sorry, Jim. By all means, take all the time you need." Lloyd was quick to respond, sympathy seeping around every word.

"Thank you, Lloyd." Jim stared out the window for a moment. Then he stood up and shook Lloyd's hand.

"Let me know if there's anything I can do," Lloyd said in the customary condolence. "Don't worry about the Deer Mountain disappearances. That story isn't going anywhere."

The news of his father's death had pushed everything else into the back of his thoughts...until now. "There's been several more disappearances," Jim blurted out. Then he told Lloyd about his run in with the sheriff and his discussion with the Lakota.

"That is so strange," Lloyd said. Jim could see the excitement in Lloyd's face and found himself wishing he could share in it. But his father's ill-timed death was a constant dark cloud that repelled any happy emotions. "When you get back and you feel up to it, I say go for it. There is definitely a story, here." Lloyd nodded his head, confirming what Jim had already suspected. "You write it, I'll publish it. As a matter of fact, I thought the other article was so good and demand has been so high for advertising space that I decided to run a special evening edition. Your article is the cover story."

"That's good," Jim said and it really would have been, if not for the shadow of his father's death looming over him. Jim shook Lloyd's hand again. He was a good friend.

"I'm really sorry, Jim. Remember, if you need anything at all, let me know," Lloyd offered again, just before Jim walked out the door.

As he walked across the boardwalk for the side street where Carlos waited with the cart, a familiar voice called his name. "Mr. Castle! I'd like a word," the sheriff's voice rang out behind him. Jim kept walking until he reached the cart.

"I'd like you to leave me alone, but that ain't happening either," Jim said, swinging himself up into the cart.

"Now, you wait a minute. What's the meaning of this?" Sheriff Ghetts called out, waving a newspaper in his hand.

Jim was about to answer, when Carlos asked, "Sheriff, any news about Anna's disappearance? Ingrid Bledsoe? The missing Lakota child?"

The sudden interrogation took the sheriff by surprise and he floundered for words. "I...er...we are...er...in the middle of the investigation," he finally blurted out.

"Well, let us know when you get to the end," Carlos answered.

"Good day, Sheriff," his brother said, then he clicked at Pearl, turning her and the cart back out onto the main road. When they were nearing the edge of town, Carlos asked, "What was that about?"

"My first article hit the streets this evening," Jim said, amazed that Lloyd had been able to get enough copies made in time for an evening edition. "I kinda called him out on the investigation."

"Good." The way Carlos said it, filled Jim with pride. But that emotion, too, was shrouded, when he recalled the package that his father would never get.

For miles, his mind wandered aimlessly through his past. He had been a trying child…a typical son. He had gotten into plenty of trouble as a child and had shared more than enough discipline at his brother's side. The punishment he endued was his own, now though.

"I should have been there," Jim said, suddenly. *I should have gone home with Carlos as soon as I knew he was sick.*

"It's not your fault, Jim. Neither of us were there, so stop it with the guilt. He wouldn't want that and you know it," Carlos said. His brother was a rock and if Jim didn't hang on, he knew the tidal wave of emotions would sweep him away.

"I know you're right, Carlos, b—"

"It hurts, I know. I'm going through the same thing. Guilt is what separates us from animals. It means we're human, Jim."

Carlos' attempt to make him feel better wasn't working, but Jim didn't want to add to his brother's burden any more than he had to. "I know," he said, even though he didn't.

The miles went by as they made their way down the road, cementing the reason for their travel. When they stopped for the night, it was late and the heat from the sun was nothing but a memory. Jim felt a chill off the wind, reminding him that fall was fast approaching as he unloaded the cart and hauled their trunk inside the small inn. Carlos had already rented the room while he took care of Pearl.

As he had stabled the mare, he had thought about Jolly and hoped that George was taking care of the horse, as he said he would. Jolly was the only thing that Jim had left that belonged to Anna. The school had sent her personal belongings home. But the matter of the horse had never really come up. So naturally, Jim had taken care of Jolly. And now the responsibility had fallen to George. He figured his worry had probably been for nothing, though. George was a man of his word in every way.

And he knew the real question his mind was trying to avoid. *How many funerals will I have to attend before the year is out?* So far, Anna hadn't been declared dead. *But, it's coming.*

The inn was minimally lit because of the late hour, when Jim made it up the stairs. He found the open door to their room, just as Carlos was pouring two glasses of whisky. Jim stowed the trunk, quickly, eager for the drink. The alcohol would help him sleep...*maybe.*

"Here," Carlos said, handing the drink to Jim.

Jim took it gratefully, barely remembering to sip. Carlos downed his. For a long moment, Carlos looked as if he were about to say something important, but then he just sighed. "We need to be up early. Are you hungry?" his brother asked him.

Jim had no appetite. "No, I'm just tired."

"Me too."

Jim kicked his boots off, turned the covers down on his bed, and slipped beneath the sheets, fully clothed. He heard Carlos blow out the candle and crawl into the other bed. After that, the hours were snails with nowhere in particular to go, a long aimless journey. And when sleep finally came for Jim, the sky was already beginning to turn from black to a dark gray.

CHAPTER TWELVE

With nothing but miles ahead before they reached their home, Carlos found his mind to be a ruthless tormentor. Several times as he drove the cart down the road, he relived the night before. He had been so close to confessing about the kiss…but it just wouldn't have been right, at least not when he and Jim needed time in order to come to grip with their father's death.

Carlos wondered how much guilt that one man could hold inside before he exploded. He was sure he was nearing the limit. *After the funeral.* If he could just make it until they buried their father, then he would tell Jim about the kiss. Scheduling a time for his confession to his brother seemed to ease Carlos' conscience. And by the time they reached the farm, he had forced his guilt into manageability.

Joe met them outside in the middle of the night and after tending to Pearl, he led them inside. A light burned within the farmhouse, casting yellow that played across the floorboards of the porch as he and Jim followed their father's oldest friend into the house.

Jackson Charles Castle, their father and mentor, lay twenty feet away…*lifeless.* Carlos swallowed a lump that threatened the air he was breathing.

The body had been washed and prepared by Lobo Joe in the customary traditions of his people. His father would have been pleased. It was the highest honor that Joe could give any man, especially a white man. The body was wrapped in deer and buffalo hides. Tomorrow, they would give his father the air burial. And then a year later, his father would be committed to the earth.

"You are his sons. It will be your duty to build his death altar. You should start tonight." Carlos and Jim had known this would be their lot, the moment they found out that their father had passed. The death altar would be their father's resting place during his air burial. In the Dakota tradition, their father's body would be left, exposed, to become one with the spirits. A year later, he and Jim would dig a grave, bury their father into the earth, and have the ground blessed by a tribal elder. *It will be a long process*...but necessary to preserve the precious bond his father had taken years to facilitate with the local natives.

Carlos held his father's hand, then kissed his forehead. Afraid to linger and fall apart, he was eager to set about the work, even though he was bone tired. So he gently laid his father's hand back at his side and turned on his heel, leaving Jim and heading for the barn.

Joe had piled the lumber and tools necessary for the task in the corner. Carlos went about getting his measurements and by the time that Jim had entered the barn to share in the building, Carlos had worked himself into a sweat, having finished the entire framework. Jim set about nailing the siding and after an hour or more, they were done. Jim carved the words, *Loving Father*, into the soft wood, while Carlos looked on. It had been a silent job, the only sounds having come from the tools or the grunts of effort on the part of the laborers.

Inside, it was more of the same type of silence. Instead of hammering though, creaking floorboards greeted Carlos as he and Jim made their way to their rooms. As they were about to part ways, Jim looked at Carlos with swollen eyes. And although there were no words to break the silence, Jim pulled Carlos to him, hugging him so hard that Carlos thought he would break. His brother was barely holding on, and he wasn't going to add his confession to the weight dragging Jim down, at least not any time soon. Carlos hugged him back, fiercely. A moment later and Jim broke off the hug, smiling through his tears. A single firm, yet fleeting grasp of Carlos' forearm and Jim turned, entering his bedroom. Carlos moved down the hall a few more steps and found the doorknob to his own room.

A candle burned low on the table beside a bottle of bourbon and fresh linens covered the bed. The window was partly open, letting in the breeze and helping with the stuffiness of a room gone unused. The last time he had been here, he had slept by his father's side or on the sofa in the living room. So crawling into his own bed was a comfort and although he didn't think sleep would come, she was a faithful bed partner that dreamless night.

The next morning when he awoke, it all came rushing back,

pounding guilt into his brain…beginning with the kiss and ending with his abandonment of his father as he lay on his deathbed. He had been so much better when he had seen him last. But that didn't matter. *I should have never left.* Carlos punched his fist into the soft bed and found no comfort in the action. He needed something harder, something that wouldn't give so easily.

But that would have to wait.

A knock sounded on his door and when he reached out with his ears, other sounds greeted him. People were already showing up. *How long did I sleep?* "Carlos," Jim said from behind the closed door.

"I'll be out in a few minutes," Carlos said. There was a tub of water in the middle of the floor and when he felt of it, it was lukewarm. He must have slept through the tub being brought in and filled. The water was cool and he welcomed a good bath, scrubbing every inch of his tired sore body with the bar of soap. Then he dressed himself, preparing for the bustle outside his door.

"Carlos!" Jim said when he saw him emerge from the hallway and into the living room. The aromas of food were pleasing and in spite of his grief, he found he had a small appetite. "Neighbors have been dropping by all morning, bringing food and paying respects."

"That's nice," Carlos said, meaning it. He found it satisfying to know that people other than just himself, his brother, and the local Dakota tribe would miss his father. Lobo Joe looked awkward, sitting near his father's body as people came by to see the unaccustomed sight. Foregoing a casket smacked against the traditions of the good Christian people who had settled in the Dakotas. But if any found it odd, they respectfully kept their feelings to themselves. *No one wants a scene.*

About two hours later and the tribe began to show up. Any white people who had lingered felt their welcome cut short, so they quickly said their condolences and ushered themselves out of the door.

Moments later, Joe told him, "It is time."

The spot was chosen facing the river, signifying that the cycle was complete. The Dakota believed they came from the river and in death, they would return. A great amount of care was given to ensure that no animals could get to the body, that it would be preserved.

Through it all, Carlos was counting the minutes, not sure how much longer he could go before his eyes would betray him and release the flood of tears that he had dammed. When he thought he could take it no longer, the haunting chant began as the tribal members formed a ring.

And then...*the ghost dance.*

**

Jim watched the members of the Dakota as they performed the ghost dance. He had never seen it before. It was a warrior's dance, representing the struggle against the white man. The fact that it was being performed to honor the death of a white man could only speak volumes for the man who was being honored.

His father had coexisted with the Dakota. He had grown to love them and everything about them. In a way, they had filled the giant void that Jim's mother had left, when she had died. And the Dakota had adopted his father into their tribe, because he had proven himself a friend and an ally on more than one occasion.

The chant was a haunting echo, which seemed never-ending, as the dancers stomped and circled the death altar. Jim felt mesmerized by the whole event. When they finally stopped, he found himself wishing the dance hadn't ended, as if a lullaby had come to an end way too soon, leaving him awake.

"Next, your father will be given his death name," Joe said from Jim's side, his voice low. The tribal elder started speaking. "He says the death name culminates a man's life," Joe translated, softly, "and a name is not given, it is earned. He says your father's spirit was strong and reliable, that is why his name will be," Joe paused, coming up with the rough translation, "Horse that could not be broken, an honorable name." Joe nodded his head in approval.

Jim agreed. It suited his father and summed up exactly how he felt about the man. It pleased him immensely that the Dakota thought the same.

They would camp for the night, by the body, and wait for the sun to come up, marking the moment that Jim's father would begin his journey to the afterlife.

That night the Dakota fed him and his brother by the fire.

Afterward, they stood vigil. For the one night, there was no difference between Jim and ny other member of the tribe. Grief bound them together…but it was more than that. It was their shared celebration of a life well spent.

Horse who could not be Broken.

As Jim looked around the camp, he felt an unexpected odd sense of family. Another thing he didn't expect was what Jim said, as he sat down in front of Jim and Carlos. The fire cast shadows across the old Indian's face. "He had me get the paper and pen for him right after you left to go back to the university," Joe told Carlos, handing him a folded piece of paper. Then he handed a nearly identical folded paper to Jim, as well. "He wrote one for each of you. He wanted me to give them to you both at the vigil."

"Thank you, Joe," Carlos said. "And not just for this." Carlos added, indicating the letter. "For everything. You were his oldest friend, Joe."

"And he was mine." Joe looked up at the sky. "There are those of the tribe who believe your father's spirit belonged to the Dakota, that sometime before he was made flesh, he was lost to us." Joe looked at the death altar and the great man who lay upon it. "And even in the wrong skin, he found his way back home."

"Do you believe that, Joe?" Jim asked, softly, clutching the letter.

"I don't know. I just know that your father's heart was big enough for everyone," Joe said, getting up. "And a man like that was at home wherever he went." Then he walked away, leaving Jim and Carlos alone with the letters from their father.

After a moment of reflection, Jim opened the letter.

Jim,

I want you to know how proud I am of you and what you have accomplished. I know that things have not always been easy for you and I know how many sacrifices you have made to remain at your brother's side. But now, you must live for you. Follow your own path, Jim. I want you to know that you are free, free to make your own decisions and free to make your own mistakes. You are your own man.

Because of this, I do not expect you to assume my role. Farming is not the life for you and your brother. So, I am deeding the land back to the people it truly belongs to, the Dakota. I've made all the arrangements with Tim Hatfield. Mr. Hatfield will handle all future taxes on the rest of the property from the sale of the actual homestead. The other 62 acres will be given to Joe and his tribe.

I do this because it is the right thing to do for you, your brother, and the Dakota.

I love you, Jim. You must remember this.

With the most sincere wish for your bright future,

Father

Jim folded the letter and held it close, laughing softly. His father had had the foresight to take care of everything, knowing that his sons would feel the call of responsibility to take care of the property at the cost of their own dreams. Giving the land to the Dakota was the greatest gift his father could have given the local natives. It was also the greatest gift that he could have given Jim and his brother. It was a gift of freedom. Jim decided right then that he was not going to return to St. James. He was going to get lodgings in Clinton and work for Lloyd at the newspaper full time. He would not waste the gift his father had given him by trying to become something he wasn't.

And Jim wasn't a doctor. *That calling belongs to Carlos. I'm a journalist.*

That was why when Jim lay down that night for his turn to sleep, his mind was more focused than it had ever been. The need to find Anna had been wrestled into submission by the death of his father. But since reading the letter, that need had returned with renewed vigor. It was the journalist in him. He recognized it now for what it was...*the overwhelming need to know the whole story.*

So, Jim decided that when he and his brother returned to Clinton, he would follow up on the only lead he had and try to draw a connection between those who were missing. When he went to sleep that night, his dreams were restless haunting visions of babes crying out to deafened ears as they were stolen away into the night.

CHAPTER THIRTEEN

Carlos woke up the next morning to hissing. He opened his eyes to see Lobo Joe pouring water over the campfire, extinguishing the glowing coals. His mind went immediately to the letter. His father had known him so well. He would miss him terribly. Carlos got up and found some coffee. Then he helped to break down the camp.

After one last goodbye, he and Jim made their way back to the farm. The chill of the night before was just a memory as Carlos stepped inside the house. It was hard to believe that the house would soon belong to someone else. He looked around taking stock of all the items that he and Jim should save. It seemed like an impossible task, especially on an empty stomach.

"How about I make us something to eat?" Carlos asked Jim.

"I can eat," Jim replied.

Carlos went into the kitchen and pulled the curtains back, letting the sun chase away the shadows. After getting a fire started in the stove, he went outside to draw water from the well. Joe was tending the chickens, throwing feed across the yard. When Joe saw him, he closed the gap between them. "You have not told your brother."

How the hell does he know these things? "No," Carlos admitted as he filled the bucket.

"Your mind will be cursed until you do." Joe threw more feed onto the ground. The chickens clucked their way over.

"It's not the right time. Once we take care of everything, here, I'll tell him." And he would…as soon as the more important matters were attended to. He knew his excuse was weak. Carlos wanted to change the subject. "I'm about to cook us up something to eat. Can you get us some eggs?"

Joe grunted, threw one more fistful of feed onto the ground, and then left for the coops. Carlos grabbed the full bucket of water and headed back inside, escaping further judgement.

The bacon and eggs were just what the doctor ordered. The lack of conversation was expected as Carlos, his brother and Joe dug in, satiating hunger. Joe went to take care of the chores while he and his brother set about going through his father's things.

After an hour of going through papers and letters and trinkets, Carlos was glad when a knock sounded at the door.

Tim Hatfield stood in his black suit with his hat in hand. Joe was taking care of Hatfield's horse as Carlos welcomed him inside. "Good day, Mr. Castle," the lawyer said, extending his hand.

Carlos grasped the man's hand in a warm greeting. "Good day to you, as well."

"I'm sorry about your father. He was a good man," Hatfield said, nervously fiddling with the hat in his hand.

"Thank you," Carlos said as Jim met them in the foyer.

"Mr. Hatfield. I figured you would be by today," Jim said, shaking the man's hand.

"Duty calls," he said. "I came here to talk about your father's last wishes. Did he happen to mention anything about that to either of you?"

"If you mean, do we know that he wanted to sell the house and farm and give the rest of the land back to the tribe, then yes. We know," Carlos told him.

Relief was visible in the man's eyes. "Good. Good. Then you know about this unusual arrangement."

"Yes," Jim said. "Why don't we go into the living room? Mr. Hatfield, will you have some coffee with us?"

Carlos led Mr. Hatfield to the living room. "Have a seat, Mr. Hatfield. Take a load off," he said congenially.

"Thank you," Hatfield said and took a seat in the high back leather chair where his father had usually sat. Carlos cringed a bit on the inside. *"Material possessions are not the people to whom they once belonged, no matter how much they remind us of those we have lost,"* These were his father's words as he had packed his mother's things after she had died and donated them to a missionary church that was passing through on the way to California. It had stuck with Carlos. It was true, but still a hard lesson to learn. The chair was nothing more than wood, padding, and fabric. His father was gone and he could only hope that his father had found peace.

Hatfield was looking nervous again after the long silence, so Carlos was thankful when Jim came back from the kitchen carrying a tray with cups and a pot of coffee. He set the tray down on the table and poured them each a cup.

Hatfield sighed, after taking a sip, "So, as I was saying before, this is a most unusual request and seeing as how this kind of strips you both of an inheritance, I am most nervous about following through, as I know I must," Mr. Hatfield said and Carlos could see how torn the man was over his predicament.

"Father left us his savings, which is more than enough to see us through until we are self-sufficient. Besides, I am sure that Jim and I both respect our father's decision. You will hear nothing against this from either of us," Carlos said, while his brother nodded his head in agreement.

The tension around Hatfield's eyes, eased considerably. "Excellent to hear. I always worry, sometimes these things can get...delicate," The lawyer explained. He took a drink of coffee and then continued. "So, first off, the house and surrounding farm will be sold at auction to the highest bidder. I need to know what to do about the furnishings. I have to confess that after drawing up such an unusual request, I missed some minor details." Hatfield said and then waited for a reply.

Jim was quick to ask, "Would it be possible to include them in the sale of the house?"

Carlos reminded himself of his father's words about material possessions. Besides, where could he possibly keep a whole house full of furnishings, anyway? *Certainly, not in the dorm.*

"Why sure. That is a fine suggestion. So you are both in agreement?" he asked hopefully, shifting his eyes to Carlos.

Carlos nodded.

"Unless the property gets rezoned sometime in the next twenty years, there should be enough off the sale to pay the taxes on the land for a very long time," Hatfield said. "Your father also stipulated that should the government ever recognize the right of the Dakota to own property that it be sold to the native residents at a cost of one dollar."

"That sounds more than fair," Jim said, letting his feelings be known. Carlos agreed. His father was nothing, if not honest. He wished he could say the same about himself. He had been nothing but dishonest with his brother ever since that night at the festival. It seemed so long ago now, that Carlos was finding it easier to put it from his mind. Of course, that task had been made easier by his father's passing.

"Good. I was a bit worried about that detail, as well. Some people may have wanted to retain the rights to the land for posterity." Hatfield smiled. "But your father knew you boys would be self-made men. He talked about you both quite a bit, when he came to me a few months ago with his affairs. He was very proud. I'll get on this directly and you can pick up the paperwork at my office tomorrow morning. Thank you for the coffee," he said and then downed his cup.

Carlos walked him to the door. "Thank you, Mr. Hatfield. One of us will be by in the morning to get the papers." He watched as the lawyer untied his horse from the post, and climbed into the saddle, before closing the door.

"That was a lot easier than I had expected," Jim called from his seat in the living room.

Carlos could only agree. His father had thought of nearly everything. He had also taken the time to remind him that although he and his brother should remain close, their paths would differ. He felt for the letter in his pocket. "Yeah," Carlos said. "I guess we had better get finished up, here. I need to get back to my classes. Are you still going on the expedition?"

**

Jim knew from the moment that Carlos had omitted him when talking about getting back to class that his brother knew he had planned to leave the medical program at St. James and devote his time to journalism. Jim could only think that his brother's letter had contained the same sort of insight he had found. He almost faltered before answering, "Actually, yes. I do still plan on going with the expedition."

"I figured you would," Carlos said, "There's still a chance that we may find something out there that will tell us what happened to her."

That was Jim's way of thinking, precisely. "I hope so. I am actually hoping to get back in time to do some digging on the missing Lakota baby. I have a feeling that all of this ties in." In his mind, he kept trying to fit it all together, but it was a useless task, give his current location. "I mean apparently, this happens more often than anyone knows. It seems to be a given of their people."

"What people?" Joe asked, coming inside to take a break from the afternoon sun. He kicked his boots off and stretched out in a chair.

"The Lakota," Jim asked and began filling Joe in on the story of the missing babe.

"The squaw is right. The babe was chosen," Joe said, leaning back.

"You don't believe that, do you?" Jim asked. Lobo Joe could often seem more like a white man than a native and Jim's incredulity belied that fact.

"I am not sure," Joe said finally. "I have often heard tales of the ancients taking their...tithes." He said coming up with a correlation that would best explain it to Jim. "The child is taken away in the middle of the night. Some return, years later, and they are very changed." The way he said it caused Jim to think that maybe the Indian in Joe did believe.

"Well, I'm going to talk with them. I can't shake the feeling that it's all related," Jim said.

"That is not a good idea," Joe said.

"Why not?" Carlos asked Joe. His brother was clearly sniffing out something to worry about.

"The Lakota may perceive you as a threat. It is dangerous," Joe answered, puling no punches.

"You could go with me," Jim said and the more he thought about it, the more he thought it was a good idea. For one thing, he knew the dialects were very close and Joe could be very helpful as a translator and an extra set of eyes. Jim was determined to go, but he had not relished the thought of going alone. He would enjoy the company. "We can have arrangements made with Hatfield in the morning for someone else to tend the farm until it is sold. What do you think?"

"Will you still go talk to them, even if I don't go?" Joe asked and Jim knew he had landed Joe like a fish. If Jim's safety were at stake, Joe would go with him, even if he didn't really want to.

Jim nodded, truthfully. "Yeah. I have to find out what's going on."

Joe sighed. "Fine."

And as easy as that, it was settled.

After making arrangements the next morning with Mr. Hatfield to keep the farm operational during Joe's absence, Jim spent the rest of the day making minor repairs around the farm and house. Both he and Carlos felt it was important that the property fetch as high a price as possible when it went up to auction. Jim knew that was what his father would have wanted.

That evening, they had a cold supper. No one wanted to clean up the mess, least of all Jim. His arms were still tired from mending the fence line and he still had to pack for the journey back to Deer Mountain. Carlos needed to get back to class and Jim finally felt that he had some direction in his life, so they would be leaving first thing in the morning.

Jim was looking forward to learning more about the missing Lakota children. He knew it was all connected and he was determined to find out how.

CHAPTER FOURTEEN

The better part of the trip back to St. James was spent waiting out inclement weather. The sky had done nothing but dump rain on their heads the whole way. *Absolutely miserable.* But Carlos had to agree that the weather mimicked his mood. He was just as miserable on the inside and according to Joe, who had felt the constant need to remind him at every available opportunity, he would remain that way until he confessed.

"Confession is good for the soul." His Indian friend said as they dried out by the fire, one evening, and midway in their travel. It was late and Jim had already gone to bed. Carlos was about to head that way.

"You're not a Christian, unless you've been converted, recently," Carlos said, snapping his head up. "Have you?" The question was sharp and ridiculous.

"It was something your father once said to me," Joe replied. Carlos had felt immediate regret. Joe was right.

"We both need time to grieve first," Carlos tried to explain his reason for delay.

"Perhaps." Joe stoked the fire. Bright embers rose up into the night sky. "Or perhaps you are punishing yourself."

After a moment or two of silence, Carlos had gone to bed, but he found it hard to sleep and the following morning came all too quickly. "Dammit," Carlos whispered as the area turned a light gray around him, promising a day of more rain.

"My sentiments exactly," Jim said, already awake, but still showing no signs of movement.

"If we push hard, we should make it back to Clinton this evening," Carlos said, anxious to get home. He thought it strange how quickly home no longer meant the farm where he had grown up.

"Right," Jim said stirring. Joe had already been up. The smell of coffee greeted him as he sat up and climbed out of the covers. There was also the smell of rabbit, roasting over an open flame. *He probably hasn't even slept.* Indians were not welcome in most parts and a smart man always remained vigilant.

And no one could ever accuse Joe of being stupid.

The rabbit was filling, if not flavorful, and the coffee was strong and hot. Twenty minutes later and they were on their way. The weather was an empty threat that blocked the sun, only sending mist where it looked like downpour. But it was still soul drenching and every mile was a gruesome chore.

Carlos drove Pearl hard that day, willing them all closer and closer to their destination. When Clinton finally came into view, he couldn't be more relieved. It meant there were only a few more miles until they would part ways. Jim and Joe would ride back to Clinton after retrieving Jolly, while he remained at St. James.

He wasn't dreading the solitude of his dorm room. On the contrary, Carlos would be glad to be alone with his thoughts for a change. He felt for the letter in his pocket. His father had given him a lot to ponder about his relationships and his responsibilities.

Jim wanted to stop at Clinton and grab a bite to eat, before heading into St. James. Carlos was against the idea, but his stomach felt differently, so he brought the cart to a stop outside one of the saloons that also served a hot meal. It would feel good to dry out in front of a fire and put something warm in his belly.

There were a few wayward looks at Joe from other patrons, but no one bothered them as they took seats at a table near the hearth. Within a few moments, a server was at the table, "We're out of beer, but there's still plenty of whiskey. The special today is beef stew," the boy said and waited for their orders.

Carlos watched as the boy's eyes kept returning to the strange Indian dressed like a white man. If Joe knew he was being scrutinized, Carlos couldn't tell. "Three whiskeys and three bowls of the stew, please." He tossed the boy a quarter dollar. "There's another one for you, if you make it quick." Carlos was tired and ready for his bed. The boy shuffled off, hastily, anxious for another coin.

A few moments later, there were three bowls of piping hot stew and a bottle of whiskey with three glasses on the table in front of them. Carlos ate the stew, letting it warm his chilled bones. Two days of travel in constant rain, makes a man appreciate warmth, even if the flavor leaves something to be desired.

"We'll leave for Deer Mountain, first thing in the morning," Jim said.

"Better you than me," Carlos noted, "I'm sick of the rain."

"Me too," Joe said and took another bite of stew. He washed it down with a healthy swig.

"At least we'll sleep in a warm bed tonight." Jim took a sip and wiped his mount on his napkin.

Joe grunted.

The boy cleared off the table, quickly, and Carlos tossed the boy another quarter, which he pocketed with nimble fingers. "Thank you, sir."

After one last drink of whiskey, they left the saloon and were soon following the road out of town to St. James University.

"I'll find out from George what steps you need to take in order to drop your classes. Might be that the school may offer a refund on some of the tuition," Carlos told Jim, logically. Although their father had left them a very good sum of money, there was no point in being irresponsible with it.

"Good. But I'm not going to worry about it if they don't," Jim replied. "I'm the one breaking my commitment. Plus, I'm making money at the paper."

That was true. Although, Carlos couldn't imagine that the pay was very good. *At least not yet.*

When St. James came into view, Carlos was beyond tired. He was dragging. Carlos could see Joe looking around the campus grounds. Even by moonlight, Carlos knew the university buildings were impressive. But after a passing look, the Indian was not so impressed as to hinder him from tending to Pearl. Jim went to see Jolly and

Carlos grabbed his trunk out of the cart, dreading the long walk to men's housing.

Carlos set his trunk outside the door to the stables, then he went back inside to say farewell to Jim. In truth, he had been dreading this, most of all. "You need to be careful out there. Let Joe do all the talking with the Lakota. You'll stick your foot in your mouth," Carlos teased his brother.

"I'll be careful," Jim told him, earnestly. "Maybe I'll come back with some answers."

Maybe. "Or maybe you'll just have more questions," Carlos answered.

**

As Jim steered Jolly onto the road back to Clinton and a warm bed, Carlos' words bothered him, immensely. What if all he ever found *were* more questions? *What if I never find any answers, at all?* These were haunting questions and just like so many other questions Jim had of late, there were no definitive answers. In the end, he would just have to trust his instincts.

Joe snoozed in the seat beside him as they passed the turnoff for Deer Mountain. The night carried with it a breeze that reminded Jim that fall was just around the corner. He was glad that he had packed accordingly. He pulled up his collar, shielding his neck from the wind. But, it didn't seem to help. A shiver ran through him, sending a chill into his bones. The hairs stood up on his neck and his eyes turned toward the mountain.

And there it was. The flash lit up the top of the mountain as bright as sunlight. Then just as quickly, it was gone. *No. Definitely not lightning.* At least no lightning that Jim had ever seen. His senses were intensified as Jim slowed the buggy, without thinking, his eyes never leaving the mountain.

"What's wrong?" Joe asked, not looking up from under his hat.

"Nothing. Thought I saw something," Jim said, giving Jolly more room to move. The horse obediently picked up the pace.

Joe grunted and shifted positions, clearly not interested. Jim began to wish he had taken Joe up on his offer to let him drive the buggy, while Jim grabbed an hour of sleep. Up until that moment, he had completely forgotten the strange light that he and Carlos had seen so many weeks before.

Now, it was in the foremost of his mind. *What can cause that?* Sure, he had been to Chicago once and saw the electric lights, but none had burned so bright as to be the cause of the flashes that lit up the mountainside. It just didn't make any sense. He simply had too many questions when it came to Deer Mountain.

"…maybe you'll just have more questions." His brother's words filled his head as he reached the town limits. Clinton was quiet for the most part. There were plenty of rooms available and soon Jolly was taken care of, leaving just him and Joe in need of rest.

The bed inside the inn was clean, if not the most comfortable. Joe had opted to sleep in the stables with Jolly, when the innkeeper had looked uncomfortable having an Indian under his roof. "We can try another inn with more hospitality," Jim told Joe as he collected his shaving kit from the cart.

Joe grabbed two blankets from the cart. One, he rolled into a pillow for his head, the other would be put to the more traditional use as cover for the chilly night. "It is no trouble. The horses never complain," Joe said as he settled in.

But it bothered Jim. "It's wrong."

"The victors get to make the rules, Jim. And you would not look as good in moccasins as I do in boots," Joe teased him.

Jim laughed. "You're probably right. You have everything you need?"

"More than enough. Sleep well," Joe said, bidding him a good night's rest.

But rest did not come easy that night and when it did, he was with Anna.

And she was terrified in his dream. "Let me go, Jim. Please don't look for me," she whispered in his ear.

Where are you? But every time he tried to speak to her in his dream, his vocal chords refused to work. He wanted to tell her that he loved her, that he was sorry for not telling her before…

But no matter how hard he tried, the words just wouldn't come. *I'll find out what has happened to you, I promise.* He wanted to tell her that, too. But just like everything else, no words were uttered.

Jim woke in a cold sweat just as the sun was coming up. A sharp knock sounded on his door. "Fresh hot water for washing." Came the call from outside. He rose from his bed and grabbed the fresh hot pail of water and fresh linens that were customarily placed outside the door of guests…*amenities.* He filled the sink and washed the sweat from his skin, then he grabbed his shaving kit and ridded himself of the three days' worth of growth that itched his face.

Even though the sun had chased away the previous day's rain, the night still hung over him Anna had been so terrified in his dream that it unnerved hi to his core. *It was just a dream.* But no matter how many times he tried to remind himself of this fact, it still jarred his center. He could still see the fear in her eyes, every time he closed his own.

Shaking hands had given him two small stinging nicks that were an annoyance as he dressed in clean, dry clothes. He was in need of coffee and nourishment and he wanted to know how Joe had fared, sleeping in the stables. So, he was quick to grab his things and exit the room, carefully leaving the door open for the maid.

Jim found Joe already awake and hooking the cart to Jolly. Jim hastily grabbed the other side of the cart, securing it to the rested horse. Jim patted Jolly's neck and grabbed an apple from the cart, which the horse took from him, greedily crunching it into bits. Jim needed more than an apple, before he started his day. "Let's go get some breakfast," Jim said.

Joe grunted his approval and together they walked back inside the inn to the main dining hall on the first floor. The smell of frying potatoes with onions and cornmeal gravy mingled with the scent of cedar coming from a fresh patch of paneling on one of the far walls.

The coffee was hot and only slightly bitter and the meal was the tastiest he'd had in days. He ate like a starved cub. "Best enjoy it. It'll be our last hot meal for days," Jim told Joe.

"Maybe," Joe said, digging in. Joe was always a man of few words. Jim expected it. He also expected the trip to be lacking in the conversation department. But, that would be fine. He needed time to think. The dream of Anna was sticking with him like honey on cold bread. "Your dreams haunt you. I see it in your eyes," Joe said out of the blue. Then he took another bite of potato and onion.

How Joe knew these kinds of things, Jim would never know. He knew better than to pretend that nothing was wrong, so he told Joe about the dream over breakfast. He honestly hoped that telling someone would make it seem less real. But it didn't. "I felt like I was really with her," Jim confided. He drained the cup of coffee and waved for another.

"White people often discount their dreams, when they should be paying attention," Joe said, setting his fork back down onto his plate. He wiped his mouth with his napkin and set it on his plate, as well, indicating that he'd had his fill.

"So what are you saying? That I should give up looking for her? Cause that's not going to ha—"

Joe shook his head, "No," he said firmly, interrupting. "All I am saying is that you should heed the warning. Take all precautions in your search, Jim." Another steaming cup of coffee hit the table and Jim wrapped his hands around it.

Jim smiled at his friend. "That's why I'm bringing you with me, right?" he asked.

Joe just grunted. Jim drained the cup of coffee, and then paid the bill.

Moments later, they were in the cart with Jolly's nose turned towards Deer Mountain.

CHAPTER FIFTEEN

Carlos woke the next morning after a troublesome sleep. He was almost sick with worry for Jim. He could only hope that Joe would keep his promise and Jim would remain safe. He shaved, dressed, and was out the door headed to find George just as the sun was coming up. The rain from the past few days might as well have been a figment of his imagination. It was already promising to be a very hot day and it was still early.

When George wasn't in his room, Carlos decided to try the library. But out of the four students reading from the vast amount of books carefully chosen to round out there knowledge, George's chubby form, wasn't one of them. *Maybe the lecture hall?* It was entirely plausible. After all, George was going on the expedition. But, Carlos wasn't so sure that he wanted to go on the expedition, anymore. Too many other things were taking up residence in his mind. For one, there were the dreams of Anna that had visited him over and over. "Let me go," she had told him. He knew from his studies that dreams were nothing more than leftover signals of the subconscious mind. He was the sole reason for his dreams. Once he had mended things with Jim, those would go away.

And for another, his father had only been dead for little more than a week. And he hadn't lied when he had told Joe, that he needed time to grieve.

So, he had more than enough reasons not to want to go on the expedition, anymore.

Carlos ducked inside the double doors and stood there for a moment, allowing his eyes to adjust. He soon spotted George talking with the professor. He slipped into a seat and waited for them to finish, not wanting to interrupt.

"The artifact you found a year ago is the most astonishing piece. But this latest find may give us exactly what we need. You are a lucky fellow, George. If you will excuse me, I need to inspect this," the professor said, holding something in his hand.

"Sure," George said, watching the professor shuffle off.

Carlos stood up and George finally noticed him. "Carlos! You're back!" George seemed genuinely happy to see him as stuck out his hand and Carlos shook it, amicably.

"Yeah, I got back in late last night," Carlos told him, smiling.

"Just you? Where's Jim?" George asked, looking around the room. His timing was perfect as always.

"That's what I wanted to talk to you about," Carlos said and then he proceeded to tell George about Jim's decision to pursue journalism full time.

"These things do happen from time to time and I do believe he is well within the cutoff to receive a small return on his investment," George said. "As long as he gets his paperwork in order."

It was good news. "Thank you, George," Carlos told him.

"I'm just glad that you and Jim are back in time for the expedition. I think old Professor Smith may just find what he's looking for this time," George said, his eyes gleaming.

"I'm not so sure that I still want to go," Carlos said, truthfully.

"What?" George asked, stunned. "Why? I thought you and Jim were still looking for Anna? Has Jim given up?" He asked, lowering his voice for privacy's sake.

Not at all. "No, Jim is still going, as far as I know. Wanna know where he's headed right now?" Carlos asked. George nodded, eagerly. "He's headed to the local Lakota tribe. Apparently, they have missing of their own." And Carlos told him what Jim had learned of the missing Lakota children.

"So, he thinks there is a connection?" George asked.

"Yeah."

"Seems a bit farfetched, doesn't it?" George asked.

"Joe doesn't think so. And he's rarely wrong." *About anything.* Carlos shuffled his satchel of books from one shoulder to the other just as the campus bells rang. "I've got to go or I'll be late," Carlos told him and then exited the lecture hall.

He walked into class for the first time, without Jim, and the room felt emptier without him. Carlos had managed a bit of studying during both stays at the farm and found that he hadn't fallen as far behind as he would have thought. Plus, classwork and tests had always come easy, and most of his nights spent studying had been for Jim's benefit and not his own. How much of his life had he given away to push his brother in a direction he didn't want to go...and shouldn't go. His brother wasn't doctor.

Carlos bit his tongue to keep it silent as he sat through class after class, tuning out the lectures and mulling over his thoughts. In the end, he kept returning to what Joe had said. *Am I punishing myself? Is that the reason I'm procrastinating?*

Perhaps. The dreams were the worst of it, though. That was the latest torture that his brain had devised. Carlos shivered in his seat, remembering. He checked the clock. Just a few minutes of class and he would be free for the rest of the day. He could finally be alone.

Suddenly, that didn't seem like the best idea. He had done nothing but be alone with his thoughts, in every class full of students. When he walked out of the building, he spotted George across the lawn and decided to see what he was doing that evening. "George," he called to his friend, waving.

George waved back and waited while Carlos trotted towards him. "Hi, Carlos. Are you through with your classes for the day?" George asked.

"Yeah. I was wondering if you wanted to go into town and get some supper?" Carlos asked.

George's eyes lit up. "Sure," he said, and slipped on his jacket. "I was just going to grab something from the commons, but I'd much rather have a hot meal, this evening. I'll be roughing it, soon enough, when we get to Deer Mountain, this weekend."

"Great," Carlos said, relieved. George was easy to talk to and good company, as well.

Soon after, Carlos was saddling Pearl, while George readied his own horse.

And Carlos pushed all the worry from his mind, while he and George talked their way through the miles to Clinton. They talked about classes and Carlos' father. They talked about the expedition and Professor Smith. Then Carlos remembered an evening that seemed so long ago, when he and Jim had been coming back from an evening out. "Have you ever seen any strange lights on the mountain at night?" Carlos asked. Just the memory of the sight made him feel as though he had seen a ghost.

A moment passed before George finally asked, "What kind of light?"

Carlos wished that he had said nothing about it now. But, it was too late. "It's hard to explain," he began. "It was strikingly bright and it was blue in tint. And it happened so fast that I wasn't sure that I had really seen it."

"How do you know your eyes weren't playing tricks on you?" George asked. "It happens, you know."

"Yeah. I know," Carlos said. "Except that I wasn't the only who saw it. Jim saw it, too."

"Well that paints the story a different color," George said, beginning to see the oddity of what Carlos had witnessed. "Could it not have been lightning?"

"No," Carlos answered firmly. "It wasn't lightning. This light seemed to come *from* the mountain." Lightning came from the sky, the last he checked.

George just shook his head, "You Castles come across the strangest things. First, Jim investigates missing Indian children. And now you tell me about this odd light on Deer Mountain."

George left out the part about Jim and Carlos being intertwined in Anna's disappearance, as well, and Carlos was glad of his friend's tact. "Yeah, guess that's our luck."

They reached the edge of town and turned their horses onto the main street, where the majority of the local establishments were interspersed along the wooden planked boardwalk. A variety of smells, wafted down the street from the various eateries that dotted the main commercial walk as Carlos and George tied their horses to the posts. Player pianos had already been set on their courses at some of the saloons and men and women walked with purpose along the boardwalk as Carlos stretched his legs, leading them into one of the many restaurants that served the populace of Clinton and the surrounding areas.

Five steps in and Carlos wished that he could turn around and go back out, but he was already committed. Sheriff Ghetts sat with two of his deputies, taking advantage of the good food and friendly service. Carlos hoped the man didn't see him as he found a table on the other side of the room and slipped into a chair, giving Ghetts his back.

After about five minutes, the waitress had already taken their order and Carlos had begun to relax. When the waitress brought him his beer he drank half, before his meal had reached the table. Roasted chicken, mashed potatoes with gravy, and creamed corn swimming in butter beckoned from the plate in front of him. He unfolded his napkin and placed it in his lap.

"This was a much better idea than grabbing some cheese and crackers from the commons," George said.

Carlos had to agree. Just as he was about to take a bite, he heard the familiar voice that grated on his nerves. "Well, I was just about to order seconds, but you Castles have a way of ruining a person's appetite."

Carlos turned in his seat. The sheriff stood behind him, his arms crossed over his chest. Pearl gripped handles rode on the man's hips. The badge on his chest held more power than the steel at his side, though. *I just don't like him.* And it was plain to see from the disgust on the man's face that the feeling was mutual. "If only you could attack your investigations with the same vigor as you attack a steak, you might actually earn your pay," Carlos said. He'd had enough of Sheriff Ghetts. Carlos stared through the man.

"I heard your brother took off towards the Lakota. I heard he had an Indian with him. A lot of folks don't feel comfortable with their kind walking the streets around here. A lot of us still remember how those savages killed off our families." Sheriff Ghetts uncrossed his arms and hung them loosely at his sides.

That was a threat against Joe and Jim. Carlos saw many shades at that moment, and they were all red. He knew the sheriff wasn't stupid enough to fire his weapon at an unarmed man in front of this many witnesses, so he called Ghetts' bluff. "That sounded like a threat against my brother, *Sheriff*," Carlos said. "I'm sure that Mr. Turner would have a field day with that story, should something happen to my brother."

Crimson rose into the sheriff's face, he was near his boiling point with unspent anger. Then suddenly, he calmed, as he realized the scene wasn't going the way he had anticipated. "It was a warning. What others may or may not do, is out of my hands."

Carlos laughed. "Doesn't the very nature of your elected position mean that the actions of others are not only in your hands, but in your hands alone?"

People at other tables began to take notice of the simmering situation. Ghetts looked around and Carlos could see the decision Ghett's had made when he turned around and placed a hefty tip on his table, a silver dollar. And to the waitress who received it, it would be a whole evening's worth of tips all in one. "It's not her fault that the place serves all kinds." The deputies who were sharing the evening meal with him, got up. Ghetts threw up his hand at them and they all headed towards the door.

When they were gone, George asked, "What the hell was that all about?"

"My brother's first article," Carlos replied. And then his mind immediately turned to Jim.

CHAPTER SIXTEEN

"I know it will be longer, but I think we need to take the route around the mountain," Jim said as they neared the fork in the road. The road to the left would be shorter, but a lot more treacherous. Had they each been on horseback that would have been their route without question. But Jim didn't want to risk it. He turned Jolly right, following the route around the mountain. "Plus, we'll avoid the frost on the mountain top."

"Either way, it will not matter," Joe said. "The weather is on our side now."

Even Joe's mood had lightened as the skies remained a clear blue, which was a stark contrast when compared to past few days of travel. *No one in his right mind would want to repeat that miserable trek.* "So no rain dances?" Jim teased his Indian friend.

Joe grunted. Clearly, the remark was not worthy of a reply. Jim laughed and stretched his legs inside the confines of the cramped cart. Conversation was the only way to pass the time and Joe wasn't much of a conversationalist.

They camped that night about fifty yards from the road and built a small fire. They had stirred a flock of pheasants on the way and Joe's quick reflexes gave them their evening meal. Jim's mind was full of questions as he tore into the pheasant. "Why do the Lakota think these Gods need their children?"

"The Gods have always needed us." Joe replied, as though the thought was common knowledge. "It is not for us to question why."

"You sound as though you've never read a book in your life, Joe," Jim said, which he knew wasn't true. Joe was educated. Jim's father had seen to that. He was still amazed at how deeply rooted the legends were inside his friend. "If we don't question these things, who will?"

"Questions are fine, Jim. Just be prepared to accept the answers," Joe said, "whatever they are. I still think there are some things we aren't supposed to understand." He took another bite of the pheasant, letting the conversation grow cold.

The next morning, they met with more clear skies. "Morning," Jim said as he emerged from his bed.

Joe saw the clear skies as a good omen. "The spirits favor us, again, today," Joe said as he gave Jolly some water while Jim began breaking down their camp. They shared a cold breakfast of jerky and two day old bread, before they were back out on the road.

Deer Mountain loomed over Jim's left shoulder, like a giant guarding secrets. *I will find them out.* His promise was rooted strong in his mind. There was something going on there and he was determined to find out what it was. His love for Anna was driving him to discover what had happened to her. And that meant that he would exhaust every lead, no matter how insignificant or farfetched.

We should have taken the pass across the mountain. It would have been another opportunity to look for Anna. But deep inside, he knew it was useless. Her trail was long cold. And the cart would make it way too hard for Jolly, especially if the freeze came early this year. It was just too dangerous. He'd made the right call.

They had been traveling a few hours, when Joe signaled for him to stop the cart. "What is it?" Jim asked.

"I'll be back in a minute," Joe said and climbed down from his seat. Jim watched him move into the tree line, where he squatted a moment at a small outcropping of rock. A few moments later, he returned, leaning against the side of the cart. "We are close. The Lakota are that way," he said, pointing over his shoulder.

"How do you know that?" Jim asked, even though he knew he wouldn't get an answer.

"We should hide the cart, let the horse graze, and walk in," Joe said. Jim was about to ask why when Joe continued, "Otherwise they may see us as a threat."

"Okay," Jim said. "It's your call."

"Just do what I tell you to do and don't stick your white foot in your mouth. Even from his grave, Jack would never forgive me if something happened to you." It was the probably the longest two sentences that Joe had ever said to him.

Jim knew it was important to Joe or he never would have invoked the memory of his father. "I will, Joe. Don't worry. You'll be doing all the talking anyway," Jim reminded him, smiling.

Joe sighed. "Let's just get this over with."

They entered the sparse tree line, walking past the outcropping of rocks that Joe had inspected when he first asked Jim to stop. Jim studied the rocks, looking for some sign of the Lakota as they moved past, but he couldn't see anything, except a very faint outline of...*something*. It rather looked like a bird with legs. *Maybe*. Or it could be his eyes playing tricks on him. It was probably a perfectly natural formation in the rock and he had missed the real symbol entirely.

When Jim turned around to take a second look, he couldn't see it all. So, he gave up. He'd have to remember to ask Joe about it later. Right then, he was supposed to stay quiet as he followed the Indian. Joe had warned him that the Lakota would be watching and listening as they moved toward their lands. He grabbed his pencil and paper and stopped briefly to make a note, reminding him to speak with Joe.

Lloyd had told him to keep his pencil and paper on hand at all times throughout his investigation, that they would be his greatest tool. So, he intended to chronicle everything he could. He put his pencil and paper back into his satchel. When he looked up, Joe was staring at him. "Sorry," Jim said.

"Keep up and don't get too comfortable," Joe warned him. Then he turned back around, leading them deeper into the rocks and crevices interspersed with the brush and small trees. The terrain on this side of Deer Mountain seemed a lot more brutal than what he had to contend with on the opposite. And he would have never thought he could get turned around, but the constant climbing and ever shifting landscape had him soon wondering exactly which direction they had come from.

In the end, he could do nothing but follow and keep up. Joe moved like a man ten years younger and Jim found that keeping up was sometimes challenging as they made their way deeper into the land of the Lakota. Soon, every crop of brush looked like the last and every jut of rock appeared to be one he had passed before. And he was getting tired of putting one foot in front of the other.

In the monotony of his circumstances, Jim wasn't paying attention and nearly ran into Joe, when the Indian halted in his steps. "Why are you stopping? Are we the—" Jim stopped short, when he looked up.

In buffalo hide, moccasins, and face paint, two Lakota warriors stepped out from behind the next outcropping. They were an impressive sight. Jim froze and his palms started sweating. Joe said something to the Indians who then looked at each other back and forth. One nodded at the other, who then took a step forward, raising his blade.

He patted Joe's chest with the butt and spoke animatedly. The other Lakota laughed. Jim didn't have to speak the language to know that they had insulted Joe about his white man's clothes. Joe said something back and Jim wished he had ever cared to learn Indian's native tongue. He felt completely out of place...*foreign*. He wanted to ask Joe what he was saying, but he knew better than to open his mouth.

Jim, especially, was an outsider and he was armed with nothing but his pencil and notebook. Joe spoke with the warriors a few moments longer, then they disappeared behind the rocks.

"Let's go," Joe said and proceeded to follow the path that the Lakota had taken.

Jim didn't know what to expect when he skirted around the rock face on Joe's heels, but it wasn't this. Acres and acres of mountainside opened up, revealing a flat spot riddled with tepees and tents. There was a section of the land where they farmed, another where they trained, and still another where they came together to celebrate.

And in the center of it all, stood the tallest tepee that Jim had ever seen. Smoke rolled from its apex and Jim was so shocked by the sudden change of scenery that he stopped walking to take it all in. If Joe was surprised, Jim couldn't tell because he didn't even slow down. He had to hurry to catch up.

"I told you to keep up," Joe whispered under his breath.

"Sorry," he whispered back. "Where are we going?" Jim asked, even though the direction was clear. They were headed straight for the tall tepee.

"We will be presented to the tribal chief. Don't speak unless you are directly spoken to. Understand?" Joe asked.

Jim nodded. The tribal chief would decide whether or not he and Joe would be welcome and allowed to move freely through their land and talk with their people. This entire part of his investigation was left solely in the hands of a man who had no reason or cause to help him. And this worried Jim to the point that he felt a bit queasy. What would he do if he and Joe were sent away? *Or worse?*

People were disappearing on Deer Mountain left and right these days.

When he entered the tepee, he was surprised for the second time since seeing the Lakota camp. The spaciousness of the inside seemed an impossible illusion, even though his mind had already noted the size of the structure. In the center was a fire pit, but it was too warm for burning logs, so it sat with smoking lemongrass as a natural insect repellent. Another unexpected characteristic was that the tent was exceptionally cool in spite of the heat outside.

The hole in the top center worked double duty as both a chimney and a skylight, allowing sunlight to fill the space below. Weapons and tools hung from the wooden framework. There was no furniture, but there were hides, blankets, and furs that made the floor a comfortable seat, for those lucky enough to be sitting.

He was not.

There were, however, three Lakota Elders sitting on the opposite side, engaged in conversation. All three looked up at Jim and Joe as the warriors who discovered them led them both for presentation. After some soft-spoken words with their elders, the warriors left Jim and Joe alone.

The man who sat in the center was an older native with silver in his hair and he had the respect of the others who sat beside him. *He's the chief.* The man studied Joe and Jim for a long moment and Jim was stunned when the man finally spoke. But not just because he had broken the silence or startled him in some other mundane way. It was because he could understand him. *He's speaking English.*

"Who are you?" The chief asked, and he wasn't talking to Lobo Joe. Deep brown eyes searched his face.

There was no point in lying to this man. He was like Joe in that respect. Jim swallowed. "Jim Castle," he said.

"Castle," the chief repeated, in deep thought, "why are you here?"

Jim could have told him about the Lakota man and woman he had seen in town. He could have told him he was there investigating the missing babe. He could have told him he was on assignment from the newspaper. He could have told him any one of these things and any one of them would have been an adequate response. *But none of it is the truth.* "A woman," he said, softly when he finally spoke.

The chief chuckled, "You surprise me with your honesty." He turned to his companions and translated Jim's response. Then he looked back at Jim, "You love this woman."

It wasn't a question. "She's missing," Jim said.

"And you think you will find her here?" The Chief asked.

"No," Jim answered, another truth. "I think that whatever steals Lakota babes from their beds at night, is the same thing that stole the woman I love from me."

The chief translated for the elders, who, in turn, shared their advice. One, he couldn't read. The other wore his thoughts on his every expression, and he was not pleased. Jim wanted someone to translate, but he knew that if Joe attempted such a thing, it would be disrespectful.

In the end, the chief was more than happy to translate. "He says that this is what comes of our women joining with white men. They seek protection from more white men, which brings white men like you to our lands. He says we should escort you back the way you came and send you on your way."

Jim didn't know what to say and he couldn't tell what the chief thought about the elder and what he had advised. He had translated it all without betraying a single emotion. Then he began to talk and his words were deliberate and long.

And not in English.

Because he isn't talking to me. Jim looked at Joe. Whatever the old chief was saying, he wasn't talking to Joe either, but Joe could understand. It was clear from the expression on his face. And the more the chief talked, the more his face betrayed him, until finally, he broke into the conversation.

A number of outcomes paraded across Jim's mind and none of them were good. Jim cursed himself for not learning the native tongue. Being bilingual would be a very beneficial skill in journalism. He vowed he would learn if he made it back to civilization in one piece as Joe spoke his peace, interrupting the chief in what could be taken as an arrogant amount of disrespect.

The chief asked Joe a question and Joe nodded. Then the chief looked at Jim. "You are welcome here. Walk my lands in peace, son of Horse that could not be Broken," the chief said and Joe was immediately at his side, pulling him away.

They stepped back outside and although there were some tribe members who questioned their presence with looks, they kept any thoughts to themselves as Joe pulled Jim along, walking away from the tepee. When they were out of earshot of any members of the tribe, Jim ground in his heels. "What just happened?" Jim asked.

"Your father's story spreads far among the tribal lands," Joe said. "You're free to investigate."

"Then why are you dragging me away like I wasn't?" Jim asked. *My father's story?* But, his father hadn't known the Lakota. And he told Joe as much.

"Word spreads quickly in peace times between the tribes." This was Joe's explanation and Jim supposed it made perfect sense. Not many white men had been so revered by the natives as his father. Jim smiled. It felt like even though his father had passed, his spirit was still a living breathing entity among the Indians he had loved. It made Jim proud to be his son.

Jim looked around. The Lakota were going about their duties. Women were farming or sewing hides and furs into clothes or bedding for the coming winter. Children ran playing from one end of the camp to the other. The men were sharpening the arrows or butchering their kills for the evening meal. "How do we start?"

"By not overstaying our welcome," Joe answered. "We'll stay for the evening meal and leave first thing in the morning."

Joe was right. Once Jim broke bread with the Lakota, they would be more than willing to share anything they could about the disappearances of the children. He would no longer be looked at like a complete outsider. At least he hoped that would be the case.

As the last rays of sun crept across the side of Deer Mountain, the cook fires were blazing and the smell of roasting venison and corn cakes filled the camp with a wonderful aroma that set Jim's mouth to watering. He followed Joe until he stopped to speak quietly with one of the natives, who was sitting on a long log laid out by one of the many fires.

A couple of words were exchanged and then Joe took a seat on the log, motioning for Jim to follow suit. Jim sat down and a few moments later, he was given some venison on top of a corn cake, which he ate greedily. The smoky flavor of the meat mingled nicely with the lightly sweet corn cakes, and when he was offered another by a young woman with soft brown eyes and braided hair, he took it gratefully. He smiled at her and she looked pleased that he took the bit of food.

He nudged Joe in the ribs. "Tell her I said, thank you," Jim told his Indian friend.

Joe obliged him. She shifted her gaze and smiled at him before she left, disappearing behind the smoke and firelight.

Jim enjoyed the tasty bits of meat and bread. As he ate, Joe talked to the man who had invited them to sit by his fire. He could only guess what they were talking about and it wasn't worth interrupting them to find out. So, he waited.

And while he did, someone handed him some more food and a cup of liquid. Jim had worked up quite a thirst. He sniffed the cup and recognized the smell of alcohol. Turning up the cup, he felt the cool liquid slide down his throat. The cough that followed was unavoidable and his throat was on fire.

"That's why it's called firewater," Joe said to him, patting him on the back. His host found the whole scene funny at Jim's expense and said something to Joe that made him smile. "He said you drink like a girl," Joe said, amused.

Jim could handle good-natured teasing. He took another drink of the alcohol, only this time he sipped and the burn wasn't quite as bad. It still threatened to take his breath. He missed the smooth bourbon that was his usual drink of choice. "I'm not a quitter, though," Jim said and took another drink of fire.

Joe translated and the Indian smiled and turned up his own cup. Then he said something, which Joe translated, "He asks why we are here?"

"To find out more about the missing children," Jim answered. "Ask him if he knows anything at all about who took them or what happened to them?" Jim felt the need to get right to the point. With the setting sun and the knowledge that he and Joe would be leaving in the morning, he felt a sudden urgency to start his investigation.

Jim waited while Joe translated. The man thought about it and shook his head, smiling. Then he said something in the language of the Lakota. "He says that you chase rainbows. The children were not taken. They were chosen, and they belong to the gods now."

Jim found it hard to identify with the Indian. The answer was an explanation he could never accept. "What if you're wrong?" Joe bunched his eyebrows together, but Jim prodded him. "Ask him." Jim was firm.

Joe translated and the man laughed. Then his tongue rolled. "He has a question for you. He asks if not the work of the gods, what else could possibly have stolen into the camp of the Lakota and made away with the child?" After Joe translated, the man swept his arm out, beckoning Jim to look around the bustling camp.

As he looked around the sprawling and active camp, Jim had to admit that the man had a point. "I don't know," Jim shrugged. There was no need for translation.

The man spoke again and Joe listened carefully, finally nodding. "He says you should talk to Kimimela, she's their healer."

"Where can I find her?" Jim asked, thankful that the conversation hadn't resulted in a complete dead end. He waited, anxiously, while Joe translated.

A few minutes later, and Jim and Joe were parting ways with their host. They thanked him for the meal, fire, and information, before he and Joe went in search of the healer's tent, which they found just a short distance away.

The healer, Kimimela, wasn't there, but her daughter was. Jim was surprised to find the pretty girl with the soft brown eyes, who had offered him the food. Jim waited while Joe spoke to the girl. "She says that we are welcome to wait, here. Her mother has gone to tend a boy on the other side of camp."

"Tell her that we'll be happy to accept her offer."

Joe translated and the girl smiled, nodding.

Twenty minutes later, the healer returned. After a brief discussion with her daughter, a steaming cup of lavender tea was produced as she set herself down on the padding of furs. She took the cup from her daughter and sipped the concoction.

Then she finally addressed her guests. "I know why you are here. But you will never find the one you seek," Joe translated the weathered woman's words.

"Ask her how she knows this?" Jim told Joe and he translated the question.

"Because I am Kimimela, the butterfly." This made no sense to Jim and when Joe saw his expression, he explained. "The butterfly is the messenger between the world of the Lakota and the spirit world." The woman spoke again. "She says her name was given to her when the gods returned her to the Lakota."

Jim was speechless. If Kimimela were to be believed, then she had been taken as a babe and returned as a girl, half-grown, just as the children in the stories that Joe had told him about. "For what purpose?" Jim finally managed and Joe conveyed his question.

The old woman smiled, sighing. "To prepare the world for their return."

It was then that Jim reached the worst realization. *Carlos was right. All I have are more questions.*

CHAPTER SEVENTEEN

Carlos was sitting in his dorm room, staring a hole through his study material.

He had several books open and turned to certain pages for easy reference. A pencil and paper along with some skeletal bones that he had borrowed from the anatomy lab were lying on the bed beside him. He had closed his door to keep disturbances at a minimum and the window was open to let in fresh air. The environment couldn't possibly be any better suited for studying. But he just couldn't stay focused. *This is useless.*

I should've just gone with them. Then Carlos wouldn't be worried about his brother. He hoped Jim would find the answers he needed...*without making any more enemies.* His mind turned to the evening, four nights past, when he'd had dinner with George. Sheriff Ghetts was a pompous ass, to be sure. But, he was also a man you didn't want as an enemy. *He's dangerous. And Jim is stupid for provoking him, needlessly.*

His father was barely gone and already Jim was risking his neck. He shouldn't have been working at the paper. He shouldn't have been investigating anything. *I should have never let him go. I should have sto—*

A knock sounded on the door and before Carlos could even get up from the bed, the door opened and Jim walked in. His anger melted away as he breathed a long held sigh of relief. "Carlos!" Jim said, excited. "I have so much to tell you."

Had he found Anna? *Does he know what happened to her?* Carlos's mind threw question after question into his mouth, but he spoke none.

Jim did all the talking. "So, at that point. I thought I was going to get nowhere with the Lakota. Kimimela was absolutely convinced that the gods had abducted her and all the other children who have gone missing. And as Joe was happy to tell me at every turn, there was no point in questioning the gods. But then she told me that animal spirits abducted the children and she gave me this as proof." Jim took a long breath while he pulled a kerchief from his pocket and unfolded it. Then he showed it to Carlos.

"It's just hair," Carlos said as he stared at the tuft of dark brown hair contained in the center of the kerchief.

"Touch it," Jim said. Carlos raised an eyebrow. "Just do it," Jim urged.

Carlos reached out to touch the tuft of mysterious hair and as soon as his fingertips touched the strands, they turned from a dark brown to match the cream kerchief. Carlos snatched his hand back. *It's not magic.* But it almost had to be.

He reached out to touch it again and he met with the same result. Five times, he touched the hair, and five times, it changed color, blending into the kerchief. Jim laughed and snatched his hand back, when Carlos made a sixth attempt. "It does it every time," he said, his eyes sparkling.

"What does Joe think about it?" Carlos asked, amazed his vocal chords could function, at all. "Where is he, by the way?" he added, before Jim could reply.

"He wanted me to give it back," Jim said in disbelief, before adding, "He's taking care of Jolly, then he's waiting for me back at the stables. I couldn't wait to get back here, this morning, and show it to you." Jim folded the tuft of hair back into the kerchief and put it in his pocket. "I want to show it to Professor Smith. After all, it's an artifact from Deer Mountain."

Carlos wondered if Jim might be right. *What if all the disappearances are connected, somehow?* "That's smart, Jim. And if Professor Smith doesn't know anything about it, then we can always let the biology department inspect it." Carlos was completely amazed by the ability of the hair to change its color. He had read about reptiles that could manage the same effect, even in striking colors. But the fact that it was hair, suggested that it came from a mammal of some sort and not a reptile.

"Let's go, then," Jim said, smiling. Carlos looked around at the pile of study material lying on the bed. But before he could give an excuse to stay, Jim said, "Don't even try it. We both know that you've read all of that at least three times and you can pass the fall exams, easily. Besides, didn't you miss me?"

"I was worried about you, if that counts," Carlos said, teasing. Then he piled all of his work together and climbed off the bed. His brother hugged him in an embrace he didn't deserve and he cringed on the inside.

Carlos was beginning to hate himself for not being honest with Jim, and if he were completely honest with himself, that was his reason for not wanting to join his brother as he took the curious contents of the kerchief to the professor. *This is ridiculous.* Carlos knew he had put his confession off for far too long. And if he'd forgotten, he knew that Joe would remind him at the next available opportunity.

But I can't tell him right now. Carlos followed Jim, who was practically running across the campus grounds in the direction of the lecture hall. They filed through the double doors and Carlos had to stop short, as Jim stood frozen in front of him, obviously, scanning the lecture hall for Professor Smith. "He isn't here," Jim said.

Carlos looked around the entire hall. "You're right. I wonder where he could be?" The expedition was leaving in two days. Most of those going on the expedition were in the lecture hall, going over maps of the terrain, preparing for the coming travel.

George was among them. "George will probably know where we can find Professor Smith," Carlos offered as a solution to their problem.

As if on cue, George looked up and Carlos waved him over. George beamed as he shook Jim's hand in greeting. "How was your trip? I bet it was fascinating."

Jim looked at Carlos and smiled before answering, "It was very productive."

"What did you find?" George asked, a bit too loudly, and murmurs came from the students who were planning the expedition route. "Let's go outside," George offered.

The moment they were outside, Jim asked, "Where's the professor?"

"He took a couple of students with him this morning to pick up a shipment of supplies," George said. Then his brows furrowed in question, "Why?"

Again, Jim looked at Carlos. Carlos nodded. He didn't see anything wrong with showing George the mysterious strands of hair. As far as he could tell, there would be no harm in it. Besides, George wasn't exactly clueless. In fact, he was very educated, as Carlos had come to learn in their conversations.

Jim pulled the kerchief from his pocket and unfolded it. Even knowing what was inside, Carlos still could not tear his eyes away as Jim held it out toward George.

George peered at the hair, just as Carlos had done no more than thirty minutes ago. "What's this?" Forever tactful, George didn't insult Jim and state the obvious, as he had done when Jim had first shown it to him.

In an odd sense of déjà vu, Jim said, "Touch it."

Carlos expected to see George's hand reach for the tuft of hair, but he didn't. When he looked back up, George had a strange expression on his face, then he broke into a big grin. "This is a joke, isn't it?"

"Just touch it," Jim repeated his command.

Annoyance flashed across George's face, but it was quickly replaced with curiosity before he reached out and touched the tuft of brown. As soon as he made contact, the color shifted and George pulled his hand back as if burned.

"How did you get this?" George asked, finally, his voice shaking. *He's scared.*

Jim appeared to think about it for a moment. Then he told George the same story he had told Carlos and George listened, without interruption. Only when Jim had finished, did he speak, "So you think it ties into the efforts of the expedition?"

"Yeah," Jim answered. "I do. That's why I want to show it to Professor Smith." Jim folded the kerchief and put it away.

"It might be hours before he returns," Carlos said.

"I guess you can wait for him," George suggested.

"Joe's waiting for me in the stables," Jim reasoned. And Carlos thought it was a tactful move on Joe's part. He had watched Joe's presence startle more than one person. Plus, it would have to be unnerving for anyone, regardless of their color, to be under constant scrutiny.

"Well," George said. "You could leave it with me and I can give it to Professor Smith when he gets back."

Carlos thought that was a solid solution.

But, Jim was silent...

**

Jim wasn't holding his tongue because he'd rather just wait on the professor. He was holding his tongue because ever since he'd shown George the strange hair inside the kerchief, he'd been judging the man's reactions.

And they weren't normal.

And he didn't know the exact moment that George had shifted from friend status to a person he couldn't trust. *But here it is.* The hairs raised on the back of Jim's neck. *Stop it.* George had never given him any reason at all not to trust him. He was Jim's friend. *Right?*

All Jim had to go on was a gut feeling. His hand touched the pocket containing his prize. "That's okay. I appreciate the offer," Jim said, maintaining all courtesies.

A flash of anger crossed George's face, so briefly, that Jim almost missed it, even though he had been looking for it. Smiling, George said, "Good. To be honest, the thought of holding onto it kind of makes me nervous."

Had Jim been wrong? Had he painted an emotion he had only hoped to see on an otherwise innocent face? "Well, to be honest, I think I need to get back to town and check in at the paper. I'll come back tomorrow," Jim said. It was one truth, if not *the* truth. He wanted to get away from George. And the part that was the most bizarre was that he didn't even really know why.

"Sure," George said and although Jim searched George's face, there wasn't a single trace of mal intent.

And what right did Jim have to even form a conclusion on such flimsy evidence? What kind of journalist would he be if he just mentally convicted someone, based on a look or a gut feeling? *The story is in the facts.* "Thanks anyway, George."

Jim didn't feel the uneasiness leave him until he and Carlos walked into the stables. He could feel George's eyes on his back as he and his brother had walked away. If Carlos had any sudden change of heart concerning George, he wasn't saying anything as they searched the stables for Joe and Jolly.

"Why didn't you leave it with George? He could have given to Professor Smith and saved you the ride," Carlos said.

"It's the only piece of evidence I have that something strange is going on. I'm not taking my eyes off it," Jim replied. He spotted Pearl, who looked antsy in her stall. "Looks like you've been saving rides at Pearl's expense." Pearl agreed, whinnying.

"Only because I don't want to run into the sheriff. I haven't been into town since the day you left," Carlos said and Jim listened while his brother told him about the ill-timed meeting with Ghetts.

"I'm sorry," Jim told him. He should have known that a lowlife like Ghetts would take the opportunity to cause a scene, misdirecting his anger at Carlos, instead of where it should be. *On me.* "When I get back to town, I'm going to give him a piece of my damned mind."

"It's okay. He's not worth the effort," his brother said. "Why take time from your investigation and waste it on the likes of Ghettts?"

His brother was right. "I'm sorry. I can't help it, Carlos. I see red every time his name is mentioned," Jim said, still boiling.

"Then forget I mentioned it."

They found Joe propped up on a hay bail in the feed room, taking a nap. Jim kicked at Joe's boots, but the Indian must have sensed him, because he dropped his feet off the bail, while Jim swiped at empty air. "You have too much foolishness in you," Joe said and stood up.

Jim laughed. "They should call you Strike of the Snake," Jim told his friend. "You have a forked tongue and you're quicker than you look."

Joe grunted. He wasn't amused. "Did you see it?" Joe asked Carlos, ignoring Jim.

Carlos nodded. And that was their whole conversation about what he held in his pocket. Jim couldn't say that Joe was afraid of it. It was more like he respected what he couldn't explain, which meant he had wanted Jim to get rid of it from the start.

Jim pulled Jolly from the stall and led the horse outside, where the cart sat, waiting. Together they hitched the cart and it wasn't long before Joe and Jim were on the bench seat, ready to depart for town. "I'll be back tomorrow," Jim said.

But already, he was beginning to rethink his decision to allow anyone else to see the color shifting lock. "See you then." His brother waved. At least he was able to see Carlos. The trip to the university hadn't been all for nothing.

CHAPTER EIGHTEEN

The following day's sun came and went, leaving Carlos as perplexed and in the dark as ever. Jim was a no show. *Where is he? He said he'd be back today.*

"Well, I'm going to bed," George said, finally.

He and George had waited nearly all day at the stables for Jim. George had been most curious about the strange artifact that the healer had given Jim. *Anybody would be.* "I guess I'm going that way, too. If he hasn't shown up by lunch tomorrow, we'll ride into town and find him."

"Sure," George said, getting up and offering Carlos a hand, which he took.

Carlos brushed the dirt from his pants. Then he and George walked back to the men's housing. "He probably had a lot of work to catch up on at the paper."

"You're probably right," George agreed. "See? It's a good thing we didn't get the professor's hopes up." Carlos had wanted to ask the professor about the tuft of hair, but George thought it was better for Professor Smith to see it, than to just hear about it, so they had waited on Jim. *Pointlessly.*

It had been a very boring day.

Carlos parted ways with George, depositing him on the second floor, while he continued to climb the stairs. When he got to his room, he crossed the small space and opened the window letting in the cool fall air. He took a deep breath and sighed as he stared out across the grounds.

He and Jim were on different paths. He was going to be a doctor. Jim was a journalist. The only thing that held them together since their father had died was the search for Anna...*the investigation.*

And Carlos was barely a part of that, anymore. He had isolated himself. And the only way out of the isolation was to be honest with his brother.

Jim didn't deserve his dishonesty. *He deserves the tr*—

Carlos' thoughts were brought up short when he spotted George, back outside, moving across the lawn in the direction of the stables. Carlos found it odd. *Maybe he left something out there on the ground.* But he couldn't see what that something would be, unless…*something fell out of his pocket.*

That was probably the reason.

He moved away from the window and moonlight poured into the room. Normally, he would have lit a candle and climbed into bed with one of his class books. But on this night, he knew that would be useless. He wouldn't be able to concentrate. He grabbed the glass and bottle of bourbon off the table and poured it nearly full. Then he drank half.

He climbed into bed and did the best he could to find sleep, hoping that if he did, it would be free of dreams.

Carlos woke the next morning and his eyes were stuck together. He had found sleep, alright. And it had knocked him out. And if he'd had any dreams, he couldn't remember them. The bourbon had done the trick. He opened his eyes and then closed them again.

Dammit. The sun was already up and hatefully glaring at him from the open window. He'd overslept. He was supposed to be meeting everyone at the lecture hall. But, he still wasn't sure that he wanted to go on the expedition. If he did, he needed to be at the meeting. Except…*I'm not.*

It was then that he made the decision not to go, which made his morning a much simpler affair. Instead of rushing, he took his time as he washed up, shaved, and dressed for the day ahead. There was no use in looking for George. He knew where George was. He was probably right on time for the meeting. So, Carlos went to the stables and saddled Pearl.

He was going to find Jim and he was going to tell his brother what happened the last time he saw Anna. He didn't care what happened after, he only knew that the before part was killing him.

He had passed some riders on the road, but none were his brother or Joe. *If Joe's still here. He's probably gone back to the farm.*

When he reached Clinton, he tried the newspaper first. He found Lloyd in his office, but there was no sign of Jim. "He's not been in this morning. I didn't even know he was back," Lloyd said. "Tell him to come in, when you find him. I want to hear all about it."

This worried Carlos. This wasn't like Jim at all. "Sure." Carlos left and hit the boardwalk, where he stopped short. It was then that it occurred to him. He had no clue where Jim was staying. *Of all the stupid things to do.* All he could do was look for Jolly and the cart.

Three streets over, Carlos spotted Jolly and the cart. He headed down the alley. When he stopped to pet the horse, Joe raised up from the back of the cart where he'd been snoozing, startling Carlos. "You nearly scared the life out of me."

"I thought you were a horse thief," Joe said. And it was then that Carlos saw Joe slip the knife back into its sheath.

"What's got you so on edge?" Carlos asked.

"Your brother. The god's lock is missing," Joe said. "And he's been searching for it all morning. Says he'd go to the sheriff if he thought it would do him any g—"

"What do you mean it's missing?" Carlos asked, interrupting. *Jim should have given the damn thing to George or else he should have come back yesterday.* What had his brother been thinking?

"He had it last night, under his pillow, he says, and when he got up this morning, it was gone." Joe swung himself down from the cart, planting his boots onto the dusty road.

"Then it's in his room," Carlos said, logically. *It has to be.*

"That's what I told him," Joe said. "But I helped him search. It isn't there."

"Well what the hell happened to it?" Carlos asked, annoyed. Getting information out of Joe was a slow and painful process.

"Your brother asked me the same thing. And he didn't like my answer."

"Try me," Carlos said.

"I think the gods take back what belongs to them." And Carlos could tell with certainty. Joe meant every word.

**

Jim thought he was losing his mind. He had been guarding the contents of the kerchief with his life and suddenly it was gone. *Stolen like the babes of the Lakota.* "Stop it," he said aloud. He was beginning to think like Joe. And that made him angry. Just because there were things he didn't understand, didn't mean that they were beyond explanation.

He looked around the room where he was staying, while working at the newspaper. It was completely ransacked. He had stripped and pulled the bed away from the wall and upturned the mattress. He had been through every drawer in the small dresser and strewn clothes all over the floor. He had even taken down the mirror and oil painting that decorated the wall. "This doesn't make any sense," Jim said, running his fingers through his hair. He wanted to tear it out. *I haven't felt this frustrated since An—*

"What doesn't make any sense?"

Jim turned to see Carlos, hovering in the doorway. He sighed, his shoulders slumping. "It's gone, Carlos." *Someone had to take it. But how?* He'd been so careful. He'd kept it hidden and hadn't shown it to anyone else.

"Obviously," Carlos said, looking around at the destruction.

"It was in the kerchief underneath my pillow while I slept, Carlos," Jim told him, doing his best to remain calm. "It's like it just disappeared."

"That's impossible," Carlos said, and then began gathering clothes. "You've misplaced it, surely."

"No. Someone stole it." *But who?*

"Why would anyone do that?" Carlos asked. Then he threw up his hand, "Wait. Why didn't you show up yesterday?"

"I changed my mind," Jim said. "And you know why someone would want to take it."

Carlos started moving the bed back into place and Jim decided there was nothing left to do, except put the room back in order. "Maybe we'll find it, by cle—"

"I should have known when Corby told me that one of his boarders had lost his marbles and started destroying his room, that it had the name Castle written all over it." Jim looked up to see Sheriff Ghett's use his pistol to swing the door open wide. Then he looked around the room. "I can see that the request for eviction is legitimate."

"I'd be angry, except that I'm too damned surprised to see you doing your job." Jim knew he shouldn't antagonize the sheriff. The last thing Jim needed was the sheriff bothering him. So he bit his tongue before he could say anything worse.

"You need to get your stuff, settle your bill, and get out. Are we clear?" Ghetts said, propping himself up against the doorframe.

"Crystal," Carlos said and grabbed the trunk. Jim started packing, gritting his teeth the whole time.

"Good. It's about time you boys learned some respect for authority," Ghetts said and then spat tobacco juice on the floor.

"When I get back from the expedition, Sheriff, I'm going to write the story that costs you your job. And when the citizens of Clinton find out that a *boy* solved the case their sheriff couldn't, how easy do you think it will be to win their vote, then?" Jim's fists were balled up at his sides and he was ready to snap.

"What expedition?" Ghetts asked. But before Jim could answer, Ghetts continued, "Are you threatening a media circus, boy?"

Jim knew he'd said too much. Provoking the man would only make his life miserable...*but only until the election.* Still, he had too much on his plate with his investigation into Deer Mountain. "No. I just plan on doing my job." Jim threw more clothes along with his shaving kit into the trunk, and then he closed the lid and fastened it.

"Let's just go, Jim," Carlos said, grabbing the trunk handle. Jim scanned the room for anything he had missed. It was torture to leave the room, knowing he could never come back and search for the strange lock of hair. But, he knew it wasn't there. He had searched everywhere. His mind still came back to the fact that someone had to have stolen it...*as I slept.* Just the thought of it made his hairs stand.

Together, he and Carlos, carried his trunk and supplies from the room, filing out past Ghetts, who was grinning, showing his dingy teeth. *He's loving this*. And Jim was hating it.

"That was the only shred of proof that I had, Carlos. All of this ties together, I'm more convinced than ever," Jim said as he stepped into the alley, heading for the cart. He could see Joe, petting Jolly. Jim stopped in his tracks and looked Carlos in the eye. "The only reason to steal it would be to hinder my investigation. And there's only one person I know who would benefit from that," Jim paused for effect, "Ghetts."

Carlos waited a moment, thinking. Then he said, "You may be right. He never has tried to found out anything about any of the missing from Deer Mountain. But if it was Ghetts, Jim, how did he do it?" Carlos had a point. Jim couldn't imagine Ghetts actually doing it. "Besides, he could just do a search and seizure. Why go to all the trouble of sneaking into your room in the middle of the night? Anyone could have seen him. It just seems like a big risk to me."

"Dammit," Jim said. He knew Carlos was making sense. Was he allowing his hatred for the man to tilt the probabilities? *Probably*.

"I suppose he could have sent someone to do his dirty crime. That way he could keep his hands clean." Carlos was thinking aloud. Jim knew when to let his brother stew on something. In fact, his brother had been stewing on something for weeks. And Jim still didn't know what it was. *Hell, I may never find out. Some things you just have to work through, alone.* And it wasn't as if their lives had been easy, the past few months. So Jim could relate and he remained silent. "The only other person who even knew about the cursed thing was…"

"George," Jim whispered. "You're right. He acted so strangely, Carlos, when I showed him the tuft of hair."

"Wait a second, Jim. He's just a suspect. He may have had nothing to do with it." Carlos sighed, thinking. "Still, we should question him."

"Let's go," Jim said and started for the cart.

"Let me do it," Carlos said. "You're out of sorts. You need a break."

"I'm fine," Jim said.

"So, we'll hear him out?" Carlos asked.

"Of course. But what do we do if we find out he took it?" Jim asked and he could tell from Carlos' expression that he hadn't thought about that.

"I guess it depends on his reason."

CHAPTER NINETEEN

"I can see why you would think that, honestly. I'd suspect me, too. But, I swear, I've never stolen anything in my life," George said and Carlos could see nothing about his friend that would make him question his sincerity. "I mean, I've turned over several artifacts to Professor Smith. I wanted you to give it to him. Why would I steal it? So that *I* could just give it to him?"

George was making complete sense, but Jim was a hard sale. "Maybe you did want to steal it and give it to him," Jim said.

"Why? For the recognition?" George laughed. "The professor has never been good at sharing recognition. The whole search for the missing link of evolution will most likely be found by a student who will never even get his name in the paper." Carlos could see that as a likely possibility, as well. *Sometimes giants stand on the shoulders of worker ants.* All of this did nothing to convince Carlos that George was the likely culprit. "Besides, look at me. I'm not exactly what you'd call agile. I sneak around abut as well as a cow."

Carlos had to admit that George was right about that. His friend was short and round. "He's telling the truth, Jim. We need to move on."

Jim sighed, relenting. "I know. I'm sorry, George," he said. "But who stole it and why? It's driving me crazy."

"I can see that," George said. "I know I might be speaking out of turn, here, but it wouldn't have been your Indian friend, would it?"

"No," Carlos said at the same time that Jim shook his head. Plus, Joe was gone already, anyway. Before coming back to St. James, he and Jim had pitched in together and purchased a horse for Joe, since Jim wouldn't be able to take Joe back to the farm and go on the expedition at the same time. And Carlos knew that Jim wasn't missing the expedition. "Joe was afraid of it. He would never have taken it."

"Okay, so that narrows it down even more." Even after standing accused, George was trying to be helpful.

Then Carlos remembered something from the night before. "Why did you go back out, last night?"

"What?" George asked, completely oblivious.

"Last night. After we came back from the stables. I saw you from the window. You went back out, heading back towards the stables," Carlos told him.

"I don't remember," George said. "I must have been sleepwalking. I've done it all my life."

"Really?" Carlos had never met anyone who had episodes of sleepwalking. Or if he had, he hadn't known. Little was understood about the sleeping disorder and no one could decide whether it was a mental or physical disorder.

"Yeah. I hate it. I'm always afraid I'll walk out a window instead of a door." Carlos could see how that would pose a problem. "Sometimes, I'll go weeks and sleep just fine. Other times, I know I've had spells, like every single day for a solid week, I'll wake up with dirty feet."

"That must be hard to deal with," Jim said, sympathizing.

"Yeah, I usually don't like to talk about it," George said. His face turned a bit pale.

Carlos imagined it would be a hard thing to talk about with anyone. He couldn't picture what it would be like to have no control over what he was doing. It made him shiver on the inside. So he understood when George changed the subject. "The expedition leaves tomorrow. I think we just need to go forward and forget about the strange lock of hair. It makes sense that whatever took the girls, took the Lakota children, too. And I've seen some strange bones and castings that have come from that mountain. We'll find answers up there, gentlemen. I just know it. That is, if you're still going, Carlos."

George had sounded convinced and with a plan of action, Jim had seemed to calm down. But at the mention that Carlos might not be going, Jim's panic was evident on his face. *He needs me.* Carlos felt sorry for his brother. He had been through more than any one person should go through. And to think, he'd been about to add to his brother's worries by telling him about the kiss between him and Anna. *It would have been a big mistake.* Jim was finding it hard to trust people, these days. "Yeah. I'm still going."

Jim visibly relaxed.

"Excellent," George said. "I'm sure that if the three of us put our minds to it, we'll figure this out. There have always been legends about the place. I've been out there more times than I can count, but this will be the first time I've been on the professor's expedition. And with everybody looking, we have to see something."

George's excitement was infectious. "I think you may be right," Jim said. "I could really use a win, right now."

Carlos could not possibly have agreed more.

**

The next morning, Jim watched as every person who had signed up for the field expedition was in the stables, well before sun up, working. Six horses had been designated to carry the supplies and nearly all were loaded down. They had tools for excavating and gathering samples. They had extra water, sacs of meal and flour, dried meats, and smoked hams. They had blankets and tents and the strange devices that could talk to each other by way of signal waves. They had a headcount and everyone was present and accounted for. They also had a long ride ahead, and with all the activity, some of the horses were getting restless.

Jim could relate.

He was more than ready to go when the professor brought his mare around to face everyone. "I think that about does it. For now it's fine, if we spread out and let the horses have space, but when we get to the foothills, I want everyone to remain in a tight formation. It is very easy to get turned around on that mountain, especially if you become separated from the group, so be safe. Everyone has a copy of the route, correct?" Professor Smith waited while everyone nodded affirmatively. As if on cue, the sun rose over the professor's shoulder, "Good. If there are no questions, then let's move out." No one voiced any concerns, and so after an adequate amount of time, the professor turned the mare east and headed for Deer Mountain.

Carlos and George filed in on either side of Jim and they chatted about all kinds of things as they rode to the first stop on the route.

"This was the easy part," Carlos said and Jim looked at the trail as it climbed ever steeper up the side of Deer Mountain. The next day would be when the real climb began.

"Yeah," Jim agreed as he unsaddled Jolly, taking the time to brush down the horse, as the group stopped for the evening. His stomach growled. It had been a long time since lunch. "I'm hungry," Jim said as he stowed the brush away amongst his gear.

"Me too," Carlos agreed, giving Pearl a good pat.

"I'll see if I can't round us up something to eat, if you guys want to get started setting up the tents," George said.

"Sure," Jim said. His stomach thought that sounded like a good idea, as well.

After setting up tents and filling their bellies, Jim shared a half a bottle of bourbon with Carlos and George, around the campfire, while they watched Professor Smith stand on a log in the center of camp, ready to address the members of the expedition. "The journey ahead will be much harder and much slower. Remember what I said. Keep a tight formation. The creature we seek is clever and smart. Eyewitness accounts report that the creature stands at nearly seven feet tall and is covered in dark brown fur. It is dangerous. We're looking for any signs that will tell us where this creature lives, its habits, and characteristics. We want to know what it eats, where it sleeps, how it mates. It is imperative that we learn everything we can about it so that we can complete our mission, which is to capture it for scientific research. I fully believe that this is the time we will find the link in our evolutionary process," The professor said. Then he stepped down off the log like a man half his age.

As Jim, Carlos, and George sat in the warmth of the fire, there were a dozen conversations scattered around the camp. Some people were joking and laughing, others had their heads together in serious thought, and some were even in spirited debate, as the night settled in around the campsite.

Jim was still wide awake when people began turning to their

beds, one by one, until finally the camp was so quiet that he, Carlos, and George were almost whispering as they sat, tending the fire.

George threw another log onto the flames, and the fire hissed, instantly drying any lingering moisture in the wood. In the distance, a pack of wolves howled at the full moon and shadows crept across the ground, reaching for the flames. "I'd hate to be out here, alone, right now."

Jim nodded, "I agree." He turned his head from the fire and stared up the mountainside, which was shrouded in deep shadows. Across the sky, darker clouds threatened to hide the moon and leave them with nothing but firelight to chase away the night. "It definitely has a certain feel about it."

"Yeah, the kind that crawls up your spine and whispers on your neck," Carlos said, shivering.

George yawned and then took a long drink from the bottle, before passing it to Jim. "I think I've had it, gentlemen." George stood up and steadied himself on wobbly legs. "Maybe I stopped, too late. I'm going to bed. Good night."

Carlos chuckled and looked at the nearly empty bottle. "Good night, George."

Jim looked up, "See you in the morning." George waved and then stumbled off towards the tents.

The silence was only magnified by the crackling of the fire.

His brother cleared his throat and reached for the bottle, turning it up. Then he passed it to Jim, who finished it off in a single gulp. It was a good batch of bourbon with a mild slow burn, warming him from head to toe. He tossed the bottle into the hearty flames. Carlos sighed, heavily, as though carrying a great weight on his shoulders. "Something on your mind, Carlos?"

Carlos sighed again, giving Jim the impression that the weight on his brother's shoulders had doubled in the space of a breath. Whatever was bothering Carlos had rooted deep in his brother's mind and Jim wished that he could take it away. His brother didn't deserve to be this tortured. *Not after everything we've been through.*

It wasn't fair. They had lost their mother when they were

children, their father less than three weeks, past, and the home they knew as children had been rightfully appropriated, but not to them. And Jim knew that he had only made things worse, when he'd lost Anna and become obsessed with doing whatever he could to find out what had happened to her. His brother's angst had only been multiplied by Jim's emotional abandonment and single-mindedness about the investigation. "What is it, Carlos?"

Again, Carlos sighed. "I need to tell you something, Jim. And, I'm sorry brother." Carlos swallowed hard. "You're not going to like it."

CHAPTER TWENTY

It was now or never. Carlos had his confession held on the tip of his tongue and the last drink of bourbon had broken the dam. He'd gone too far to back down now. He looked at the empty bottle as the flames danced around it. He wished it had been more than half-full when the expedition team had stopped for the evening to make camp.

"Just tell me, Carlos. Whatever it is, it's been bothering you for weeks. Out with it," Jim said, sternly. Guilt washed over Carlos. He thought he'd been managing to hide his demons, but Jim had seen them the whole time.

"The night Anna disappeared. I didn't tell you everything," Carlos said and waited for that to sink in.

Jim took a moment, before he spoke. "What didn't you tell me?"

"I kissed Anna." There he'd said it. He studied his brother's face and a myriad of emotions rose to the surface, highlighted by the flickering light from the fire.

After trying on a few different feelings, Carlos could see that Jim had settled on anger. His brother's dark eyes narrowed into slits and his jaw rocked back and forth, as he ground his teeth, chewing on all the words he wanted to say.

Carlos had been right. Jim hated him. And he had every right. "Why?" Jim finally asked.

"I don't know. It was a mistake. You have to believe me, Jim. I didn't mean it," Carlos said.

"You didn't mean it? Is that supposed to make me feel better, Carlos? You're my brother and I loved her," Jim said in a harsh whisper, attempting not to disturb those trying to sleep.

Carlos felt about two inches tall. He should have been honest from the start. "No. I know nothing will make you feel better. All I can say is that I'm sorry, Jim."

"Did she kiss you back?" Jim asked Carlos the question he should have asked Anna. *If she were here.*

Carlos closed his eyes and the guilt he'd seen on Anna's face, that night, at the moment of their betrayal, materialized in his field of vision. *Yes.* She had returned the kiss. "No," he said, lying. He opened his eyes. It was a small untruth that would save his brother added grief. And it was one that Carlos would be happy to live with. "I told you. It was a mistake. I drank too much." Carlos remembered the round after round of Gibsons. And she was too smart, too pretty and in the end...*too close.*

"You drank too much? That's a sorry excuse and you know it. You've had weeks to come up with better lies."

Jim's words were deserved, but that didn't keep them from cutting Carlos like a knife. "I know it's a sorry excuse, but it's the only one I have, Jim. You have to know how sorry I am," Carlos pleaded for understanding.

But it was too soon. "Just leave me alone, Carlos." Jim threw a heavy log onto the fire and the bottle broke apart inside the flames.

Carlos hated to leave things as they were, but his brother needed time. And he would give it to him. "Okay," he said and stood up. After fighting back, a final apology. Carlos turned to head back to his tent and in a blaze Jim pummeled Carlos to the ground, Carlos was caught off guard. He never lost a fight to his younger brother, but this time Carlos had no fight left in him. He wanted Jim to see his sincerity. Jim balled his fist, Carlos could see the rage in his face under the dim light of the fire as he left loose and landed two solid punches on his face. Carlos left his face unguarded and took each punch, showing no anger.

Jim stopped his assault, a look of confusion washed away his rage. "What the hell is wrong with you? Why won't you fight back?"

Carlos pulled himself to his feet and said, "I done enough damage brother, it's been killing me inside. I blame myself for Anna being missing. If you have to hate me, hate me. At least now you know the truth."

Carlos turned his back to Jim and headed for the tent he would share with his brother. *If Jim ever comes to bed.* Carlos had given his brother a lot to wrap his mind around.

As he walked away, he felt tons lighter. He had finally told Jim the truth, or at least enough that his burden of guilt had been lifted. His step was light when he entered the circle of tents and his heart was even lighter.

Of course, Jim was angry, now. But maybe Joe was right, and in time, Jim would find it in himself to forgive Carlos for his betrayal. If Jim needed space, then Carlos would give it to him. Whatever it took to get his brother back is what he would do. With the confession over, it was easier to be positive.

Carlos rubbed his chin when he reached the tent, *my little brother has a nice right hook* he chuckled to himself. "Now that's a Castle," he said as he smiled. But just as he stretched his hand out for the flap, a shadow moved on the outside of his peripheral, and he turned to see a familiar shape moving up the slope.

George.

He could be going to relieve himself. But Carlos didn't think so. Afraid that George was sleepwalking, Carlos let the flap of the tent fall and went scrambling after. He needed to catch George before he hurt himself. The thought of George walking over a cliff, gave his feet wings as he sped up the slope.

When he topped the rise, he scanned the valley below. Shades crawled across the valley floor as the clouds moved in wisps, blocking the moonlight. As he stood there, chasing shadows with his eyes, he spotted George moving behind an outcropping and going up the next slope.

Carlos had never seen anyone sleepwalk, but he was certain that George was doing just that. If his friend had simply wanted to relieve his bladder, he could have done that as soon as he had put the camp out of sight. *He's going to get hurt, if I don't stop him soon.*

Carlos skirted down the side of the hill, sending rocks to cascade in front of his path. "George!" he called out when he reached the valley below. Carlos honestly didn't know if George were even capable of hearing him in his condition. So he kept moving, heading for the outcrop where George had disappeared from his view.

When he rounded the turn, he froze as his mind tried to make sense out of what his eyes were seeing.

Professor Smith was right. Not only was the damned creature absolutely and completely real. It was also fearless of humans. Carlos knew because it was standing in arms reach of George as he was in deep conversation…*with the strangest looking man Carlos ever lay eyes upon,* something seemed off about the small figure, but he had trouble keeping his train of thought about the strange man, when he could clearly see a real, living and breathing Bigfoot standing guard over the two from the best he could tell. He wished the Bigfoot was the strangest part, but as he strained his ears to hear the two conversing, they were speaking in a strange dialect that was eerily unfamiliar, he had heard many of tongue in his lifetime, but nothing seemed remotely close.

***

Jim was angry. *And hurt.* He tossed another log on the fire and listened while the green bits hissed and popped. What the hell had Carlos been thinking? But Jim knew the answer to that. His brother hadn't been thinking. *At least not with his mind.* Kissing Anna was selfish. And selfish was a word Jim had *never* used to describe Carlos. He had always been the selfish one. It must have been exactly how his brother had described it. *A terrible mistake. An accident. Carlos probably did have too much to drink.* He was good at telling when his brother was sincere and he had no reason to doubt him after Carlos refused to fight back. Any other time Jim knew his brother would have given him a good beating, because Carlos had always been the strongest of the two.

None of these thoughts mattered, though. Because they didn't change how Jim felt. He was still angry. Hot tears gathered in his eyes, brought on by the fact that he could change nothing. He could *do* nothing…except stew in his own anger. He wished he had never come on the expedition.

"But then I'd never find answers," Jim whispered to himself.

He was so torn. Part of him want to apologize to Jim for blindsiding him and another part still wanted to fight, the feelings twisted around in his mind like two snakes constricting each other.

What I ought to do is march into that tent and punch him right in the damned nose. But when he balled up his fist, it was his own leg he struck this time. *Damn it! Why?* His mind kept asking the same question, over and over again.

Jim didn't know how long he sat there after Carlos left, but he was tired when he finally left and the fire had dwindled to little more than hot glowing coals. There was even a hint of light grey peaking from behind the mountain, overhead. The sun would be up in no more than a couple of hours.

Jim stretched and then went in search of a blanket and a good spot of ground where he could rest before the camp came to life. He was in no mood to see his brother. *Not yet, anyway. Maybe tomorrow.* For now, he would avoid the tent where he knew his brother slept.

Even when he couldn't find a blanket, he still couldn't bring himself to crawl inside the tent. *I'm not cold, anyway.* His anger was keeping him warm.

***

The next morning, he woke in the exact position he had fallen asleep, with his back leaning against a knotty tree. His neck was stiff, and he couldn't hear anything for the thunder rolling in his ears. His tongue felt as if it had doubled in size, searching for moisture. His throat was so dry, he knew he'd have to find some coffee before he even tried to speak. *And I have a lot to say to Carlos* Jim thought to himself.

Jim rubbed the soreness from his neck and he could feel the blood returning to his brain, breathing life back into the thoughts of the previous night. He still had some words to share with his brother, but that would have to wait. First thing, he needed coffee.

His whole body felt sluggish as he walked to the camp, and Jim was slowly realizing that he'd only punished himself by not sleeping in the tent in his own bedroll. There were several small cook fires going and it was easy enough to find a cup and a fresh pot. Someone handed him some warm bread and ham, as he took a sip of coffee. Jim scanned the campsite for signs of Carlos, but he was disappointed when he didn't spot his brother. *He may still be asleep.*

Jim devoured the bread and ham and washed it down with the rest of his coffee. Then he headed for the circle of tents, where he figured he would find his brother sleeping. But when he flung back the flap, the tent was empty. Carlos wasn't sleeping. And wherever he was, he wasn't in his tent.

Jim walked back to the cook fires, where he expected to find his brother sharing a meal. A quick look around, and although he could see a multitude of faces going about their mornings, none belonged to Carlos. But he did find George, holding a cup of coffee and laughing with a fellow explorer.

Jim wasted no time. "Have you seen Carlos this morning?" he asked George, when he could speak to the man without needing to yell.

"No," George said and shook his head. "Haven't seen him since last night." George turned up his coffee and downed it.

"He never went to bed last night." Jim recalled the untouched condition of the tent.

"What?" George asked, his eyebrows rising in question. "What do you mean?"

"Exactly what I said. He never came to bed." *And I would have known that a lot sooner, if I'd gone back to the tent.*

"He's around here, somewhere." George set his cup down with the others in need of rinsing. "We'll find him. He's probably just answering the call of nature." George said, offering a smile.

"Maybe." Then Jim had a sudden idea and took off in the direction of the horses.

"Where are we going?" George asked, trying to keep pace at Jim's side.

To see if Carlos left. But Jim wouldn't say that out loud. *What if he has left?* His gut started twisting into knots. The ridges were dangerous, especially at night. "He might be with the horses."

"Right." George's shorter legs moved quickly as they both covered the distance across the sprawling campsite. When they rounded the bend, Jim spotted both Pearl and Jolly, right where they'd been hobbled for the night and that surprised him. He hadn't actually expected to find both the horses. Somehow he'd *felt* that Carlos was far away that Jim had told him to leave him alone and his brother was doing exactly that. But if that were the case, he would have taken Pearl. The horse whinnied as though it was listening in on Jim's thoughts and was in agreement. Jim patted both horses and then left them to graze.

"Where are we going now?" George asked.

"To talk to the professor." Jim quickened his pace. The feeling in his gut travelled to the back of his throat. He was beginning to worry. *Where is he?* What if he's hurt? What if he'd done something stupid? The questions of the morning were becoming very different than the ones he'd been asking himself in the night and that irritated him. Instead of searching for his brother, he should be having it out with him. This made him even angrier with his brother. When had Carlos become so selfish?

He and George found the professor instructing the group while the students broke camp. Jim didn't even let the professor finish. He jumped up on the stump that the professor had used the evening before to address the expedition crew. "What are you doing?" George asked, whispering.

Jim ignored him. "Has anyone seen my brother, Carlos Castle?" Jim asked, not caring if Carlos suddenly appeared, making him look like a fool.

"What's going on, here?" The professor looked annoyed at being interrupted. Jim didn't care. All he could see were people shaking their heads.

No one had seen his brother. "Not since last night," one student replied and Jim swung around to see a redheaded young man still bearing the freckles of youth. "I saw him walking out of camp. Up that way." The man pointed up the slope. "At least I think it was him. It was dark."

Jim recognized the young man from a couple of his classes, but he couldn't recall his name. He climbed down from the stump and the man met him halfway. "But you think it was him, right?"

"I think so." The man shifted on his feet, and Jim could see the man second-guessing himself behind his eyes. "Yeah. I believe it was him. Tall and slender, dark headed." The man looked as though he was trying to convince himself, as well.

"Wonder what he was doing up there?" Jim asked, but he didn't wait for a reply. He made for the slope.

Worry was increasing inside Jim's mind, gnawing at him. He scrambled up the slope, hoping to see Carlos at the top of the rise...but he could only see a nearly empty landscape of rocks, slopes, and shrubbery that insisted on growing. "Jim!" He heard George calling out to him. But he didn't stop. He just kept going, picking his way down the shorter slope and to the next rise. Still, he saw nothing. But what did he honestly expect to see...*Carlos squatting behind a rock? Or at the bottom of the next slope in a lifeless heap?* Jim's thoughts were scaring the hell out of him. Regardless of how angry he was with his brother, an untimely demise would literally crush him. *Stop it!* This line of thought was helping no one.

"Jim," George said, nearly out of breath. "He's fine. He's probably wandering back into camp while we're out here." George said logically.

Jim didn't want George's logic. He wanted to find his brother.

"If you insist on doing this, right now and not waiting, then we should get the horses. We'll cover more ground."

It annoyed Jim that George was probably right. "Okay." Jim ran his fingers through his hair, scanning the landscape one more time. Then he followed George back to the camp.

The others stared at him and whispered among themselves as he and George made their way back through the camp towards the horses.

"I'm sure he's alright," George said.

But Jim had this sinking feeling that George was very wrong.

CHAPTER TWENTY-ONE

Carlos was more confused than he'd ever been in his life. He knew he was lying down, unable to move or see, but he didn't know how he'd came to be there. He tried to work his jaw, to cry out for help, but it was a useless effort. He strained to hear and somewhere, singers were humming a single chord. It was a constant thrum in his ears. His throat was raw and he would give anything for a drop of water. He felt a wave of heat that burned over every inch of his skin, then he lost control of his stomach and vomited. A foul odor greeted his nostrils and he fought back another round of heaving.

Rough hands jerked him upright, and he swayed back and forth, as he felt himself lifted and carried away. *Where are you taking me?* He wanted to scream the words at his captors. But he had no voice. He searched his mind, trying to remember what had happened, why he was there, but his memories felt like clouds that were well beyond his reach.

Flung down like a sack of grain, Carlos fell to the floor and his head smacked against the smooth metal. His stomach twisted in knots and he heaved again, gasping for air. Why was he so sick? *Am I dying?* Fear whispered through him. Was that why he couldn't see? Why he couldn't move or speak? *Because I'm dying?* And then an even more terrifying thought occurred to him. *What if I'm already dead?*

More wrenching in his gut told him that was not the case. *I'm not dead, yet.* Carlos forced himself to take long deep breaths. It was a calming exercise he'd read about in a book, but he couldn't remember where. The trick was to mimic the natural rhythm of sleep in order to control anxiety. So that's what he did. He counted in his head as he drew each breath in and held it, exhaling moments later. Over and over, he repeated the process until finally, his head felt a bit clearer and his heart felt a bit calmer.

What was the last thing he could remember? Carlos dug into the corners of his mind, but he came up empty. He blinked his eyes, trying to see…*something…anything.* But the world was a gray blur, interrupted by the occasional flash of light. *Like stars flickering…*

What bothered him most as he stared at the twinkling lights in the sea of gray was that he knew nothing. He didn't know where he was. He didn't know how he'd gotten there. And he certainly didn't know who had taken him. *Or why.*

"Then focus on what you do know, instead of worrying about what you don't." His mother's voice filled his head, comforting him, and although he couldn't feel them, he knew tears spilled from his eyes. Yet he knew his situation was far too urgent for tears. So he got his emotions into check and did as he was told.

He started with the easiest of facts, first. *I'm still alive. And I can still think…*even though he was having trouble remembering all the details.

A sudden rush of pain shot up his spine and settled in his head, right behind his eardrums. He fought back another round of nausea as his ears popped and the song flooded in, penetrating his thoughts. A moan escaped his lips when he realized the song he had heard being sung by a hundred voices sounded more like the screams of death. Men, women, and children cried out like a howling wind…and again, Carlos wept. Only this time, he cried out of frustration. All he could do was wait…*and listen.* He knew he had never been as helpless in his life as he was lying there, paralyzed, in the strange metal room with the blinking lights.

Minutes passed, while Carlos attempted to gain control of his muscles. In his mind, he was working his limbs back and forth, loosening them, but in reality, he knew his limbs barely flinched. But a flinch was a start, so he'd take his small victory. And then a strange thought occurred. Was that how his life was going to be measured, now? In small victories against his captors? And who were his captors and what the hell did they want?

Carlos had so many questions. And no answers…except the never-ending screams from beyond his world of gray.

It would be easy to fall into the clutches of self-pity, but Carlos had never been the type to wallow. He liked to act. And yet he was facing challenges around every turn in that respect. *It's hard to act when you can barely move!*

The familiar sensation of pins and needles began crawling the length of his skin and under any other circumstances, Carlos would have remained still until the feeling passed, but these were not normal. With every move, Carlos was rewarded with the seizing sensation that comes from attempting to move a limb that has only begun to regain feeling.

His flinches soon became concentrated action as his hands felt down his body, feeling for broken limbs, seeping wounds, or any other sign of injury. All he could feel was the fever that had a clear hold on his body. He was sick, but...

"I'm whole," he whispered in relief, and it startled him to hear his own voice. "Hello?" He cried out, but he knew no one would answer his calls. Just like there was no help for the others he could hear crying out.

Moments later, his vision began to clear and he could finally see more than just shapes and colors. It was frightening, but he moved his head slowly, taking in the gray room and trying to get a handle on his situation. So far, there was little more to see than what he imagined in the blurry landscape. Gray walls with mysterious blinking lights. *There has to be more.*

Carlos turned himself over to see what was behind him, expecting to find more metal walls with strange lights. But instead, he froze, realizing...

...I'm not alone.

On the floor in front of him, was a mangle of limbs and fabric. *And long blonde hair.*

***

Carlos was gone.

After two hours with the whole camp on horseback, searching, Jim had to reach that conclusion and it killed him. It felt like the worst defeat of his life.

"The creature is the culprit," Professor Smith said for the third time. "Find the creature and you'll find your brother." Jim watched the man hold the strange listening device up, but he came away shaking his head. "There's still no signal."

The professor had insisted that each explorer be equipped with one of the black boxes, but so far, Carlos' signal could not be detected. "He might not even have it on," he reasoned.

"That would be a problem," Professor Smith said.

"He had it on last night when I went to bed." George scanned the valley below. "I think I see something."

Jim's eyes trained in the direction of where George squinted and after a few moments, he saw it, too. "You're right." There were disturbed rocks and broken shrubbery at the bottom of the hill. "Something happened there," Jim said and he urged Jolly down.

Jim led George and the professor down the slope until he came to the spot that George had spotted from above. A trained tracker would have seen it much sooner and Jim cursed the fact that he hadn't paid more attention to Joe on their hunts. *Dammit!* He knew he'd been over the same spot twice, himself.

"It looks like a struggle," George said.

"It does to me too," Jim said squatting and trying to envision what had happened.

"There!" the professor said, excitedly. Jim looked at where the professor was pointing and lying just a few feet away on the ground, was a small shred of fabric.

George was closer, so he snatched it up. Jim crossed the short distance between them and George held it up for inspection.

"This was his." Jim knew, as he fingered the cloth. He recognized his mother's stitching.

"He's been abducted by them," The professor said, convinced, and all Jim could think about were the animal spirits, the god's lock, and...*Anna*. Had she been abducted the same way that his brother had? *Probably*. And he'd been searching for her for months, now.

George must have seen the volley of emotions trying to overtake him. "It's okay. We'll find your brother."

"How can you say that, George?" Jim asked, bitterly. "Did we find Anna?"

"No, but Carlos isn't Anna." George pulled himself up into the saddle. "And Anna wasn't wearing a tracking device."

George was right. Plus they had plenty of people and supplies, so a thorough search could ensue. It was then that Jim focused his helplessness into action and began organizing the search along with George.

The Professor sent riders in all four directions, while he and George searched the immediate vicinity for further clues. But by late afternoon three of the groups had returned empty handed and Jim and George weren't having any better luck.

"I think we need to move the whole camp up the mountain until sunset, then we camp and expand the search, further up, tomorrow. What do you think, Jim?" George asked.

"It's better than what we've been doing. As soon as the others return, we'll set out." Jim made the call to move camp. And then he watched George scurry up the slope to spread the word.

Jim stood up and stretched his sore muscles. He'd spent all afternoon combing the ground for any indication of where he could find his brother. The anger he had felt all night and into the morning had been replaced by a nagging dread that he would never get to see Carlos again.

Jim blamed himself. If he hadn't told Carlos to go away and leave him alone, then his brother would probably still be alright. But he knew he was going to get nowhere worrying about what could have been, when he knew he should be focusing on the issue at hand. *Carlos is miss—*

"Jim!" he heard George yell from above. He looked up the slope to see George waving at him. "They spotted the last set of riders coming this way," George said as Jim gained the top of the slope. "And they have someone with them."

Jim knew it was too much to hope that the extra rider was Carlos, but he did it all the same. As he and George trotted back to camp, the riders brought their horses up hard, sending a cloud of dust into the air. Jim held his breath as the dust cleared and when it finally settled, he exhaled in mix of confusion and disappointment.

The extra rider was Lloyd. "Jim!" Lloyd said, when he spotted him from the saddle. Then he quickly climbed down and handed off the reigns to one of the students to care for the horse.

Jim reached Lloyd with his hand outstretched. After a quick shake, "What are you doing here," Jim asked, still bewildered by Lloyd's presence at camp.

"They have your Indian friend," Lloyd said. *Joe?* "Ghetts arrested him yesterday morning and threw him in jail."

"What?" Jim asked trying to take it all in. "Joe should be close to home by now."

"Well, he's not," Lloyd replied. "Right now he's an honorary guest of the sheriff. Once I heard, I tried to see him, but the sheriff said that Indians didn't deserve visitors. Then he said he'd be willing to make an exception for you."

Jim didn't know what to say, much less what to do. "But Carlos is missing," Jim said.

"I know. I heard. I'm sorry Jim. Is there anything I can do to help?" Lloyd asked. Jim wanted to bury his head in the sand and forget all his problems. *How much can one man take?*

His bad luck had started a long time ago. And at the end of it, he'd lost his mother, his father, the woman he loved, his brother and now his best friend was being held against his will. And there was literally nothing he could do to stop it…*except*…

He looked at George. "I need you to go with Lloyd." Then Jim looked at Lloyd. "Do whatever it takes. Take George with you. Get Joe out and bring him here. If anyone can track Carlos, Joe can."

"Jim, how the hell are we supposed to get him out of jail? Ghetts won't even let anyone see him. Weren't you listening to me?" Lloyd asked, his eyes growing wider. "I can't be involved in a jail break."

"You won't be. Cause you're gonna tell Ghetts exactly what he wants to hear. If he'll release Joe, I'll never write another article for the Clinton Weekly." If the man was afraid of a media circus revolving around him, then Jim would take that fear away. "But tell him if he doesn't, I'll make it my personal business to become his worst nightmare."

"You sure it wouldn't be best if I stayed here and helped with the search?" George asked.

"There is no search without Joe." *There's just me and you and the rest of the expedition. And not one of us is a real tracker.*

"Are you sure about this?" Lloyd asked.

Jim nodded.

"I can find work at another paper. Tell the sheriff whatever you have to," Jim told Lloyd. "Just get Joe here."

His brother's life may well depend on it. *Joe will find Carlos.* He had to. The sheriff's prejudice may be exactly what saved his brother's life and Jim would have found it amusingly ironic, if the situation hadn't been so dire.

"Hurry. Because I'm not waiting around." Jim had decided to stick with his and George's original plan and move the campsite further up the mountain.

"We will," Lloyd promised.

George nodded.

Jim could tell by the look on George's face that he'd rather stay and continue searching for Carlos, but Jim knew that it was more important for Joe to be freed. And Ghett's might believe Lloyd about Jim's promise, if George were there backing him up.

Jim watched them ride off in a cloud of dust. *Three days.* That's how old the trail would likely be when Joe finally arrived. And even a novice knew that was a trail gone cold. But Jim had seen Joe track the week old trail of a wolf that had been killing off livestock. But this creature of the professors was more elusive than a wolf.

"Remember to stay close and keep your signal boxes on you at all times," the professor said from the back of his horse. Jim mounted Jolly and fell in line with the other riders while he led Pearl. The mare's burden was lighter by a rider, but someone had logically thought to put the horse to use, carrying supplies.

For three hours, they travelled. Then they managed to find a clearing large enough to camp and keep the horses close. But Jim didn't linger around the campfires as he had the previous night. Instead, he turned in early. It felt wrong crawling into the tent. Did his brother have a warm bed? *Is he hungry? Is he hurt? Is he even alive?*

Each question hurt more than the last. And what hurt most was that he'd asked them all before...*when Anna disappeared.* And he still had no answers.

He stretched out in the tent and waited for sleep, which proved to be an unreliable visitor, checking in and out. Twice he'd fallen asleep, just to wake up again, moments later, with worry feasting on his brain. So he abandoned his bed.

By the time the sky had gone from black to gray, Jim had disassembled his tent, cared for the horses, and made a fresh brew of coffee, while the rest of the camp began stirring to life. And by the time the sun rose from behind the mountain, the expedition had already set out and was well under way.

Jim kept expecting to find Carlos. *Maybe he's just lost.* But then he would remember the broken shrubbery and the scuffs in the dirt and his heart would sink into his stomach, causing him to dig his heels into Jolly's side and urge the horse at a faster pace.

He didn't talk to anyone unless he had to, as he pushed them all forward. Mainly, because he was tired of hearing condolences. Everyone was sorry for him. And if he listened too long, he'd start to feel sorry for himself. The only person who didn't offer condolences was Professor Smith. And that's only because the man was too excited about using his specialized equipment. But so far his *specialized equipment* had found nothing.

"While the others make camp, you and I will scout ahead with your machine," Jim said to the professor as he brought Jolly up beside the wiry little man.

"Absolutely," the professor replied. "We shouldn't waste a moment."

"I'm glad we agree." *Otherwise, we'd have to do this the hard way.* Jim was more determined than ever to find Carlos and he'd decided that no one was going to stand in his way.

"How far can that thing listen?" Jim asked, wishing he'd paid more attention to the man's lectures.

The professor tapped the device, which rode in front of him in the saddle. "Quite far, actually, but it depends on the terrain, too, you see." The professor waved his hand out, taking in the mountainous landscape. "These are not ideal circumstances."

"So what's the short answer?" Jim asked, tired of hearing the man talk.

If the professor was offended, Jim couldn't tell. And that was a good thing, too. The way he saw it, he didn't have time for lectures. "About a half a mile," the professor said smiling. "But over open water the signal has been detected up to a mile and a half. Don't you find that astonishing?"

"Up until a few weeks ago, I didn't think any of this was possible. Consider me amazed." Jim said.

"It *is* incredible," the professor said wistfully. "It's the game changer, in fact." Then he began doing what did best. *Another lecture.* "And after studying several different animal species, I fully believe that the abducted are taken back to the creatures' dens, for lack of better terminology, which is why I believe that if we find your brother, we will find where they live. And then perhaps, we can turn the tables on them and capture one of their own. Wouldn't that be something, Mr. Castle?"

Jim didn't care about capturing the damned creature. He cared about finding his brother. *Alive.* And the way the professor talked, Carlos could have been last night's dinner. "How do these creatures move around without detection?" Jim asked. That was the most important question.

"That is one of things we will study once we locate the den. There are a few different theories. Did you know that nearly every culture has a myth about similar creatures? Don't you find that interesting?"

"Yes, but I'm more interested in hearing some of those theories you spoke about," Jim said, steering the professor back to the most pressing topic. If he could figure out how the damned thing hides then he could follow it and find Carlos. And he still had two days, at the earliest, before Joe would join him in the search.

"Yes, yes. This one is possible, if not probable. There are some who believe the creature is not of this world, that it has the ability to move itself from one location to another. Instantaneously. Can you imagine?" the professor asked and Jim honestly couldn't.

"I think I would have to see that for myself," Jim said.

"Ah, yes. You like facts. Well, this next theory is based on scientific evidence. You may or may not know that some species of animals have the ability to blend into their environment, lizards can look like tree bark, while some fish can take on the appearance of rocks."

"Of course," Jim whispered to himself. The reason it could move around without being detected was because it could camouflage itself. The hairs raised on Jim's neck as he remembered the god's lock and how it had changed color every time he touched it. The professor kept rambling, but Jim was no longer listening. As soon as the professor mentioned the theory, his wheels had started turning.

Jim was absolutely convinced that everything he had been investigating was tied together, now. It made too much sense. And then his heart jumped into his throat. *How do you track something that can't be seen?*

He knew the professor's answer to that question. But so far the signal boxes and devices had been pretty much useless. *Maybe Joe will know Jim thought.*

After five straight hours of scouting the surrounding area with Professor Smith and his black boxes and wires, Jim was ready to drop and he was no closer to finding Carlos, than he was to finding Anna. He'd had little to no sleep in the past two days and what sleep he'd managed to find had been brief and restless.

Carlos looked over at the professor, "Let's return to camp professor, will start again at first light…I think your black box would have picked my brothers location up by now if he was in this direction."

"Yes, it is highly improbable that we will find him in this direction, we already traveled a great distance and my box is tracking a good distance ahead of us, so I feel it is safe to call it."

***

Jim sent riders out again, to scan the surrounding area for any sign of a trail or nesting ground, but he didn't have much hope. He and the professor had been fairly thorough. *Still, the more people looking, the better the chances of finding Carlos.*

Jim crawled into his tent, found his pillow, and was asleep before the riders returned. He knew if they returned with any news, someone would find him.

CHAPTER TWENTY-TWO

Carlos stared at the blonde hair attached to the limp body. As the feeling returned to his arms and legs, he crawled across the cold metal floor, stopping only once to heave up yellow bile. His stomach was entirely empty and that was fine with him. He couldn't abide the thought of food.

Water was a different story. He was so thirsty he'd gladly drink from a mud puddle.

Carlos crawled around the girl's body, angling himself forward until he could see her face. He held his breath as she came into view. *It's not Anna.* Carlos exhaled, whooshing. He had let his imagination go at the sight of a female form with golden hair. Now, he was relieved.

From his angle, he could see the girl's chest moving up and down in the soft rhythm of sleep. He reached out and touched her shoulder.

Immediately, her eyes flew open and she shrank back from him. "Don't touch me!" she screamed.

"It's okay. I'm not going to hurt you." Carlos felt as though he were dealing with a wild animal. He watched her blue eyes dart around the room and back to him. "It's okay," he told her again.

"I thought you were one of them," she said, wrapping her arms around herself. Then she narrowed her eyes at him. "Who are you?"

"I'm sorry." Carlos had never intended to scare the young woman. "My name is Carlos Castle."

"Maggie," she said her one word introduction. Then she rubbed her arms, as if she were cold.

"Do you know where we are, Maggie?" Carlos asked, and then hastily added, "Do you know who took us and what they want?"

"You don't remember," Maggie laughed and there was nothing funny about it. "But you will," she sang the words to him.

"What is that supposed to mean?" Carlos asked, irritated.

"Your memories are the last to come back. At least it was that way for me," Maggie said. Then she whispered, "Even if you don't want them to."

She's losing her senses. "How long have you been here, Maggie?" Carlos knew he needed to know the answer, even if he couldn't remember why. He looked at her dress. It was dirty and worn although he could tell that it had been of fine quality some time in its past.

"Months, maybe years," she whispered, staring at something that wasn't there.

"You've been here alone all that time?" Carlos asked, recognizing the symptoms of severe isolation.

"Most of it." She looked down and began picking at her dress like a nervous child. "There were others."

"What happened to the others, Maggie?" Carlos asked, not certain he wanted the answer.

Maggie smiled around dirty teeth, making him shiver on the inside. "The white demons, with glass faces came for them, as soon as they were all better. But not me." She laughed as though she had told a funny joke. "They don't want me."

The white demons came for them?

And that's when Carlos started remembering.

***

When Jim woke and stepped from his tent, the moon was as full as his mind. He'd slept the entire evening away and half the night, as well. But he was wide awake, now. *Awake and alone with his thoughts.* And his thoughts were weights on his chest, making it hard to breathe.

Jim was terrified for Carlos and for himself. What if he found his brother and it was too late? Or, what if he couldn't find his brother at all? Could he live with another person he loved, gone without

167

answers? He didn't even want to think about it. It was too much.

It had already been three nights and two days since Lloyd brought news about Joe, and gone back to Clinton with Jim's offer to Sheriff Ghetts, the days were occupied with Jim and the others searching for Carlos. Jim felt like they had clambered over every rock and every gully of the mountain, from the low foothills to the rocky peak. That wasn't true, of course. The mountain was much too vast.

The scope of the search and treacherous terrain were the least of Jim's worries. What gnawed at his conscious the most was his choice to search for his brother in the first place. Jim feared that the very act of searching was a mistake until Joe arrived. None of the members of the professor's expedition were trained trackers. Any attempt they made would be amateur at best. What if, in searching for signs of Carlos's trail, they erased it, or contaminated it with their own tracks? Jim's stomach churned as a horrible thought seeped into his already fragile mind…what if Joe mistook their tracks as signs of Carlos's passage? Jim tried to shake these horrible thoughts away, but deep down guilt crept up his spine.

Why did he get angry with Carlos? He was trying to apologize, he had felt horrible about what he did. It's not like he would ever wish any harm come to Anna, Jim thought aloud.

At first Jim had insisted that the company leave alone the immediate area around camp, to preserve the trail for Joe. The professor had had the members of the expedition cast about for clues on parts of the mountain slopes that were some distance off from camp, and told them to move in slowly expanding in spirals, as Jim instructed. But soon Jim began to fear that even this would hinder the search when Joe arrived, and Jim had self-doubts about his own ability to track, and didn't want to chance it, he knew Joe was the best, and his brother's life might very well depended on them finding him. He and the professor issued new instructions: Only search areas high up on the mountain side, or down at the bottom of the foothills, or a mile off at the same altitude in flanking direction. Also, they were to use only narrow trails when coming and going from the search areas.

Jim suspected that the others were grumbling behind his back. Part of it, he felt was due to his impatience and his inexperience, and uncertainty when giving instructions. But part of it might have to do with the way the search was a distraction from the real work of the expedition, the search for fossils. He thought he sensed it in the way the others looked at him and stopped talking when he was near. *It's his fault we're not getting work done*, he imagined them grumbling to each other. *If only he and his brother hadn't come along we could be doing serious scientific work*. Jim felt shame at these suspicions, which were completely without merit, and he told himself it was just his guilt getting the better of him. But then one evening he overheard the professor say something to another member of the expedition in a sharp voice: "What if it were you or your brother?"

But if the days were occupied with the search, the nights were occupied with fears and anxieties. Naturally, Jim's greatest worries were about Carlos. He tried desperately to put away those terrible images of Carlos lying dead somewhere. But of course the longer the search went on without sign or evidence of his brother, the harder it became for Jim to ignore the likelihood that he had not only lost his father and the girl he loved, but that he had lost his brother as well…also Joe weighed on his emotions causing added anxieties.

Sheriff Ghetts had jailed him on trumped-up charges. The Sheriff had no love for the tribes in the area, that was plain, and he had a grudge against him that much Jim was certain of. Maybe it was his imagination, trying to avoid creating morbid fantasies about Carlos. Jim's mind was hard at work giving him vivid scenes of the Sheriff to worry about at night. Jim imagined Sheriff Ghetts laughing in a long, slow and lazy way at Lloyd and at George as they pleaded with him to accept Jim's offer. He imagined the Sheriff telling them that he would have to sleep on it, that he would have to investigate the precedents for receiving and making such an offer, that he would have to write to the county seat or the territorial capital. He imagined Sheriff Ghetts telling them that he would be happy to consider Jim's offer, but that he couldn't take it seriously unless Jim himself returned to Clinton to offer it himself. He imagined Lloyd and George returning after these delays, and telling Jim that he would have to return to Clinton with them. And he imagined, at the end of all this tortuous filibustering, the Sheriff telling him, "No."

Jim bolted up from his sleep…was I dreaming? He thought aloud. It was getting to the point where he didn't know if the visions that tormented him were memories of nightmares or inventions welling up into his consciousness directly. Jim lay awake for quiet sometime, waiting to see if sleep would return, then he impatiently crawled from his tent. He walked quietly around camp, not caring whether he woke himself up more fully, or tired himself out. Either would be preferable to the mental and physical twilight he found himself in.

He had made halfway around the camp when he caught sight of a figure huddled atop a rock. Cautiously he approached, and saw it was a man bent over some kind of work. He heard a voice mutter, and recognized it as Professor Smith's. Before Jim could speak, his foot slid over a rock, and he stumbled.

The professor looked up. "Who's there?" he hissed. "Oh, it's you, Jim. Can't sleep either, my boy?"

"I woke up. Why are you awake?"

"I couldn't sleep, saw the moon was bright, thought I might fiddle a little with a signal box. But it's too dark after all."

"You could light a lantern."

"Ah, well, it doesn't really matter. I was only satisfying curiosity about them."

Jim leaned against the same rock the professor was perched upon. "How did you come by these things?"

"An inventor named Hertz. Have you heard of him?"

"No."

"Well, it was a foolish question, he's rather a mysterious fellow, I gather. Likes to tinker and dabble in things, but doesn't like publicity. Not like Edison." He laughed. "It was George who brought him to my attention, in fact."

"How did George know about him?" Jim thought it odd that a student, and not a professor at the college, would have penetrated whatever veil surrounded this inventor.

"He worked for him as an assistant before becoming a student. Hertz trusts him, and George apparently gave me a good reference or something. Ha ha, that's quite a turnabout, isn't it, the student recommending the teacher? George arranged for me to test some early prototypes of these, and now I'm testing some more advanced models."

"How do they work?"

"I've no idea. I'm a doctor, not an electrician. More's the pity, since I really am impressed by them."

He put the signal box back into a small pack. "Well, I can't see anything by moonlight, and it wouldn't have done me much good anyhow." He craned his neck and looked up at the sky. "If I thought I'd be passing more than one sleepless night, I would have thought to bring a telescope."

He continued staring upward and didn't stop. Jim glanced up at the sky, it was peppered in stars, if it were a time before his brother or Anna went missing, he would have cared more, taking one last glance at his favorite constellation Orion, he picked up the pack and tossed it from hand to hand thoughtfully. It was a remarkable device: Give it to a person to carry, and you could use another device to locate them. And yet what good had it done. Carlos had been carrying one, but in the days since his disappearance they had not been able to get a signal from it. That, more than anything else, was what convinced Jim and the professor that one of the mysterious creatures had carried Carlos off. If Carlos had just slipped into a crevice or fallen down a hole, the signal would have taken them to him. But it seemed far more likely that he had been carried off.

It must have taken him a fair distance, too, which was the awful thing, for that made the search area so much larger. And there was no guarantee that the signal box would even have remained on Carlos. Suppose the creatures stripped him before disposing of him? Jim shuddered horribly at *that* new thought of Carlos being torn to bits by some wild, eldritch monstrosity that was neither human nor inhuman. If that had happened, then even if they were to catch the signal from the box Carlos was carrying, it might not lead them to him. It might lead them to *it*.

Lead them to it. Jim felt the hairs on the back of his neck start to rise.

"Well, I should try to get some sleep," the professor said with a sigh. "I suggest you get some too, Jim."

He started to get up, but Jim grasped him by the arm. "Professor

Smith, do you have any extra signal boxes on hand?"

"A few," Professor Smith said. "Why?"

Jim felt as though someone were shouting an idea at him, but he couldn't quite make out the words. He tightened his grip on the academic's arm. "Do you think the creatures are still about, still watching us?"

"It wouldn't surprise me. Though, to be perfectly honest, I am trying not to dwell on the possibility."

"Suppose, just suppose, professor," gasped Jim. "If one of the creatures took one of the signal boxes, it might take it back to where Carlos is? Mightn't it?"

"It's a possibility," Professor Smith said, though he sounded doubtful. "Although I'm not certain what good it would do. If it took the box to where your brother is, then we wouldn't be able to find the signal box the thing carried off, any more than we can find the one that is on your brother."

"Unless the one Carlos was wearing was broken in a struggle," Jim said. "It's worth a gamble, surely!"

"Yes, I think it might be," said the professor after a moment's thought. "But how do we put one of the boxes onto a creature?"

"We don't," said Jim. "We entice it to carry the box away!"

"How do we do that?"

"I haven't thought *that* far ahead!" Jim said.

"Shh! You'll wake the camp!" Professor Smith hissed.

Jim pondered the matter furiously. What did the creatures want that they kept carrying people off? There was one obvious answer, and Jim recoiled instinctively from it. But if this idea was going to work, it would have to be faced. They would have to dip into their stores of dried and salted beef and pork.

But maybe there was something else about the human victims that was attracting their attention. "I don't suppose we could make a kind of scarecrow as bait," he mused aloud. "Give it a fake person it might carry off."

"We could give it the makings of a scarecrow, perhaps," Professor Smith said.

Jim decided that it was better to make the attempt than to continue musing on it. Impatiently, he plunged back into camp, to the tent where the supplies were housed. The professor joined him, and after lighting a lantern they started going through the stores.

It was a poor excuse for a scarecrow when they were finished: a pile of dried meats and fruits tied up in a bundle of shirts that were themselves tied together by lengths of stout cord. One of these cords was knotted onto one of the spare signal boxes; they also attached some shiny belt buckles to the rope, in case it was the glint of metal that appealed to the creatures. The entire smelly pile of bait they placed on a rag that was placed on a rock and smeared with a paste of wet coffee grounds and beans. Jim thought it very unappetizing, and his spirits sank after they had it propped up. Now that the bait was set, it seemed to him an unlikely sort of thing to be carried off. And as he crawled back into his tent he resolved not to expect any great success from the experiment. At best, he decided, they would wake the next morning to find it undisturbed. More likely, some other wild beast prowling the side of the mountain, would make off with it. At worst, the bait would be torn apart, the food devoured, and the signal box trampled to ruins. And as he closed his eyes he couldn't help telling himself that his desperation was making him foolish if not outright crazy...but the mere fact that he'd tried something new seemed to have settled his spirit, for he was almost instantly asleep after closing his eyes.

***

Jim awoke to someone or something, violently shaking him from his sleep. He instinctively balled his hands into hard fists ready to fight for his life. As his eyes came into focus he realized it was just the professor, so he disarmed his fists and sighed a breath of fresh air.

"I think it worked, my boy," Professor Smith said excitedly. "The signal box, the bait, all of it! It's been carried away!"

CHAPTER TWENTY-THREE

A quick investigation showed that the professor was right. The mess of food and rags had vanished from its rock, and the signal box had gone right with it. Everyone in camp swore that they hadn't touched it. That meant either a coyote or some other scavenger had dragged it away, or that one of the creatures carried it off.

Jim tried not to get his hopes up as the professor and another student warmed up the receiving instruments that would allow them to locate the missing signal box. But the professor seemed to have no doubts.

"I rather doubt an ordinary wild animal would have made off with it between the time we set it out and when I rose at dawn," Professor Smith said. "I think it much more probable that one of the creatures was watching us, and, perhaps impelled by some sense of curiosity, took it shortly thereafter."

It didn't exactly comfort Jim to think that the entire time they were setting it up, they were being spied upon. But he was soon distracted by another cry from the professor. "I think we have it, gentlemen! This way!" And with enthusiasm hardly less than Jim himself could have felt, the professor jogged out of camp while holding the receiving instrument before him.

Jim didn't know how the signal boxes worked, so he just hurried along behind the professor. Another dozen students, caught up in the interest and excitement, chasing after them. But for most of them, the initial burst soon faded, and they returned to camp for breakfast. The four or so other students also began to lag as the first, easy dash over level ground gave way to a trickier and more strenuous climb up the slopes of the mountain. When the professor came to the foot of a sheer cliff and craned his neck to gaze up at it, all that had followed, except Jim, turned back to watch at a distance.

Jim tried to ignore the hunger pangs that gnawed at him as he and the professor tried to find a way up the cliff. They finally found a narrow crevice in the side of the mountain, parallel to the cliff, which through a combination of steep slope and handholds held promise of a path to the top. The professor hung the receiver across his back with a sturdy strap and left Jim lead the way up. It was hot, hard, and dirty work, despite the cool morning air, and it took them nearly twenty minutes to get to the more level space at the top of the cliff. They were quite dusty when they reached the top. Jim started to brush the professor off, but the latter seemed oblivious to anything except the promise of catching up to the signal box, and the professor was on the trail again as soon as he had caught his breath.

Almost immediately, Jim and the professor found themselves peering into a dark, narrow cleft that opened up in the mountain side just a few dozen yards from where they had come out onto the shoulder of the mountain. Jim felt his heart beat excitedly, for he was certain that none of the expedition had investigated this spot yet. But his excitement soon fell to crushing disappointment. Just under the lip of the cleft lay the signal box they had been following. It was still attached to the pile of rags and food and shiny bits of metal, all of which were still intact.

***

Jim was hot to organize an intensive search of the mountainside near the cleft, but such thoughts were driven from his mind as soon as he and the professor got back to camp. George was waiting for him.

"I've got good news, Jim," he said after clasping the other in a hearty embrace. "Your friend is on his way, he will be here by noon at the latest I'm guessing."

"Ghetts released him?" Jim cried out. After the dread he had felt, this news was an unexpected joy.

But George's expression wasn't entirely clear of anxiety. "Not exactly," he said. "Ghetts is coming along too. He says Joe is still his prisoner, but he says that he's willing to let Joe help out."

This extra bit of news of course infuriated Jim, and he was privately resolved to see that Joe was fully released. But it gladdened him considerably to know that his friend would be arriving to help, and that he'd be arriving almost as soon as he could have hoped to see him.

There was nothing else to do but wait, and with the promise of Joe's arrival Professor Smith released the other members of the expedition to start preparing for the work they had come intending to perform, and he guided them to a point almost a mile off in the opposite direction from camp, so that any work they did would not interfere with the search for Carlos.

But the professor himself returned soon after. "They can carry on without me for a little while," he told Jim and George, "and I am more anxious to help find Carlos. Of course if, God forbid, your Indian friend can't help us find his trail, I will summon them back and we will plunge into the search again."

Jim told the professor, "I hope that that is not necessary, I need a win…things been spiraling out of control, we have to find my brother."

An anxious few hours passed, which Jim did his best to burn with some light hiking and desultory exploration over terrain he'd already combed over, but a little before lunchtime two men on horseback rode into camp. Joe was hunched up on the back of one, looking like he wanted to disappear. Sheriff Ghetts sat on his horse with more confidence. "I was told you might have a use for this fellow," he drawled at Jim.

"Yes, sheriff, thank you, I'll take charge of him," Jim said as he reached up to help Joe from the horse. He was most anxious to see the back of Ghetts's horse as the lawman rode back to Clinton.

"Now hold on," said the sheriff, and he reached over to grasp Joe by the shoulder. "I said nothing about releasing him into anyone's charge, least of all a fellow I came near to arresting earlier myself." His smile had an ugly gloat inside it. "That's why I came out, to ensure that no false representations or assurances were being made."

"I swear to you, sheriff," Jim hissed impatiently. "The promises that I conveyed through George Kinley and Lloyd Turner were absolutely truthful."

"And what were those assurances? We would like us both to be certain, wouldn't we? That we both understand those assurances in the same way, right?" Ghetts said, smiling broadly.

Jim gritted his teeth. "That if you released Joe I wouldn't write any more articles for the Clinton Weekly," he said. "Of course, since you *haven't* released Joe, I am still perfectly free to write another article tonight and send it by messenger to Mr. Turner."

Sheriff Ghetts snickered. "That would be clever of you. And what would you write? That I was failing to do my duty by undertaking a search for missing persons?"

"An excellent suggestion, sheriff," Jim said. "Perhaps *you* should take a part-time job working for the paper, as you have an intuitive grasp of what would make for a good story."

But the sheriff continued to look serene. "I wouldn't like to see such an untruthful report published in Mr. Turner's fine gazette."

"*Untruthful?*" Jim exploded, and he shook off George Kinley's restraining hand. "Do you deny that you have failed to search for a missing girl, and for abducted children, and to investigate reports concerning their possible whereabouts?"

"I do not deny that I have regarded such reports as mere rumor-mongering, or that I have deemed it, on the basis of my professional opinion, that certain investigations would have been premature. Nonetheless, in light of new reports I have come to a new judgment." He glanced at Professor Smith, who had been coldly regarding this conversation. "You've already lost one student, professor," he said to the doctor. "How careless do you have to be to lose a second one? But as I say, in light of this second, er, incident, I have decided to take your advice, Mr. Castle." The sunlight practically glinted off his smile. "I have accompanied the prisoner so that I may supervise the search."

***

Jim regarded the presence of the sheriff with stark horror, but of course there was nothing he could do. The sheriff insisted that everyone consume a leisurely lunch from the expedition's stock of supplies before allowing the search to begin. Now new fantasies began to crowd into Jim's already crowded mind. Fantasies in which the sheriff destroyed evidence, hindered Joe, and misdirected the search alternated with fantasies of murder and burial.

But perhaps the sheriff only intended to torture Jim with his presence, as he only watched with a casual curiosity as Jim, the professor, and George showed Joe to the spot where they had last found evidence of Carlos. Joe squatted and examined the scene for a very long time, and when Jim grew impatient he only raised his hand and frowned at him. But finally he had something declare. "Too many footprints."

"Then is it hopeless?" Jim said.

"Nothing is hopeless," Joe said. "But from here I see nothing useful. Is there no place else you can show me?"

"There is a cave," Jim started to say, and he glanced at the sheriff, fearful the man would object to changing the location of the search. But Ghetts just chawed on a leaf of tobacco that he stuffed in his cheek a moment earlier, seeming to have no real opinion.

So Jim and the professor led the other three up the mountain slope to where they had found the signal box. As they went, the professor explained the nature and use of the device. The sheriff listened with what appeared to be vague interest. Joe only grunted and remarked that a man would have to have sharp eyes indeed to follow an invisible trail through the open air.

But they were still almost half a mile away from the cliff face when Joe called for them a halt so that he could study the ground.

"What is it?" Jim asked excitedly.

"I don't know," Joe said after long thought. "If it is an animal, it is not one that leaves a trail like any other I've seen."

"Could it be a man?" Jim asked.

"Something leading or carrying a man." Joe said.

"I cannot read such things as that," Joe retorted. He looked uneasy. "I would give it a wide berth if I found such a thing while traveling. But for the sake of your brother, Jim, I will follow it."

So the five of them pressed forward, slowly winding up a slow and painful trail, up the side of the mountain. The track diverged from the easy trail they had been following and went up at a steeper angle. But Jim grew more and more excited as he saw that despite this, it was veering in the same direction they had been heading. The professor noticed this as well.

"This may be the tracks of the creature that took our bait last night," Professor Smith said.

"I'd rather it were the track of the one that took Carlos," Jim said.

"At any rate, if our guide is correct, we were not following the trail of any ordinary wild animal."

By taking this route they were able to come to the top of the cliff without having to clamber up the same steep gully that Jim and the professor had had to traverse that morning. They still found themselves at the opening of the cleft. And this time, since they had intended to come this way, they had lanterns with them, and could plunge more deeply into the cave than they had before.

It was narrow and dusty, and they made so much noise going that even the sheriff, who did not appear to be a naturally cautious man, said some sharp words about not being so loud. The floor gave way from dirt to bare stone, but Joe, when examining the cave entrance, had said it showed signs of traffic in and out. For that reason, and because the sheriff insisted that no weapons be given to the prisoner, Jim led the way while keeping a pistol at the ready. He wondered how much good it would do in the dark against creatures that could camouflage themselves in broad daylight.

For a quarter-hour or so they went, with boots shuffling over the rocky floor making echo's throughout the cave, flames licked the walls from their lanterns, casting their shadows on the rock-walls as they made their way through the pitch-black void. When Jim called for them to stop. "We'll have to go back and get some rope," he declared. The others pressed forward to see what the issue was.

A wide chasm, so deep its bottom was invisible, split the cave in two. On the other side, barely visible in the light of their lanterns, they could see the passage way continue, but to their left and to their right, as far as they could see, a gorge cut across their path. There was not even a ledge along, which to explore. Experimentally, Jim dropped a rock into the deep. No sound returned, even after they had counted to twenty.

"I don't understand," said the professor. "Something came in, we know that. There were no other caves branching off of this one. Did it fly across?"

"Spirits need no wings," Joe said.

"It wasn't a *spirit*, my dear fellow," Professor Smith retorted. "These things are flesh and bone, just as much as I am."

"If we could see what is on the other side of this chasm," Jim said, "maybe would understand how they crossed it."

"If we could see the other side of the chasm, we'd be on the other side and would have no need of a hypothesis!" Professor Smith said.

"Give me your lantern, boy," the sheriff said impatiently. "If we can't get across, we can maybe get it across."

"What are you going to do?" Jim said as Ghetts yanked the oil lantern from his hand. He cried out as the sheriff sent it in a soft arc across the gap to the other side. "It'll just shatter!"

"It certainly will," Ghetts said, as that's exactly what happened. "But at least we can see a little of what's over there until the oil burns out."

Indeed, the burning oil ran out of the shattered lantern and spread in a bright pool on the other side. They could make out very little, though, except for the fact that the cave pierced the wall on the other side.

But then a very curious thing happened. The lamp had landed on a shallow slope, and as it rolled down that slope, leaving a stream of burning oil, it gathered speed until it shot over the lip of the chasm and plunged downward. But it fell only a few feet before bouncing off something hard. Sparks and flame leapt out, and seemed to hang in the middle of the air. The battered lantern continue to roll in a straight line in defiance of gravity, until it came to rest in the middle of the chasm, right next to a large stone. The flame leaped and guttered for a few seconds, then went out.

No one said anything. Then the professor dropped to his stomach and extended his own lantern as far over the chasm as he could. With his free hand he picked up a loose stone and dropped it. It fell perhaps ten feet for fetching up in the middle of the air, to hang there illuminated by the light from above.

"Help me down there," Jim said.

"You're crazy!" Ghetts exclaimed.

"You'd like to be rid of me once and for all, wouldn't you?" Jim yelled back at him. "This way you can and it'll be my fault."

"This is the work of bad spirits, Jim," Joe said. He glanced uneasily at Ghetts. "The sheriff is right. We should not be here."

"I'm afraid I have to make it three to two," George said. "I know what you're thinking, and it's too dangerous."

But before the professor could add his own cautions, Jim leaped into the chasm. Four voices shouted.

Then a fifth voice laughed as they fell silent. Jim stood only a few feet below, looking up at them with a wild smile. "It's solid!" he shouted back. "See!"

"I have to see this," Professor Smith said. The others tried holding him back, but he too scrambled over the edge, and dropped.

"Why, this is remarkable," he said when he was standing next to Jim. He crouched and felt the ground with his hands. "It's some kind of spongy surface. Perfectly solid, and perfectly black!"

***

If it hadn't been for the others, the professor probably would have been perfectly content to explore and examine the "chasm" for the rest of the day. It was more of a shallow trench, actually, whose floor was only about dozen feet below the floor of the cave, and whose walls could, with some difficulty, be conquered from below. The illusion of its being very deep was a consequence of the thick, lichen-like substance that covered its bottom. This lichen was so dark in color that it showed no gleam or highlight, as even coal would, when set next to a lantern. And of course, its sponginess had dampened the sound of the rock Jim had tossed into the trench.

On the other side they found that the cave they were following broadened out, and its floor became smooth, so that soon it appeared they were following a corridor that had been cut into the rock. From farther ahead they soon made out a dim light. "We can't possibly have gone all the way through the mountain," the professor mused.

"The pathways of the spirits are not easily measured by the feet of men," Joe said darkly.

Ghetts muttered, "What was I thinking following this idiot to my grave."

Jim didn't know if Ghetts was referring to the professor or himself, but he honestly could care less what the lawman thought, he was here to rescue his brother, and nothing would stand in his way of that not even the sheriff.

They approached the new cave entrance cautiously, it seemed too easy, and that was unsettling to Jim, although they had met nothing during their dark trek through the mountain that didn't mean something wouldn't be waiting for them on the other side, or worse another impassible obstacle.

But nothing had prepared them for what they saw when they stepped through, the light of the sun was blinding, after walking through the dark cavern. Jim couldn't stop blinking, as he walked into the daylight on the other side.

"What th— " Jim said, pointing skyward.

CHAPTER TWENTY-FOUR

Jim and the rest of the company crept cautiously out of the cave into the landscape beyond. Jim didn't know how it was with the others, but he felt a shudder that began somewhere down in bowl holding his guts. It then rippled upward until it grasped his throat like a cold hand.

Looming above the northern horizon was a vast and unearthly object, a cylinder of gargantuan size, hanging in the midst of the air. It rose perpendicular to the earth, and it rose so high that its upper curves, Jim thought, must rise nearly out of the atmosphere and into space itself. Its surface seemed nearly featureless, but that might have been on account of its great distance: its outlines were softened by the same haze of dust and humidity that softened the outlines of the mountains beneath it, and it had a bluish tinge that surrounded the object, if you stared close enough.

But did it loom over those mountains? Or were those peaks actually between them and the object? From this angle the bottom of the cylinder looked like an oval, but Jim was certain it was perfectly circular. To show itself as that fat of an oval ... Jim blinked and shook a painful head at the implication. The thing might be hundreds of miles away; and if were yet so plainly visible over the horizon, it would have to be larger than an entire mountain range.

No one said anything for a very long time. Certainly Jim didn't know what to say. His head hurt and his mind felt fuzzy. It seemed inconceivable to him that a thing like what he was seeing should have gone unnoticed and unreported by the citizens of this state. And surely it was visible in Canada. But what could he say to the others that wouldn't sound foolish? *Do you see it too? What is that?*

Professor Smith finally broke the silence. "A camera," he muttered. "I want a camera very badly. Fortunately I have one at the camp." But he didn't make any move back toward the tunnel.

"We should go back and not return, this is the spirit realm...the gods will not be pleased with us coming uninvited," Joe said.

Jim turned sharply on him. "What about Carlos?" he demanded. His shock of coming out of the cave vanished in his renewed concern for his brother.

Joe lowered his eyes. "The gods have him. And the gods have come. We may join him soon enough."

"I think the professor's right," George said. "This needs documenting." He took a few steps back toward the cave, and the professor fell in beside him. But they stopped when none of the others moved.

"We're looking for a missing man," Ghetts said. "I don't see anything that's changed that fact."

Jim nearly jumped with astonishment, both at the sheriff's words and by the wave of startled gratitude he felt wash over himself on hearing them. Did he hear right? Was the sheriff actually saying they should continue the search? Did Ghetts actually have that much of a conscience? Had he actually roused himself to do his job -- and to do on behalf of Jim's own kin?

But Jim was too cautious -- and still too skeptical of the sheriff's good intentions -- to express himself in words. "We could split up," he said. "Some of us can follow the track, and the others can return for a camera and more witnesses." He looked at George and the professor. "You could also bring back some horses."

"We couldn't get horses through the cave," George said.

"We don't need to bring them through the cave," Professor Smith said. "We can simply come around the side of the mountain, over the eastern shoulder." He scanned the horizon, and pointed to a well-defined knoll. "There, if you and the others will wait at the edge of that foothill, I'll be around with a company of men and horses by sundown."

It seemed to make the most sense -- pursuit on horseback would be preferable to pursuit on foot -- but George changed his mind about going back to camp, and the professor returned into the cave alone. The others -- Jim, Joe, George, and the sheriff -- set off along a track that wound off in the direction of that enormous object in the sky.

Jim found himself tongue-tied as they progressed. He didn't want to distract Joe, who was bending his entire concentration upon the ground, moving slowly to and fro and pausing for long stretches of time as he tried to tease out the scattered hints of the trail. Jim also felt guilty for forcing Joe upon a track that he clearly didn't want to follow.

Nor did he have anything to say to Sheriff Ghetts. He hadn't spoken to the man, except under duress, since leaving Clinton, and he was still hot with fury about the cavalier and cruel treatment he had received from the lawman in the past, but those feelings were now slightly complicated by the fact that Ghetts alone had seemingly backed him in wanting to continue the pursuit of Carlos's trail. He still didn't like or trust the sheriff, but he couldn't make up his mind whether Ghetts's laziness, corruption and arrogance were actually leavened by a small -- a *very* small -- sense of responsibility, or whether the man was pursuing some ulterior motive in driving him and Joe and George farther from camp.

That left George as the only one he might comfortably converse with, but the only subject of conversation, he felt, would be that bizarre object dominating the northern sky. And concerning it, Jim felt baffled. No, it was worse than that. His very brain felt oppressed by the sight of it, and he found that he couldn't bear even to look at it, and he shied away when his eyes happened to rake across it. As he could not comprehend it, and as he could not even speak of it, he sought inwardly instead to discover the reason for that sense of oppression.

After much pondering, he decided it was on account of its sheer improbability. Were it an enormous mountain -- a mountain the like of which no man had ever seen -- he could easily accept it as a prodigy of nature. Were it a demon or a monster, some vast and devilish creature spreading its wings and horns against the sky to blot out the stars and sun and moon, he might have cowered with his face in the dust, but his Bible reading would have forewarned him of such horrors. Against the natural and the supernatural he was in some sense prepared.

But against the artificial, the manufactured, as this thing appeared to be. That should have been an easier matter to accept, and Jim tried

185

to convince himself that although he might have been startled or even frightened by the sight of a locomotive or a steamship or even an Egyptian pyramid floating in the air, his own mind would not have rebelled against the sight of such. But the thing ahead, it was unnatural in its shape and aspect, and had all the hallmarks of being engineered, was like no manufactured object he had ever seen. Its blank simplicity -- it was only a cylinder --this was another cause for fright, for it gave the eye no detail to seize, leaving only the thing's size as an object of contemplation.

And so there it was: an artificial object of inscrutable aspect and incomprehensible size, occupying an impossible space.

But was that really all there was to it? Jim began to watch the others out of the corner of his eye, and he noticed that they too seemed to avoid looking at the object. Joe, of course, kept his eyes firmly on the ground. But Jim noticed that his friend, when crouched with his head ducked as he studied some clue, more often than not kept his back turned on the thing. Ghetts, too, seemed to keep his head lowered, and when he did raise them it was more often than not to squint at the horizon to the east or to the west. George alone kept erect, but at no point did Jim catch him gazing at the mysterious thing in the northern sky.

After they had made a very slow mile into the valley on the other side of the mountain, Jim caught Ghetts looking to the south with a deep frown, muttering to himself. Before he could reconsider, Jim blurted out a question: "What is it?"

The sheriff turned sharply at him with a troubled and preoccupied eye. For a moment he stared at Jim, then looked between Deer Mountain and the eerie monstrosity. "Thing oughta be visible over the top of the mountain," he said gruffly.

"If you're on the foothills," George said, "the peak would be high enough to obscure it."

"I wasn't on the foothills this morning," Ghetts retorted. "I was on the road leading up to the foothills. And yesterday I certainly would have been able to --"

He clapped his mouth shut.

"So it's appeared in the last few hours?" Jim suggested. "Moving down from the north?"

"It doesn't appear to be moving," George said. "It just appears to be hanging there."

"I haven't been watching it close," Ghetts snapped. Jim wondered if the man wasn't embarrassed at having to make the confession, and that's why he seemed so angry. "I don't like looking at it."

"I don't either," Jim said. "It's intolerable." Again, the words came out before he had intended them to. Maybe it was a relief to make that confession. Or maybe he was groping for a shared connection to the sheriff. Under an increasingly alien sky, he found himself thinking more kindly of the man, as he at least shared something with him, even if it was only membership in the same species.

"Vertigo," said George. The other two looked startled. "That's what you're feeling. Have you never stood at the foot of a tall tower or wall -- one a hundred or more feet tall, I mean -- and stared straight up the face of it?

"I've never been near anything so tall," Jim said.

Ghetts said nothing.

"It gives you a queer feeling of vertigo," George said. "You become dizzy, and have a feeling that you're going to topple over, and maybe the wall or tower is going to fall over onto you. That thing, by its size and location, is creating the same feeling. That's all."

Jim looked up at it, directly, something he'd not done since coming out of the cave.

Then he had to look away. George was right. The thing made him dizzy.

* **

For the next hour the company scrambled down the lower flanks of the mountain. On the other side of a small rise they came down into a valley that flanked a long spur of the mountain that trailed to the north. A gully -- dry now, but a sign that rainfall collected here -- cut between them and the spur, and the grass was somewhat thicker and lusher. Eventually they came to a kind of wide, grassy bowl where a lone tree stood. The sun was sinking toward the western horizon as Joe crouched under the tree. "We should stop here," he said in a low voice.

Jim looked back the way they'd come, but saw no sign of the professor or the rest of their company. "We're supposed to meet the others farther up, at the end of that ridge."

"We should stop here," Joe repeated. "We're being watched."

The others glanced about uneasily. Jim thought he had felt a gathering sense of watchfulness as they had descended the mountainside, and Joe's words quickened his heart rate. Ghetts rested his hand on the grip of his pistol and leaned back casually on his hips and heels.

George looked about anxiously.

"Lakota?" Jim asked, for they were on the side of the mountain facing the lands occupied by the tribe he and Joe had visited earlier.

"No. Lakota will have gone. They would not have stayed under -- " Joe didn't finish, but Jim knew what he meant. The Lakota would have fled at the appearance of the thing over the northern horizon. Jim looked at it from under his brows. Under the high midday sun it had had the appearance of a massive figure painted onto a vast backdrop -- the way the moon or distant peaks will resemble the backdrop decorations for a theatrical performance. But under the slanting afternoon sun it looked more real somehow, like a thing with genuine height and depth, and that made it seem even more frightening. If it weren't for the fact that Carlos's trail led toward it, he would have joined Joe and the professor and the others in hurrying back to the cave. Even now, like a slithering tentacle up his spine, he felt the fearful temptation to bolt.

"Ain't no one in these parts 'cept your kind," the sheriff said to Joe. "Everyone else is smart enough to stick to his own. The way it ought to be, too."

Jim saw Joe stiffen, and for a moment he thought he was reacting to Ghetts's comment. But by the expression around his friend's eyes, he knew Joe was reacting to something else. Jim sank to the ground and brushed at it thoughtfully, as though he were absorbed in the grass and soil. But he looked in the direction that Joe was also surreptitiously staring.

At first he took it for a bush or a stunted tree standing on the ridge above, silhouetted against the sky. But if it was a tree, it had two trunks that joined into a bushy mass. Slowly, casually, Jim stood up, watching the "tree" closely. As he changed his position, the bush seemed to sink beneath the lip of the ridge -- and to seemingly vanish. Where he looked there was now only a lip of bare rock. Jim sank back to the ground, and the "tree" once more rose against the sky.

"Stop," Joe whispered. "It will see you, will know you have seen it."

"You saw it?"

"It moved."

"What moved?" Ghetts asked.

"Hush!"

But as Joe spoke, Jim saw the "tree" abruptly drop and disappear.

"If you'd said something, we might've shot it!" Jim hissed at Joe.

"It's not alone," Joe said, as he spoke, a rush of footsteps broke out around them.

The first that Jim saw was a figure looming behind Ghetts. For a moment Jim could only gape, and then for a moment he wanted to laugh out loud. It was like a tall feather duster, with long, draping hair or feathers fluttering behind it. But then it raised its arms, which were immensely long, and which ended in strong, grasping fingers, and lifted its head. Jim saw dark, saucer-like eyes in a flat face, and a mouth that showed a crimson interior as the thing opened wide. No sound came out, but Jim felt a pressure on his ear drums.

Jim just had time to see this when Ghetts shouted at him and raised his pistol. For a moment Jim thought the sheriff was aiming to shoot him, then -- almost too late -- realized that another of the creatures must be behind him. He threw himself down. Ghetts's pistol made an ear-splitting crack. Jim looked up from the grass in time to see the sheriff's boots lift almost a foot off the ground and go flying. A hand clapped him on the scruff of the neck, and Jim yelled and scrambled away.

The hand did not let go. Jim screamed and rolled over.

The hand slid down the back of his shirt.

Screaming like a maniac now, Jim rolled around for all he was worth on the ground, trying to free himself from his captor. The sky and earth reeled all about him. Then something heavy landed on him, and he felt a stinging blow across his face.

"For God's sake, be still!" George yelled at him.

Jim blinked and squirmed under the weight of his friend's body, for he still felt something down in the small of his back, like a rat that crawled between his clothes and skin.

George looked over his shoulder. "Is he going to be alright?" he called. The reply -- from Joe? from Ghetts -- was inaudible, but George made a face.

"Patch him up as best you can. We should get back to the tunnel before they -- "

The words died on his lips, and Jim saw a change come over his face. It looked like a mixture of surprise, relief, and fear.

Jim twisted around to see what George was looking at. It took him a moment to see it correctly, since adrenalin was still coursing through him, his wits were not as sharp as normal, because of the attack. But it soon resolved clearly.

It was a man with a thin, tanned face and long, reddish-gold hair. He was dressed in something that looked like buckskin, and in his hands he was holding the strangest-looking rifle Jim had ever seen.

CHAPTER TWENTY-FIVE

Jim craned his neck and stared at the stranger. He had seen plenty of white men decked out like Indians before -- it wasn't an uncommon sight on the frontier -- but something in the man's demeanor seemed to place him in neither camp. He didn't have the patient, dogged and hardened look that Jim associated with the Lakota or the Dakota, and his gear didn't look right for them either. But he also didn't have the look of a settler or city-dweller. This man looked both wary and relaxed.

Then, too, there was that rifle in his hands. It had a strange sheen to it, not at all like oiled metal, and it had a large, gray canister attached to it like an undercarriage. Small tubes connected this canister to its barrel.

The man didn't brandish the weapon, and when he spoke his voice was soft. But his eye was keen. And when no one replied, his eye sharpened, and he spoke in a louder, harder voice.

Jim didn't understand his words.

George got up, and Jim gingerly sat up. Whatever had fallen down the back of his shirt shifted about, but since it didn't seem to be alive, Jim only grimaced as he stood. The stranger spoke again and gave Jim a strange look as he carefully pulled up the back of his shirt and let the thing fall to the ground.

It was a leathery hand, cut off at the wrist, and smeared with blood. Jim raised his own hands, and saw that his fingers were smeared with the same. He raised his eyes and met the stranger's gaze. The man barked a short laugh and chattered out another string of nonsense syllables.

Jim looked around. Ghetts was on the ground and Joe was kneeling beside him. Jim took a step toward them, but stopped at a sharp word from the newcomer. He glanced at George, he was

191

looking more than slightly ill. "What's going on? Did we just get rescued, or did we just get captured?"

"Maybe both," George said. He hesitated, then turned toward the other man. To Jim's surprise, he loosed a string of words in what sounded like the other man's language. The other replied, and George spoke again, gesturing as he did.

"Jim!" That was Joe calling, and since George and the other were deep in some kind of conversation, Joe went over. He found Ghetts on his back, grimacing hard. "He broke both his arms when he fell," Jim said.

"You mean when it hit me," Ghetts said through gritted teeth. He hissed as he inhaled.

"We'll need splints. Here." He handed Jim a large Bowie knife and nodded at the tree.

Ghetts's eyes widened. "Where did you --? That's *mine!*"

Joe smiled faintly. "I took it last night while you slept."

"I had you tied up!"

Jim smiled as he left Joe and the sheriff to argue. He could imagine the scene of the night before, Joe slipping his bonds and stealing the knife, then putting some fake knots about himself again; the sheriff cursing as he searched the ground all about for the missing knife, and unable to conceive that his prisoner had made off with it but not used it to escape. If Joe hadn't wanted to join Jim the search for Carlos, he could have done terrible things to Ghetts and made off without anyone being the wiser until it was far too late.

And as he glanced at the edge of the blade he understood how he came to have that paw down the back of his shirt...there was blood on its edge. As one of the creature grasped him, Joe must have slashed at the things wrist, lopping its hand clean off. Jim shuddered at the memory of the attack, and as he sawed at and stripped some of the smaller branches from the tree he looked about warily. The things were able to move about almost invisibly, which is what had allowed them to get so close before. They might be closing in on them again.

"Do you know what kind of man that is George is talking to?" he asked Joe when he was again kneeling by him. Joe had his shirt off and had already torn most of it into strips. Together they began to expertly set Ghetts's broken bones.

"Do you understand what they're saying?" Jim asked when Jim shook his head.

"No. But they are using the language of the gods." Joe said.

"The gods?" Jim looked over Joe's hunched form at the two men. "George? How would he know the language of the gods? And how do you know what it sounds like?"

Jim had never felt skepticism for anything that Joe had said or done. He had grown up around Joe, and he thought of his father's friend as the wisest man he knew or was ever likely to know. Even when Joe spoke of the "gods" and the "spirits," Jim accepted what he said as simply the best way of thinking or speaking of something that was likely very real.

But now he was beginning to feel irritation at what Joe said -- despite his respect and affection for him, Jim regarded the gods and spirits as superstition. *Not everything we don't understand is on account of the gods,* he wanted to yell. *Sometimes it's just something new or strange.*

Of course, right now he would have to admit that almost everything they had experienced since coming to Deer Mountain was very new and very strange.

"I have heard it before," Joe said. His words and tone were very plain, shorn of all emotion. "I told you that some the gods take my people and later send them back. They have learned the language of the gods. They do not speak it willingly after they return. But the spirits come to them at times, and they must converse with them. When they speak, they sound like *that.*"

"George never told me he had been taken by the gods."

"Did you ever ask him?" Joe said.

Why would I ask him something like that, Jim wanted to retort. But it was probably just Joe making a very dry joke.

But it looked like he would be getting something like an answer, for George knelt beside them as they were readying the slings for Ghetts's arms. "How is he?"

"Two broken arms."

"He can walk?" George said.

"Of course I can walk," the sheriff barked. "It broke my arms, not my legs."

"He will still need help," Joe said.

"Keep your opinions and your hands to yourself," the sheriff grumbled.

"There's a camp about a mile to the east," George said. "If we can get him there we should be alright."

"Professor Smith and the others should be along any time," Jim said.

"No they won't," George said.

"What do you mean?" Jim said.

George had spoken calmly and matter-of-factly, and that calmness made his words all the more shocking.

"Help me get him up." George said.

Jim put his hand on George's shoulder and pushed him back. "No. What you do mean?" he demanded again, and he felt the hair at the top of his scalp began to crawl as anger crept over him. There were many things about George that had been bothering him lately, and only the need to help Sheriff Ghetts had kept him from exploding at the sight of George conversing in a strange language with the strange man. Anger began to build into fury as George turned a blank expression on him. Jim gripped his shoulder more tightly, and almost without realizing it he bunched his other hand into a fist.

"I'll explain when we get to the camp -- "

"You'll explain now!"

Joe tried to step between them. "Jim."

"All of you!" That was the sheriff, glaring up at them from the ground. "Maybe I can't give you all the beating you deserve, but whatever it is that needs saying had *best be said! Now!*"

George licked his lips and looked deeply vexed and embarrassed. "There is only one way into this valley, and that's through the tunnel we came through. The professor and the others will be coming over the shoulder of the mountain that way. Coming that way -- " He grimaced hard. "There they won't see any of this. They won't see us, they won't see this landscape, and they won't see *that*." He gestured at the monstrosity to their north.

"Why not?" Jim asked.

"Because that tunnel is not only a crack running through the mountain. It is a crack running through *time*."

***

Sheriff Ghetts had allowed Jim and Joe to help him to his feet, but he gruffly refused to let them help him as they walked along. Fortunately, the ground was fairly easy, with only a few low ridges to interrupt ground that fell gently and steadily away. So Jim had lots of time to puzzle over what George had said, both as they stood in that grassy bowl and after they began their trek to the promised camp. Looking around Jim knew that Gorge spoke the truth, it was starting to finally sink in. Everything looked somehow different, but his mind refused to accept the smaller details, like even the ground color felt off, and the sky…when was the last time he'd ever seen a blush sky mid-morning that lasted the whole day, not to mention the hovering monolith the made him dizzy.

"You know what a time line is, Jim," he'd said. "You've taken classes in mathematics. Just imagine that time is like a line, a line stretching back into the past and forward into the future, and we are carried along it from moment to moment. But imagine now that it isn't a straight line, that it is like a rope and it lies in coils. Two points in time may be very far from each other along the length of the rope. Hundreds or thousands or even millions of years may separate them along the rope. But they might lie directly next to each other as the rope curls about. If you could only hop across that short distance, you might find yourself hundreds of years in the future. Or, if you go the other way, you would find yourself hundreds of years in the past." George said.

Jim thought about what George had said, the theory seemed possible if you thought of time this way, so he did not rule out the possibility.

"But hopping over the gap is a terribly hard thing," George had continued. "But what if there were a bit of fiber that bridged it? Or what if one length of rope actually touched the other part, so that you could step across if you just knew where they touched? Then, like an ant walking along the length of the rope, you might unwittingly step across that breach, from one year into a very distant year. It would be very disorienting at first. But you might learn to find your way back and forth, as easily as a man crosses a stream by using a fallen log."

"Is that what the tunnel is?" Jim asked. He alone had questioned George. Ghetts had listened, but not said anything, and Joe seemed wrapped in his own thoughts. "A way to get from -- " He had stopped, puzzled, for it seemed to make no sense to think of a year as a place. *A year is a time. It is not a "here" or a "there." It is a "then."*

"Yes. It is a road leading from the year where we were to the year where we are. As it happens, the gap between the two times is always constant. If we return through the tunnel tomorrow, we will not find ourselves back on the same day that we left. We will find ourselves on Deer Mountain on the day *after* we left. If you stay here, and the rest of us return through the tunnel, and remain there a week before coming back, you would tell us on our return that we have been gone a week by your reckoning as well. I cannot say how wide the gap in years is, exactly."

"Calendars --"George had hesitated. "Calendars have changed, and I am not sure how you would reckon what year it is here. But I could estimate that it is 2749 and I would not be off by more than four or five decades in either direction."

Jim had doubted that George's words really made much of an impression upon the others, for they didn't make much sense to him, his mind refused to accept the year George suggested. The number was just an abstraction. The landscape and the shape of the sky -- that was concrete.

"That is why Professor Smith and the others won't find us when they come riding down the side of the mountain. When they come over the shoulder of the mountain, it will be 1899. But where we are standing, it is not 1899. It is a year and three-quarters of a millennium beyond 1899."

"We walked here by following Carlos's trail. How did he come to be here?" Jim said.

George had looked miserable. "He was brought here against his will."

"He is a prisoner?" Jim's heart had begun to beat very hard, with both excitement and with dread as the topic of his brother returned. "And how do you know all this?" he demanded.

"Because this is my year and my world," George said unhappily. "I was born here, in 2724. I know it because I helped open that tunnel, and went back to 1899 to find help."

"Help? Help for what?"

"Against what, you mean." George's tone had turned truculent, and he'd bent his head.

"Alright, against what?" Jim insisted.

George had marched along for a dozen yards with his head down before answering. Then he'd jerked his head in the direction of the celestial cylinder. "Against that."

Jim had paused to stare at it. The sky behind had turned violet as the sun sank, and the thing itself had begun to glow a shade of pink. Jim shuddered at the sheer size of the thing, a large cloud sat between him and it and the object dwarfed the cloud.

"What is it," he'd said after hurrying up to rejoin George. A cold breeze had sprung up, and he shivered.

"The *Mayflower*," he had replied, and declined to say any more.

CHAPTER TWENTY-SIX

Their destination looked nothing like what Jim would have expected of a campsite in the year 2749. Of course, he reflected, he really had no right to have any expectations for a camp in the year 2749.

It was circular, with a diameter of maybe a hundred yards, and surrounded by a coil of thin wire at waist height that had been looped through the top of a series of short posts. Every twenty yards or so was a much taller post atop which was a broad, shallow cone that opened like an immense flower toward the darkening landscape without.

"Defense lights," said George when he caught Jim staring at them.

"They're not lit," Jim pointed out.

"Yes they are. They don't illuminate the landscape, though. Only anything that might be out skulking in the landscape. Things that ordinary lights wouldn't pick out," he'd added with a meaningful glance. They passed through an opening into the camp

Within the perimeter were things that looked more familiar to Jim: teepees. They came in all different sizes, with the tip of the tallest rising almost thirty feet above the ground. When he got closer, however, he saw that they were not made of animal skins, but of some other material he could not identify.

As for the people, they were dressed like the man who had led them here, in something that looked like buckskin. Their dark dress lacked ornamentation, however, and put Jim in mind of the severe dress of the classic Puritan.

But mostly what Jim noticed were the children. Children in short pants, children in shifts; some in shoes but most of them unshod. Toddlers who could barely walk, and sober-faced adolescents. Some were white, others black or brown, and he thought he saw some who looked Chinese. All of them had been darkened by the sun.

They scampered about outside the perimeter and inside it too. They huddled in groups and played games, and they chased each other. The younger ones, it looked, were being minded by older ones, who were minded by children older still.

Their guide led them inside one of the larger tents, whose floor was covered in thick, soft rugs. A box like a lantern gave off a warm, natural glow that caused Jim to look around in puzzlement. For a moment he had the impression the teepee had vanished, for the box gave off a glow nothing like the light lantern oil, and nothing like electric light, either. Its glow was much more like sunlight. The man who had led them said something to George, then ducked back out of the tent.

"This is the medical tent," George told the others in a soft voice. "He went to find the, uh, doctor. She'll look after the sheriff." He patted Ghetts gently on the shoulder, and though the man looked doubtful, he sank to the ground.

"Why do you hesitate to call her a doctor?" Jim asked.

"To your eyes she might look more like a medicine woman," George said. "The hospitals in the cities don't look much like this tent, and the doctors have a great deal more equipment at their disposal. But she will be as fully trained as any physician -- as fully trained as anyone who graduates from St. James -- and her skill will be more than sufficient to see to the sheriff."

They didn't have long to wait. The flap to the tent opened and their guide stepped back in. He was followed by a woman who Jim thought looked very familiar but whom he couldn't quite place. She was a beautiful woman, with an expression that was grave but not severe as she knelt beside the sheriff, who drew back a little from her. As she turned, Jim caught the expression on Joe's face: one of shock. At first Jim thought Joe must be reacting to the way she almost instantly set about undoing the wrappings on the sheriff's arms. But when Jim looked again at the doctor, he recognized her, and understood Joe's reaction.

It was Kimimela, the healer he and Joe had met when visiting the Lakota.

George saw the look that passed between Jim and Joe. "Is something wrong," he asked.

"We've met her," Jim told him in a low voice. "She's the healer at a Lakota settlement near here." Then he remembered where -- or *when* -- he was. "In 1899, I mean."

"She's my sister," the doctor said without raising her head. Her voice was very clear, and she had only a trace of an accent. "Kimimela," she added. "How is she?"

Sister? It took Jim a moment -- for he was still reeling in recognition -- to catch the implication: Kimimela had a twin sister, and this was her. "She's well, I suppose," Jim stammered.

No she isn't, she's dead and she's been dead for almost a thousand years, a voice screamed in his head. Jim wondered when -- or if -- he would ever become used to what he had experienced since waking up. He grasped George by the elbow. "I wish you would explain a few more things to me," he said through gritted teeth.

But George didn't, and only gave him some soothing reassurances that it would be best to wait until the morning. "You're hungry, right?" he said. "I know I am." Jim didn't admit aloud that George was right. "Some food, some sleep, and tomorrow we'll find Carlos. I'll tell you more, too. Right now you've heard enough."

But instead of releasing George, Jim tightened his grip on him. "You know where my brother is." That seemed to be the implication of the other's words, and the thought that George had been keeping that a secret sizzled in Jim's head like a droplet of water on a hot pan.

George winced and tried to tug free. "Yes I do," he said. "I was taking you to him. Well, more or less." He glanced at Joe, who was also giving him a very hard look. "I was letting you track him, going to let you find him."

Something hot was beginning to form behind Jim's eyes. "You knew what happened to him, didn't you?" He shook George.

It probably wouldn't have gone well for George if Joe hadn't interceded. "Let him go," he told Jim as he slipped an arm between him and George. "You're tired and hungry. We'll talk about this tomorrow."

Jim knew that Joe was right, but still he bared his teeth at George even as he let him go.

George took them to another tent, and pointed to some rugs where they could sleep. He himself left for another tent, but Jim and Joe didn't have this tent to themselves. The man who had guided them to this tent joined them. He pointed to himself and said a word a few times, by which Jim guessed he was giving his name. "Jacob" seemed the nearest approximation to it that Jim could say, and the man assented when Jim tried it out.

Nor was Jacob the only person they would have to share the teepee with. A woman came in, and also a small clutch of children. Jacob only had to say a few words to them and they settled down almost immediately, then they left with the woman. When they returned, it was with bowls of a thick, beefy stew that Jim and Joe gratefully and hungrily ate. Once these were cleared away, the entire company began bedding down for the night.

Sleep was soon stealing over Jim, but he forced himself to remain alert enough to listen to the conversation of the others. He was amazed that English should have died out in North America. Or, he was amazed until he did some backwards comparisons. Imagine, he told himself, that an Englishman from 1250 should find himself at the court of Queen Victoria. Would he be able to understand the language when he came from a world where Chaucer had not yet been born? So Jim listened more closely to his hosts, and now that he knew what to listen for --

He still could not make out what they said, though he thought he caught a few particles -- possibly an "and" or a "the" in their speech -- but he could allow that there was something familiar in it. It sounded a bit like Dutch, he decided as he began to drift off to sleep.

***

Jim woke early the next morning, but he also felt much more rested, and after eating another bowl of stew for breakfast he felt even better. He still didn't feel very well disposed toward George as Jacob led him and Joe out of the campsite, but he thought he would be able to control his temper.

They went about a half mile or so before they came to pasture where a small herd of horses were eating and trotting. George was waiting for them. There was a small teepee here as well, and from inside it Jacob and George removed three sets of saddles and bridles. "Faster than walking," George said. "You'll like that, won't you?"

"I'll like it better when you start answering my questions."

But George waited until they had saddled and mounted three horses. He led them on a slow and easy walk to the east as they talked.

"First of all, I'm sorry it had to work out like this," George said. "I didn't want it to, and it wouldn't have except that Carlos saw something I didn't want him to see."

"What was that?" Jim said.

"Me." They walked on a bit further while George plainly tried to organize his thoughts. "I was -- Well, I was talking to someone, and it would have been very hard for me to explain to Carlos why I was talking to that person. So I had him kidnapped."

Jim gave George a very hard and sharp look, but held his tongue.

"That's a rough way of putting it," George said. "But accurately. I had him carried through the tunnel to this side, taken to the place I'm leading you to now. Explanations would have to be given to him before anything else got decided."

"Would you give me those explanations now?" Jim said impatiently.

"Well, the first thing to understand is *that*," George said, pointing to their left where that strange cylinder still hung in the sky. "And where it came from. It came from the stars."

"The stars?" Jim said.

George ignored Jim's interjection, and leaned forward so he could speak to Joe. "When I say 'the stars'," he said, clearly speaking to both his companions, "I don't mean the gods or the spirits. A star is just another sun, like ours, but very far away. Some stars have planets, like the sun has planets, and some of those planets have animals and plants on them, as the Earth does."

Joe gave George a dark look. The meaning behind it wasn't clear, but Jim would have gambled that Joe resented being spoken to as if he were a childish savage.

"We don't know where they came from," George continued. "Which planet and which star. They never told us. They never told us anything, for they have no words to spare for us. But one day they arrived. That day was closer to 1899 than to today. But with the confusion about calendars, it's not worth trying to pin a date down. Not that it matters anyway."

"Is that a craft, a craft that carried them," Jim asked as he contemplated the vast cylinder.

"Yes. One of dozens. They are scattered about the globe, and it is possible to travel many thousands of miles without seeing one. Those who do not have one in their sky are the lucky ones."

"You called it the *Mayflower*," Jim said. He glanced back at the rise that obscured the settlement where they'd slept. An uncomfortable thought was trying to form in his mind, and he was trying very hard to push it away. "Did they come as settlers?"

"No," said George. "They came as hunters. They came to Earth the way Cortez and Pizarro came to the Americas. But they didn't conquer empires and they didn't found kingdoms. Or maybe they did, up there, in their ships. But down here, on the surface, they acted as hunters, the way –" He paused. "The way those who made trailed across the prairies hunted and killed buffalo and bison. Except in this case they hunted *us*."

It took Jim a moment to realize what was encompassed when George said "us." He thought at first it only meant "people like George," but then realized it meant --

"You mean they hunted people? Humans?" he asked in a quiet, horror-struck voice.

"Exactly. They smashed all the great nations of the world -- all their armies and navies, all their advanced weaponry. Anything that tried to fight them, they destroyed. After that, they were content to sweep in and capture people in great herds. We found out later that many of these were put into camps, the equivalent of cattle pens, to be bred and raised. Most of these are in the temperate zones, but there's one to the north." George glanced to his left. "They keep their ships near these."

"What do they do with these ... prisoners?" *Eat them*, he expected the answer to be.

It was almost as bad. "Harvest them for parts. It appears that there is a market for human parts out in the stars." George's tone turned wry. "We are like the rhinoceros, whose horn, when ground into powder, is supposed to act as an aphrodisiac. But in this case, sadly, the medical facts are against us. Whatever it is that we possess, it actually does have value to the harvesters."

"Is that what you call them? The harvesters?"

"We've got lots of names for them, many of them impolite, as you can guess. 'Harvester' is as good a descriptive name as any, and seems a reasonable translation of the word used by their own servants."

"What servants?"

"You met them yesterday. They're the ones that broke the sheriff's arms."

"The creatures we were looking for?" Jim said.

"Yes. They don't have a word for themselves -- they are very self-effacing, in lots of ways -- but we call them the Maorong. It's from the Chinese for 'hairy things'. We have no dealings with the harvesters, but we've lots of dealings with the Maorong, and it's from them that we've learned what little we know."

"You said they put people into camps. Is that one of them back there, where we spent the night?"

"Oh heavens, no. The breeding camps are much vaster, much more comfortable. Arranged like barracks, with regular feeding times, regular exercise areas. Very powerful security, too, impossible to escape from.

Jim looked at George. He was soft and fat, not at all like the lean, weathered inhabitants of the camp where they had slept. If anyone looked like a head of "human cattle," it would be George. "So how did you escape," he asked bluntly.

George looked at him in surprise. "I didn't. I didn't come from a —"He smiled tightly. "There are, more or less, three types of human society in our world. The first lives in the breeding camps. We don't know what their population is, but it is probably in the millions. Millions more live in the second type of society, where I come from. You might call us the 'wild animals'. Just as there are herd cattle and wild cattle, domestic horses --" He patted his mount's neck affectionately "and wild horses, there are the domestic, breeding humans and wild humans. We're the descendants of the nations and civilizations that remained after the initial invasion and round up. The harvesters seem content to let us be, for the most part. We still have cities and politics and marketplaces. Universities and science and art and all the rest. We don't have any wars, of course. The Harvesters do not tolerate any kind of large-scale armed groups among us, and at the first evidence of any kind of systematic armaments manufacturing or stockpiling, they sweep in and destroy whatever cities are nearby. Even beyond that, it's a nervous existence for us. We have no idea how long we might be tolerated, for the Harvesters can destroy us, instantly, any time they feel like it. They also sweep through our own cities, occasionally, to harvest even from us, as a hunter might sweep through a herd of game animals even when he has farm animals of his own. Which brings us to the third type of society, the one we slept with last night."

"Jacob's group. Are they outlaws? Outcasts?" Jim said.

"On the contrary. In your world you would call them Rockefellers and Vanderbilts."

So the elite members of society? Jim giggled.

"Yes, what is funny about that?" George said.

"Not much...outside of them living like a bunch of Indians. I would expect them to be living more luxuriously than that...there must be so many advancements in this time."

Jim looked over at Joe, "Sorry about the comment, it's nothing personal, and I don't think there is anything wrong with how Indians live."

Joe sighed.

Everyone mounted up, Jim was happy to be on horseback since they could travel faster this way, also it made him feel safer from being attacked, and he doubted the creatures would attack them on horseback as easily as they did when they were on foot. Jim took the reins of his horse and nudged the paint, "Come on boy lets go find Carlos, yaw." He said, gently spurring his horse.

CHAPTER TWENTY-SEVEN

The company of Jim, George and Joe had been riding eastward for most of the morning as they talked, but they had now bent south and were riding around the flank and shoulder of Deer Mountain.

"There is still art and science, as I think I mentioned," George said. "And much else hasn't changed. In some ways the Harvesters are more of a nuisance than a threat. At worst they are like a plague that sweeps in periodically. But we still have relative wealth and relative poverty, we still have businesses and government and taxes." He paused thoughtfully, and by his manner it seemed to Jim that George was in danger of waxing philosophical. But if he was tempted, he overcame it.

"But what counts as wealth and what counts as poverty have changed somewhat," he said then he continued. "When you live under the threat that you might be swept up in a raid and butchered, or when you fear that your children will be then your safety or their safety becomes extremely valuable. There are bunkers and safe places beneath our cities, and most of our cities have infrastructure is beneath the surface. But there is no guarantee of safety, and there have been raids carried out underground. The safest place, especially for children, is away from the cities, actually.

"There are farms, still, of course, scattered across the landscape, and land in the countryside is very valuable, because it is isolated and there is less chance of being raided. But even there it happens. So the safest places, actually is the wilderness, where you can live a nomadic existence. It is much harder for the Harvesters to catch a group of wanderers. Harder to locate them and harder to herd them. For even the Harvesters time is the same as money, and a camp that moves and that can scatter in an instant is more trouble than it is worth. So the very richest families place their children with tribes like Jacob's."

Jim said nothing, but George shrugged anyway. "Did I just call them a tribe? I know that's what they look like to you, and they carry on much the same way that the Lakota or Dakota did, er, a thousand years ago. They hunt wild game and keep herds of cattle and do a little farming. It's a hard existence but a reasonably safe one. It's also a subsidized existence. That's the price that the parents pay. Some food and medicines and supplies they can't make themselves are dropped off at designated spots. In case of serious injury, a tribesman will be transported to a hospital at the nearest city, and sometimes they will even take holidays in the city. But their life is the most survivable, when you fear being harvested."

A question had been forming in the back of Jim's mind ever since George had begun talking about ways of escaping the Harvesters. He hesitated to ask it, for fear of introducing an idea that he shouldn't introduce. But he asked it anyway. "You have a tunnel connecting this year to a year where there are no Harvesters. Why don't people seek exile in -- Well, in the past?"

George smiled tightly. "The thought has occurred to some, but no government would allow it. At least, they would not countenance it." He turned and squinted back toward the camp they had left. "Of course, you will have noticed that Jacob's camp is not far from the entrance to the tunnel. They do not go in and out of it, but it is a kind of bolt hole if worse comes to worse. One of the perquisites of being very, very rich."

Jim looked over his shoulder. The camp where they had spent the night had long since vanished behind several ridges. But Jim remembered what it had looked like and smelled like. Its rough simplicity and lack of ornamentation. *That,* he marveled, was this world's equivalent of ... Buckingham Palace?

Joe's eye caught his as he turned back around. For the first time in a long time, his father's old friend looked in high spirits.

"But we don't dare use it for mass migration," George said. "Even if we leave aside what it be like on the other side, in 1899, if all the people in this year started pouring through, it would risk calling the Harvesters' attention to them. Would you like to see the Harvesters coming through into 1899? Not to mention the possibility of contaminating the time lines, or introducing a disease that could potential kill off a large portion of the past human population, and create a whole new future."

"Would they?" Jim said.

George shrugged. "Who knows? They are inscrutable."

"What do they look like? Are they like the -- What do you call them, the hairy things?"

"The Maorong? No, the Harvesters are very different. They look like enormous insects or enormous lizards." George struggled for words, then gave up. "They are very hard to describe, and I hope you never see one. I've only seen one, briefly, at a distance. But we don't want them coming through into 1899, or any other year. They have the capability, if they wanted to, and we don't want to give them ideas."

"How do you know they have the capability?"

"Because we opened the tunnels using devices stolen from them. The Maorong, I said, they are their servants. But they are unwilling servants. 'Slaves' would be a better word. We cannot treat the Maorong as our allies, not exactly, but they do help us when they can. With their help we were able to steal something from one of their craft. They must be able to travel immense distances in a very short period of time, and they do this by making a hole through time itself. We used the device to create a tunnel here, leading back to 1899. And if we could do that, then they could too."

"If you don't use the tunnel to migrate, why did you open it?" Jim said.

"As part of a desperate plan to defeat the Harvesters. We hope to change the past, even though we are not certain that we can."

"You mean that you hope to defeat the Harvesters in battle when they invade?" George's meaning was very unclear to Jim -- as it always was when the matter of traveling between years was before him.

"In a matter of speaking. What we hope to do is secretly and indirectly prepare the nations of the world to better resist the invasion when it comes. They did not have the weapons that could resist the Harvesters. The technology was simply not advanced enough. But what if we advanced the technology for them?" George's tone grew warm with excitement. "What if we introduced certain technical advances in 1899 that were not actually introduced until, let us say, 1950. Then the world of 1899 would be fifty years ahead of where it had been. And by the time 1950 came, and we had introduced more technical advances, it might be where it was in 2100. By the year of the invasion, the world might have become so advanced that they could repel the Harvesters."

Jim pulled his horse to a halt. "Hertz!" he cried. He felt as though he had been struck by a bolt of lightning.

George smiled. "Exactly. Those signal boxes that so impress Professor Smith," he continued as Jim spurred his horse to catch up, "were provided by one of our agents who has taken up residence in 1899. The wheel of progress advances slowly, but we are giving it a gentle brush, speeding it up."

"How will you know you have succeeded?"

George's expression turned troubled. "We don't know. We don't know how the changes propagate. We don't even know that they are visible. It might be that the changes occur and we don't even realize it. Inventions that we possess now may be as a result of our own interference with the past. But interference in the past would alter our own memories of the way things had been." He laughed dryly. "It may be that success will come when there are no harvesting ships in the sky, and when our history books tell us that an invasion from the stars had been turned back. And we won't even remember that it was by our own efforts that we did it."

Jim tried to imagine how it would be possible to not remember something very important that you did. He finally had to give up. It sounded as though George, who was much more used to thinking of these things, was just as puzzled by it.

"But now," George said once he saw that Jim was paying attention again, I think I can finally explain where your brother is and why we took him."

Jim pulled his horse to a halt, and did not continue until the dizziness had passed. It was guilt, he realized once he was cantering along again. He had gotten so wrapped up in George's explanations that he had quite forgotten where they were going -- and why he had been so angry at George.

He didn't feel that anger now. Partly it was because he was still suffering the after-pangs of confusion. But partly it was because he had a better sense of the pressures that George and others of this thousand-years-into-the-future world were suffering.

"Traveling from one year to another," George said, "is not like traveling from one state of the Union to another. That's bad enough, because the customs of the North are not those of the South, and neither are the customs of the West. If our agents are to 'pass' in 1899, they have to be educated and trained in the languages, the customs, the habits, the mores, the intuitions of the year they are traveling toward. They have to swim in it as naturally as though they had been born in it. And that requires teachers and a school."

They crossed a small ridge, and the valley on the south side of Deer Mountain came into view. Jim sucked in a sharp gasp. That valley in this year was populated.

At least five small towns were crowded onto the plain. The nearest could have been Clinton or any other village on the high northern plain. Beyond it, though, were towns of greater population and buildings of greater height. Most of these he would have described as neighborhoods in larger towns, but the largest -- the one that sprawled out the most and was situated at the greatest distance, was composed of tall brownstone houses and office buildings. It took him a moment to realize it looked like the city he had seen in photographs of Manhattan.

And all the streets were crowded with people, horses, buggies, and children. All were dressed in the fashion that he was used to, and going about the kind of business he recognized. He even saw a steam locomotive chugging in the distance.

He gazed at this scene wonderingly for several long minutes, until he caught George's expression. It showed quiet pride. "Are those --" he started to ask, but didn't know how to finish.

"Those are our schools," George said. "And our students. Well, most of them are students. A handful are teachers. People like myself who have already been trained and are training others. Some of them are also, well, people we have taken. Err, *kidnapped*, if I'm going to be blunt about it."

"That's why you kidnapped Carlos, to be a teacher in that school down there?" Jim was beginning to feel his temper again. However

211

much George and his friends needed "teachers," it hardly seemed right that they seize and carry them off. Especially when they seized and carried off Jim's own brother.

"No, that's not why," George said, "although we could easily find a use for him as a teacher. I told you, he found me talking to someone I shouldn't have been talking to."

"Who?"

"A Maorong." George spurred his horse, and Jim and Joe followed as they rode down toward the towns.

"I told you that they are unwilling servants of the Harvesters," George continued. "Many have even tried to escape, and some have succeeded. There is a small group of them that lives near Jacob's camp, and cooperates with them and with us. They, at least, I can call our allies. They keep a watch for us, on both sides of the tunnel, because they can so easily blend into their surroundings, and when we ask them, they bring us, um -- "George turned very red. "People," he finally said.

"Children," Jim said. "My brother." He suddenly stood up in his saddle, and if he had been standing still he would have grabbed George and hauled him to the ground, his temper boiled like a steam kettle. "Anna!"

Maybe George thought Jim really would launch himself from horse to horse and try to unseat him, he opened a space between him and Jim. "Anna is a special case," he said. "She's my colleague, another one of our agents."

"What?" Now Jim really did have to halt, and he swayed in his saddle. Joe rode up next to him and put a steadying hand on his shoulder.

"I'm sorry, Jim," George said as he turned round again and joined the other two. "I know I could have spared you a lot of anguish if I had been able to tell you. She's perfectly safe, perfectly healthy. You might be able to see her at some point. But the night she left you she went to the tunnel and returned here. I'm not certain why. She might have received orders. The point is that you can't blame me for *that* disappearance." His mouth curled in a sour frown. "If you don't mind me saying so, I am getting a little tired of you constantly trying to hit me just because I'm doing my job."

That didn't exactly thrill Jim, and he once again felt a bout of anger in his stomach, just like the night before. "But you are to blame for Carlos's disappearance. What happened?" He followed George as the other resumed his march.

"He followed me out of camp and caught me talking with one of the Maorong who had been watching us. Then we caught him. As it would have been at the very least embarrassing and very likely impossible to explain things, I had my companion bundle him across the tunnel to this side. Someone will have explained things to him."

"If you and these Maorong are such great friends, why did they attack us yesterday?"

"Because they were the injected ones from the Harvesters. They must have sent them here anticipating something is going on, they watch us from the sky, when the Harvesters inject their Maorong they instantly go into a killing frenzy and don't stop until their hearts can't take it any longer and they just fall over dead. The Maorong that work with us would have assumed we were exactly what we appeared to be, interlopers from the other side of the tunnel who had stumbled through to this side. The natural things would have been to take us prisoner, as they take prisoner almost anyone on the other side who comes too close to the tunnel. They understand the stakes involved. But they are gentle and would never harm anyone."

"What would they have done with us if it was the nicer Maorong?"

"Taken us to Jacob. It's just that he came upon our company at almost the same time as they did. Lucky for us he did, the gun he was carrying was a Death Ray, it incinerated the junked up Maorong, he thought he recognized me and that is why he assisted us. I gave him a bit of a scare by not answering his challenge right away."

***

And in this way Jim found all of his questions answered right up to the point that he and the others had been captured the day before. He asked a few clarifying questions of George as they rode the rest of the way into the town below, but for the most part he felt satisfied. Unhappy, but satisfied.

He felt a bit irritable as he rode into the town below that he and Joe didn't get any second glances, no more than they would have gotten if they had ridden into Clinton. After all, he and Joe didn't belong here. But it only stood to reason that their appearance wouldn't cause any reaction. The people in this city of false fronts were themselves false fronts, and they would assume that Jim and Joe were another set of false fronts. It amused Jim slightly to see Joe stiffen at the sight of a Lakota stepping out of what looked like a hardware store – Joe's eyes ratcheted onto the single imposter, he looked more annoyed than the time he saw a street full of them. But maybe it was on account of the Lakota being such a singular instance of one.

He was a little more disturbed when George called at the sheriff's office to inquire after "Carlos Castle," but relaxed when the "deputy" out front said that he was at "the schoolhouse." *Of course*, thought Jim. If Carlos was to be a "teacher," that is where they would have him.

Jim rushed into the rickety old school house, with a quick scan he located his brother, curled up at a desk that was much too small for him and listening intently as a middle-aged woman at the front pointed to pictures of cats, dogs, cows, chickens, and people while reciting odd-sounding names for each. Seeing his brother again made him burst with joy, the flood of emotions were stronger than he anticipated.

"Carlos!" Jim yelled, interrupting the teacher.

"Glad to see you brother, seems nothing has changed still interrupting educators." Carlos said, smiling wide.

Jim ran over and scooped Carlos out of his chair giving him the biggest hug, he had ever gave anyone in his life.

CHAPTER TWENTY-EIGHT

Jim and Carlos smiled faintly as they stared at each other across the table, nursing mugs of coffee. The saloon had the oily smell of any saloon in Clinton, and it had the same set of rough-looking customers in one corner. But the coffee had a different taste. George had said something to the bartender, and the man had disappeared into the back to make a special brew. "It's not authentic," George had told them as they sat down. "But I hope you'll like it."

And over the coffee that the brothers had exchanged news. Jim had the most to say, and had told it with some corrections and amplifications from George. Carlos had comparatively little to relate.

"The girl -- Maggie -- got taken to one place. I was taken to another," he said. "They explained things to me. I yelled at them." He gave George a sidelong glance. "I probably would have had a lot more to say if *you* had been there."

George squirmed.

Carlos was glad the man was uncomfortable. Carlos did not think of himself as a violent man -- it ran against all the instincts that had led him to study medicine -- but in the hours after being separated from the girl and put into a solitary confinement unit and then hauled out to get a stern and bewildering lecture, he probably would have lashed out hard against the man who had brought him to this place. Even in the days that followed it was less that he had cooled down than that he had hidden his temper.

It was a revelation to him, in a way, learning just how much sustained rage he was capable of. Had he been introduced slowly to this world of the future and its problems he might have reacted with more sympathy and understanding. He might have even volunteered to help them, as he did feel genuine horror at the stories they had told him, and the scenes they had shown him on the moving picture screens and in the living dioramas.

But whatever wrongs they had suffered, he felt, did not justify the wrenching wrong they had done to him and to others. The anger festered still within him.

He hadn't said anything to his captors and educators, of course. He knew that would do no good. So he had smiled and pretended to accept his new situation and with a deeply insincere enthusiasm he had agreed to help them. And his feelings were unmovable, they refused to soften at all, after arriving in this cardboard city, and he had seen Deer Mountain rising before him. The knowledge that he was walking on ground he had walked over before, almost a thousand years in the past, was nearly intolerable to him. And so the flame, instead of being banked and extinguished, had grown hotter.

And now here was his own brother talking enthusiastically about the challenge of defeating the "Harvesters" and what might be done to combat them. Here was his own brother treating the man who had kidnapped him as a genuine companion.

At least Carlos had the satisfaction of knowing that George could read his mood, for George kept more to Jim's side of the table than to his. He noticed, too, that Joe kept on the other side of the table from George, and sat closer to him than to Jim.

At last, with a murmured word, George excused himself, leaving the trio of exiles alone for the moment. "What do you think they'll do with the sheriff?" Carlos asked. He avoided the others' eyes as he sipped the dregs of his coffee.

"I don't know," Jim said. "I have to confess I've not given him much thought since last night."

"Can you imagine him here, playing secret schoolmaster without any bullets in his gun? I can't imagine they would let him have a loaded weapon."

"It's not really our business, is it?" Jim said.

"Why not?" Carlos asked. "I know you don't feel any love or respect for him, but he is, after all -- "Carlos set his mug on the table with a hard thump. "One of us."

Jim didn't like the expression on Carlos's face. It had been growing uglier and uglier as the afternoon wore on. His brother had been glad enough to see him and Joe when they had walked into that schoolhouse, and crowed over him. But Jim didn't have to be adept at reading his brother's emotions to see the change come over him as they had talked in the saloon. Carlos was rarely angry, and so he was very bad at hiding it when he was. "What do you mean, 'one of us'?" Jim asked.

Now Carlos fixed him a very dark eye, almost as if he was looking at a stranger. "What do you think I mean," he asked softly.

Jim felt his own blood beginning to pump. He wasn't used to being challenged in this way by his brother, and he especially didn't like the implication -- and for what reason he didn't know – why Carlos put him in the crosshairs, since he been nothing but grateful for finding his brother. Didn't the fact that he had moved heaven and earth to find and catch up to him, not show how much he meant to him? As for Ghetts --

He tried controlling his anger. "I know what you mean," he said.

"Then you tell me what I mean," Carlos replied. He wasn't in the mood to let Jim wriggle away by pretending to agree to anything he said.

But George returned before any more could be said. "I've arranged for you to have a room at the hotel," he told them. "Naturally, there won't be any charge. It'll be a violation of the rules, but you haven't got any --"

"We want to go back," Jim said. He also visibly relaxed.

George reacted as though he'd been slapped. "Go back? Go back where?"

"To St. James," Jim said. The anger he had felt building almost instantly drained away as he held his brother's eye. He knew he was surrendering, but he preferred the peace that would follow an immediate surrender than the ill-will that might follow a sustained argument, no matter how it turned out. He remembered too well the anger he had felt at Carlos after his confession about Anna, and he didn't want to go through that again.

"It's where we belong, you know," Jim continued as George sat dumbstruck. "I have to thank you for reuniting us, but my brother, Joe, the sheriff, and I don't fit into this place in time--." And yet he had to hesitate instead of continuing.

This was the easiest way of telling Carlos that he thought he understood what his brother meant. There was no place for Sheriff Ghetts in this world. Ironically, he thought there wasn't much of a place for Ghetts in any world, but the man clearly would not adapt well to this town or to these people. He was too old and set in his ways, and far too used to being the man of authority. Far too used to be being the bully.

And though Jim would have been happy enough to see the back of Sheriff Ghetts while he remained here, he was also sure that there was only way to see to it that the man was returned safely to 1899. He would have to go with him.

That's what Carlos wanted, he could tell that much. The ugly reference to "us" made it clear to him that he did not identify with these people, and would want to return as well. And after reuniting with Carlos, Jim didn't think he had it in him to part again.

Nor did he want to be left alone in George's world, for Joe would certainly want to go back as well.

It didn't seem like he needed to finish the thought, however. George spread his hands on the table. "It's not my decision," he said. "But I know who to talk to. It's not a decision that can be made right away, you do understand?"

"I understand," Jim said. "As long as you understand too." But he said it while looking at Carlos, for the message was meant for him too.

Carlos allowed himself a smile as he and Jim held each other's' eye. He was glad that he and Jim had successfully "communicated," but he was also certain that there was more to be said. Jim's words, he was sure, were not a simple acquiescence. And Carlos could well guess part of the attraction that George's world had for Jim.

Anna. Carlos hadn't missed the way Jim's eyes had lit up when he related that she was here, somewhere, and that she was safe and healthy. Carlos certainly hadn't forgotten the argument he and his brother had had when Carlos confessed to kissing her. Jim might speak now of returning home, but it was clear that he would want to see Anna before he left. And it was also clear that Jim felt -- or would feel -- resentment at being forced to choose between his brother and the girl he had fallen in love with.

"You will all want to talk," George was saying. "I'm sure there are things you'll want to say outside of my presence." He rose. "So I'll take you to your hotel now."

But they didn't make it that far. They had crossed the dusty street and were nearing the telegraph office when they heard an excited explosion of voices ahead. Jim and Carlos couldn't understand the words; George stopped the company where they stood. "Someone just broke character," he said with a grin. "You might want to see what comes next."

They didn't have long to wait and Carlos felt like his ears were drowning under the din of noise, it sounded like complete nonsense to him.

An urchin playing marbles in the street turned around and frowned into the telegraph shop, then drew himself up very sharply and marched to the doorway. "Excuse me, sir" he said in a very loud voice. "I don't want you to think I'm eavesdropping, but I couldn't help overhearing you. Do you need me to fetch the sheriff?"

"Little prig," Carlos muttered.

"Hush," said George.

But the voices continued in the same unintelligible tongue, though here and there Jim and Carlos could make out English words and phrases. The boy stared intently into the office, and his cheeks paled. "I don't think that's much of an excuse," he stammered. "And I will still call on the sheriff unless -- "

Jim noticed that George had tensed. It was over a set of English words, too. "Denver" and "most of the municipal district."

The boy swallowed hard, then ran across the street.

"Well, nothing more to see here," George said. "The law will be along in a bit, that's all. Come on."

"What was that about Denver?" Jim asked.

"You heard most of it, didn't you?" George said in a clipped voice. "The Harvesters raided it this morning. Nearly ten thousand swept up. That was the news that just came through. Naturally, it has upset people."

Although Jim understood in the abstract what George was saying, and he well understood why George and the others would take the news so badly, it was still the case that it didn't mean nearly as much to him as it did to the people of this time and place. "I'm sorry," he said.

"Yes, you're *sorry*," George snapped back. "It's not *your* affair, is it? It's only *ours*."

Jim and Carlos exchanged a glance. "I'm sorry," Jim said again. "But you're right. It isn't. It doesn't have the same reality for us. But that doesn't mean we can't give you our sympathies."

"Maybe it would have the same reality for you," George said, and in the heat of his obvious anger a trace of an accent crept into his voice, "if I told you that Anna has been stationed in Denver since her return." He closed his eyes, drew out his handkerchief and covered his mouth. "Now it's my turn to say I'm sorry," he told them after the shocked silence had hung in the air -- like discharged lightning -- for several moments. "I've worked with Anna for several years now. So this raid has a little more *reality* for me."

***

It was a train, George told them, but it was like no train Jim and Carlos had ever seen. It was underground, to begin with, like the subways on the east coast they had heard of. It also lacked windows. And wheels. And a locomotive to pull it. It was a metal cylinder, completely featureless, and Jim and Carlos looked at it doubtfully.

"Hurry up," snapped George as he approached its end, where it was open. "Unless you want to stay behind with Joe." Their friend had elected to remain at the hotel. So Jim and Carlos hustled along in George's wake.

They were several hundred feet below ground level: George told them that most transportation systems in the world were dug into the bedrock, in order to keep their locations and connections as secret as possible from the Harvesters. That was only the first of several surprises as they descended into the earth. When they stepped onto what George told them was the train platform, they stopped to stare in stupefaction at the roof, which seemed to open out directly onto a cloudless sky when it should have been at the bottom of the very deep pit. "It's a illusion," George told them as they and two dozen other travelers waited on the platform for the special train to be loaded into the tube. "Like the flat screens I showed you earlier. It shows an image of the sky that is transmitted from above. It makes the platform feel less 'closed in'." Indeed, Jim glanced several times back at the foot of the steps, to confirm that he actually was deep underground.

He also noticed that he and the other two were drawing curious looks from the others on the platform, but he and the other two ignored them.

The three of them were the last onto the train, and Carlos froze as he stepped into it. "I know what this is," he said. George only nodded impatiently. Carlos turned to exit the train, but the door slid shut in his face with a soft hiss.

"I want out," Carlos called in a loud voice.

"Quiet," George said. "It's too late for that."

"What's wrong?" Jim asked. He felt a spasm of sudden alarm.

"There's nothing to be afraid of," George said. "It's only a train."

"The screaming," Carlos said. "I heard -- "

"You heard machinery, that's all," George said.

"What are you two talking about?" Jim demanded.

"Your brother was on a train like this when he recovered consciousness," George said. "There's a field hospital about fifty miles south of here. He would have been transported there as a precaution after being brought over. Examined and released. He regained consciousness on the return trip. Now if you want to stand here," George said, indicating the small, empty compartment with a sweep of his arm, "you can. There are seats in the next compartment up." He slid open a door opposite the one they had come in through and walked through like the rest of the passengers had, and disappeared, leaving Carlos and Jim by themselves.

"Was it really that bad?" Jim asked Carlos quietly. Carlos did not have the sense of adventure that he did, but Jim also thought of his brother as remarkably level-headed and not prone to panicking.

"I'm not sure," Carlos said. "Maybe it was my imagination playing tricks on me. But it sounded like thousands of people screaming. What's that?" He and Jim felt it at the same time: a very gentle tug from the rear of the train, and a feeling that the floor was sliding out from under their feet. There were no vibrations, though, so it was a moment before Jim could figure it out.

"Acceleration," he said. "That's all. Just like on a normal train. But there are no tracks under the carriage, did you see? Just smooth, polished metal. So no jolting or bumping to go with it." He laughed nervously. "No derailments either."

Carlos put his palm against the curved inner surface of the compartment, and he felt only the slightest tremble. But as he and Jim listened, a low, distant hum began to sound.

To Jim's ears it sounded vaguely musical: a vibration that sounded like a cross between a low, throaty cello and a clarinet. Dozens or even hundreds of them playing the same note simultaneously. But he also heard what George had said it was: the hum of machinery, or the sound of the train car as it slid at an ever-rising speed through the tunnel. But he also saw Carlos pale. "Is that what you heard before?" he asked. His brother nodded. "It's just a vibration," he said.

Carlos closed his eyes. *Jim's right*, he thought. *It's just a vibration.*

But it had also been his first introduction to this new world, and he doubted he could ever forget what he had heard that first time: thousands of voices screaming in unison.

***

It would have been a journey of at least two or three days if they had traveled from St. James to Denver by train. But an hour of constant acceleration on one end, and an hour of constant deceleration on the other, with a short period of comfort in between, had sufficed to bring them that same distance in the space of only a few hours. Jim wanted to ask George about the enormous amounts of rock that had been removed to make a tunnel that long. But mindful of the passengers, who did not realize that he and Carlos were not from their time, he kept quiet.

Besides, he was beginning to think there was would be a lot more time to come to ask such questions.

When they poured out of the train at the other end they found a station much like the one they had used at their embarkation point, even to the skylights that showed a soft evening sky. But there were many more platforms and walkways to cross before they came to a wide set of stairs leading up. Foot traffic was heavy. Jim tried not to stare at the wardrobes of the people they passed, though he noticed the odd looks that he and the other visitors from Deer Mountain were drawing.

The trio emerged into a wide plaza in the midst of a district with buildings all about. They looked very odd to Jim's eye, because although they rose many stories into the air, almost all of them were lacking walls. Instead, the spaces inside seemed to open directly into the air, giving them the appearance of skeletal boxes that had been stacked atop each other. Again, he held his tongue instead of asking pointless questions, but the hypothesis naturally came to him that the walls were made of a perfectly translucent material in place of windows. It gave the buildings a cadaverous look, though, one he didn't much care for. But he was sure he would get used to it in time.

But George had stopped in his tracks as soon as they were in the open air, and a soft moan escaped his throat as he looked about. "What's wrong," Carlos asked.

"Don't you see?" George said, and spread his arm slowly about. "The Harvesters have been here!"

Neither Jim nor Carlos were quite certain what he was referring to. Horseless vehicles were moving about, and lights were flashing, but that was the only activity.

George buried his face in his hands. "I've only ever seen it on the news reports," he said quietly. "To actually see the wreckage of a raid directly -- "

"What wreckage?" Jim asked bluntly. He knew he sounded rude, but if he was going to give George any sympathy, he would have to know what George was referring to.

"What wreckage?" George yelled, raising his head again. His face was red. "Look at it!"

"We don't know what we're looking at," Carlos said gently.

George's eyes bulged. "The walls, you fools! They tore the walls off all the buildings so they could get at the people inside!"

CHAPTER TWENTY-NINE

It was early evening, so instead of taking Carlos and Jim with him, George left them in a hotel with strict orders not to move while he checked on the whereabouts of Anna. He did remember to order food delivered to their room before he left. Both the Castle brothers were relieved that -- unlike the city they had glimpsed as they were silent and smoothly whisked to the hotel -- it was homey and familiar, being a supper of steak and vegetables.

They ate it in silence as they studied the room. It was immensely comfortable, decorated in muted colors with a floor that was bare of rugs but nonetheless yielding beneath their feet without being soft. The beds -- there were two of them -- were large, and in a separate room they found a large tub, though there was no obvious way of getting water to pour from the faucet. They were only a few stories above ground level, and as the sun sank behind the mountains they looked out at the skyline of Denver. Few of the surrounding buildings rose higher than their own, and they had an unobstructed view as lights came on. The air was very clean.

Only after they had finished eating did they speak. "I'm sorry that I was angry with you about Anna," said Jim.

"You had every right to be," said Carlos. "You still do. And I'm sorry for that."

"Then let us forgive each other and put it behind us," said Jim, and extended his hand. "If you forgive me, that is."

"I'm not sure I do, since I'm not sure you have wronged me in any way," said Carlos with a small smile as he clasped Jim's hand. "But I will pretend you have, and will forgive it, if you forgive me."

Jim kept hold of Carlos's hand as he stood, and he pulled his brother up into a hard embrace. "I lost Anna. And then I lost you. I would tell you which hurt and frightened me the most, but I think you know." He tightened his grip on Carlos as he fought to keep back the tears that suddenly welled in his eyes. "I nearly made myself ill."

Carlos too held his brother tightly, and squeezed his own eyes shut. "I would have been ill at losing you as well, but I was too angry at those that tore us apart." He released Jim, and the two stood apart though they still held each other loosely. Each smiled a little to see the wet cheeks of the other. "We will go home, won't we," he asked. "After we have seen to it that Anna is -- "

He broke off when he saw the shift in his brother's eyes.

Jim tried pulling Carlos back into another embrace, but his brother resisted. "We know where the tunnel is," Jim said. "If one of us returns to St. James and the other stays here, we would not be parted any more than if the other returned to the old home with Joe."

"You want to stay?" said Carlos. "Why?" he asked, though he knew the answer perfectly well.

"I don't want to have to choose," Jim said. He also knew that Carlos knew his reasons, and didn't feel the need to say Anna's name. "We don't even know that they'll let us go back. George has said that they let some return, but only after many years have passed."

Carlos said nothing. He didn't know what to say, because Jim was right. He and his brother -- and Joe and Sheriff Ghetts -- were now privy to a great secret, and it seemed deeply unlikely that George's masters would risk seeing that secret revealed to the people of 1899. He had been given no hint that he would be allowed to return to his home.

It settled heavily on him now, the conviction that he would not be returning, but now it smothered that flame of anger he had nurtured. That was another consequence of Jim's arrival. When it had only been himself he could nurse the sense of injustice, feeding it with a lonely resentment. With companionship, though, it seemed that exile would be easier to bear, and that made it harder to maintain that sense of rage.

"I suppose there will be time enough to worry about it later," he said at last. "Although I should like to see them try to keep Joe here if he gets a mind to try going back," he added, and smiled at Jim. "If I were them, I'd worry more about what mischief Joe could get up to here if he had a mind to make trouble, than about what mischief he might cause if they let him go." Jim also chuckled at the thought.

They fell to talking lightly of this and that for a bit, with Carlos asking Jim for more details about what he had seen while making the search. They had plenty of time to talk, for night had well and truly fallen by the time door opened and George, looking very tired, came in. Jim was instantly on his feet with an anxious feeling.

George shook his head. "There's no sign of her. The building she was working in was one of the ones that was raided. Top to bottom, including the subterranean levels. There were a few casualties, but they think they have recovered all the bodies." He sank onto the foot of one of the beds. "They might have been the lucky ones," he said in a sunken whisper.

"Where would they have taken her," Carlos asked, for Jim was too horror-struck to speak.

"Their raiding ships fly cloaked. Invisible," George added. "So we don't know the direction in which they were headed. We are nearly equidistant from four of their breeding colonies. And even if we did know which one it was -- " He stared at his hands. "If we were able to track cloaked raiders," he said in a rush, "we would not advertise the fact by giving pursuit. There's no point anyway. The camps are impregnable.

"I'm sorry," he said a little later, when the silence had stretched out intolerably with no one speaking. "I'm sorry for all of us, but mostly I'm sorry for Anna. She was a lovely girl."

He rose a little after that and left them for the night, saying he would collect them in the morning for the trip back to the towns clustered at the foot of Deer Mountain.

***

Conversation was a desultory affair the next morning, even over an excellent breakfast. Jim and George were wrapped in thoughts of Anna; Carlos too thought of her, but he also, with some trace of guilt, thought about his own future and how to broach it with George. But by ten o'clock they had returned to the train station, and their gear drew even more stares than it had the day before. Some passengers even came up to ask questions. These George fielded. "I told them we're actors," he murmured to Jim and Carlos. "We are, after all, in a manner of speaking."

The return trip by train passed slowly. Where Jim and Carlos had spent the first journey in a state of tension, not knowing how the journey would evolve or climax, they passed the second one in a state of torpor. There were no windows, so there was no scenery to study as there would have been in more familiar train. The compartment was comfortable, and George showed them a device that appeared to contain hundreds of pages of a book while still being as small and thin as a chalkboard slate. But they couldn't read the text. So while George confined himself to the strange book, the Castle brothers passed a restless sleep almost all the way to their destination.

And when they arrived, almost the first thing they learned was that Lobo Joe was in jail.

∗

"Can't you stay out of trouble," Jim asked him in a teasing tone after the sheriff had released him into their custody. "The sheriff said he found you sleeping in a wagon again. We left you in a good hotel room."

"I liked the wagon better," Joe muttered.

"And it wasn't personal," George said in Jim's ear. "It's part of the role-playing. It's what would have happened in Clinton."

"It *did* happen in Clinton, remember," Jim said. "By the way -- " He stopped when he caught the sheriff looking at him narrowly. Acting out of character, he remembered, could get a man arrested in this kind of town. How funny it was, he thought, that he, a genuine man of 1899, might get arrested in 2749 for not acting like a genuine man of 1899, even though he was genuinely acting as a man of 1899 would act in 2749. "I don't much hold with these tin-starred Tsars," he said in a loud voice. "Let's talk outside!"

"You'll keep a civil tongue in your head wherever you take it," the sheriff growled.

"They're all the same wherever you go," Jim retorted. "I knew a man much like yourself who held a job much like yours. Then he broke both his arms and discovered what a lack of neighborliness had cost him. At least, I hope he did," he added thoughtfully to himself. He wondered now what was happening to Sheriff Ghetts. And since that reminded him of what he wanted to say to George, so he now pulled the others out into the street.

"We're back where we started," he told George. "In more ways than one. When we left we were debating what was to become of us." He swept his arm around to encompass himself, Carlos, and Joe.

"That's one reason I was so late returning last night," George replied. "I spent most of the evening with the commissioners that I report to, pleading your case. They are not used to giving people the chance to return, not until after they have undergone extensive training, and feel that we can trust them as agents on the other side of the tunnel. But I told them that I knew you and that I trusted you. I told them that if you gave me your word -- "He hesitated as he gave Joe a wary look." "That if you gave me your word to return and say nothing about what you've seen, I would vouch for you."

Jim and Carlos looked at each other. Both were surprised and impressed with George's words, though too different extents. Of the two brothers, Jim was the better disposed toward the man, for he had spent more time in his company and had seen him in a much better light. Carlos, on the other hand, was more inclined to snort and to take the offer in a grudging spirit of deserved recompense for trouble given rather than as a gracious offer to stand surety. "What did they say," he asked George.

"They said they would consider it," George replied. "Which was a great victory in itself."

"How long until they decide," Jim asked.

"They decided this morning and informed me while we were on the train." He rolled his eyes as the others looked puzzled. "Call it 'wireless telegraphy'. Their reply appeared in the, er, *book* I was reading."

Jim felt a sudden spasm of excitement. Messages communicated by book through the very ether? Again, he had the thought that this was a world well worth exploring. And guiltily, he hoped that the commission had decided against him and the others being allowed to return. He was inclined to believe that this would be their answer, for George looked unhappy.

"They said my word was not sufficient," he said. "But that my word along with the word of three others could stand for another. One, if he gives a promise of silence, can return immediately as a kind of junior agent on probation. But three others must remain here."

Carlos, Jim, and Joe stood mutely in the street. Then Carlos looked around with a distracted glance. "I need a drink," he said. So they repaired to the saloon.

For each of the brothers it was a matter of calculation. For Jim it was a straight-forward matter. No one could trust Sheriff Ghetts to keep him mouth shut on the other side, and he would be useless as an agent for George and his government. Nor would Joe be inclined to act as an agent, but in his case Jim was sure that Joe would rather die than to speak of what he had seen and heard. But he also knew that Carlos wanted to return. He suspected that it would come down to an argument between Carlos and Joe, with each trying to yield the promised return passage to the other. If he had to act as tiebreaker, he didn't know what he would do.

Carlos reasoned similarly about Ghetts and about Joe. He also shrewdly guessed that Jim would want to remain. And he was shrewder than his brother still, for like a chess player thinking several moves ahead, he saw how to play the board. "Well," he said in a loud voice after they had their drinks and were seated in a dark corner. "I think we can all agree on who should not return." He lifted his glass. "To Sheriff Ghetts. May he enjoy the rest of his life here!" He knocked the drink back in a single swallow, but no one else followed him. "Does anyone disagree with me? No? Then there is only one more question to be answered." He turned to Joe. "Do you want to return home this afternoon or tomorrow?"

Joe started like a fox that has just realized it has been caught in a trap, and his eye glittered as he stared at Carlos. He opened his mouth, but no words came out.

"Come come, Joe" Carlos said expansively. "You have been our best friend since we were boys, just as you were our father's best friend. I know you too well, and know that you would never separate two brothers just so you can remain in this world of marvels by sacrificing your own happiness and returning to the miserable year that we left, so that my brother and I can remain together."

Joe opened his mouth again, and closed it again with a snap. So did Jim, for he saw clearly what Carlos was doing, but saw no good way to stop it. Carlos was giving Joe the chance to return while also giving him the excuse that it was a "sacrifice" he was taking on himself so that Jim and Carlos could remain together.

George just stared at Carlos as though the man had just become violently and loathsomely drunk.

"If you say it like that," Joe finally said, after looking around the table and realizing he was not going to be rescued. "I think we should all stay. Send the sheriff back. Or we should all stay."

"Don't be an ass, Carlos," Jim exclaimed. "You want to return. And our separation would not be permanent. Visits through the tunnel would still be possible."

"I doubt that," George said. "You've forgotten Professor Smith. How would you explain your return to him? I think whoever returns is going to have to move far away from Clinton and St. James." But before he could expand on the point, he rose, for a man dressed as a member of Jacob's tribe was beckoning to him from the door of the saloon.

The three exiles began to argue harshly as George talked with the visitor, and continued even after he had returned with a frown on his lips and a packet of letters in his hand. He sat and studied the names on the envelopes and ignored the heated words flying about him. Then he raised his own whisky, tossed it back, and set it with a sharp report on the table. The sound caused the others to fall silent and to look at him expectantly.

"This may change matters," George told them. "That was a messenger from Jacob's camp. A messenger came through the tunnel this morning and left these letters with a request that they be brought here. To this very saloon, in fact, where he anticipated we would be. He asked that they be delivered to us."

Jim and Carlos blinked at him and at each other: *How could someone at Jacob's camp know where they would be?* Joe just frowned, probably on account of the harsh words that were still echoing from their argument.

"A letter for Carlos," George said, and passed it over. "A letter for Jim." He passed the second letter. "And one for me." He kept the thickest packet for himself. "You will recognized the handwriting, I trust, and understand who these letters are from."

It took Carlos some time to place it, and he was only sure after seeing the expression on his brother's pale face. For Jim had recognized the handwriting immediately.

It was in Anna's hand.

CHAPTER THIRTY

Carlos, Jim, and George weighed the three letters in their hands. It seemed impossible that Anna should have been able to send them letters, or that she would have sent them by way of the tunnel or by Jacob's camp. And yet the handwriting was unmistakably hers. They exchanged uneasy glances, then simultaneously tore them open.

Silently, they read them.

Jim was the first to finish his letter, and he read through it quickly. An expostulation came to and died on his lips as he reached the end of it, and he looked up sharply at George, who was frowning deeply under a creased brow as he pored over the bundle that Anna had left for him. Jim then shot a worried glance at Carlos, who had sunk into his chair and read the letter he had received with a very grave countenance. There seemed little doubt that the letters to the others were of a longer nature than the one he had received, so Jim read his again with bewilderment and fear:

My dearest, it began.

As you are reading this, you will have learned much about me: truths which I kept from you because you would not have understood them, and would not have believed if I had told them. But now you have seen with your own eyes the secrets that I hid, and I know -- because I know you, my sweet and beloved Jim -- that you have accepted and comprehended them. And I know too -- for unlike me, you never veiled yourself from others -- that as you accepted them, that you will have accepted me despite the mysteries that I hid from you. For you are large-minded and great-hearted, kind, noble, and forgiving of the greatest wrongs you might ever suffer from those who love you as dearly as I do.

I know, then, I need not say more to you than this: that I am in desperate danger for reasons that my friend and companion, the man you know as George Kinley, will be able to well explain after he has digested the report I have sent to him. You and you alone can give me the succor that I beg. George may violently deny that there is anything to be done for me. I will only say that the true heart may see farther than the keenest eye, and that yours is the truest heart I know.

Adieu, my sweetest Jim, for I cannot bear to say farewell.

Your ardent Anna.

Thrice he read this, burning his eyes and his mind with its terrible hints and unbearable inscrutabilities. When he saw Carlos lay his letter aside he leaned forward eagerly. "Well?" he cried out. "What does she say in yours? Here is mine!" He thrust at his brother his own letter.

But Carlos turned it away. "She tells no great secrets," he said as he tucked his own letter into an inner pocket of coat. "But she closes by saying that I may show it to you only if she gives me permission. Which she doesn't, in the body of her letter or by postscript."

"All the more reason to go her," exclaimed Jim. "As though we hadn't reason enough," he added, for he realized how his words had sounded. And yet it there was more meaning and truth in that exclamation than he would have wanted to admit. A wild pang of jealousy smote his heart at the thought that Anna -- the girl he loved and who called him "beloved" -- should have imparted secrets to Carlos.

So he looked impatiently at George, who was still reading. "Well, what is the news? She speaks cryptically to me... of what she says to you, and says that you will explain more."

But George only raised his hand to stop Jim's outburst, and continued to read. His face lost most of all of its color as he did so, and the lines of his face had sunk so that he looked as though a weight of years had in that afternoon wasted him.

When at last he had laid aside the last sheet, he leaned back and closed his eyes with a groan. "It is impossible," he said, more to himself than the others. "It is a trick. A trap. Or a mistake."

"What does she say to you," Jim demanded.

"It doesn't concern you."

"I think it does." Jim flung his letter onto the table in front of George, who quickly read it.

"It is still not a matter for you," George said. He rose and turned to the door.

But Jim rose swiftly in turn and blocked him. "Anna would not have sent a message to me if she did not mean for me to act on it."

George turned red. "You have no right and no standing to -- "

"I think he does," Carlos said, and joined his brother in blocking George. Joe, seeing his two friends rising together in this way, joined them too.

"You would do something very foolish if I told you," George said to Jim. "I wouldn't have it on my conscience."

"You already have a great deal on your conscience," Jim said with a faint smile. "You would hardly be adding to it."

"As the man said when he laid a straw upon the camel's back," George retorted. But as he looked at the three determined countenances bent on him, he relented and sank back into his chair.

"A plague has broken out in the camp where she was taken. But it is no innocent plague, or else the Harvesters would have stamped it out themselves. It is a plague that they themselves have created and introduced. They mean to use it to eradicate most of the human population."

Jim and Carlos both made loud exclamations at this. "How does she know this?"

"From the Maorong. I told you that they are slaves, and have no great love for their masters. Some at the camp know Anna, and they told her of the Harvesters' intentions."

"But how did she get word back to us so?" Carlos asked. "And by means of the tunnel?" He shared Jim's horror, but he had the presence of mind to attend not only to George's words, but to the way this news had reached them.

"That is what I do not fully understand, and why I worry that it is a trick of some kind," George said. "She writes that the Harvesters have opened a tunnel of their own to 1899, and that she entrusted these letters to a Maorong in the hope that through it the letters might reach us here."

"I don't follow," said Jim.

"Nor do I, clearly," George said. "I believe she intended that the Maorong should use the Harvesters' tunnel to return to 1899. Then, after slipping from his masters, he would use our own tunnel to bring the messages here, to Jacob's camp, and thence to us." He tugged his lip and stared intently into the air. "It's a scheme fraught with risk, and there are a hundred ways it might go wrong --"

"But clearly it went right," Jim said. "For here they are!"

"That's just it," said George. "Here they are, and yet they shouldn't be. That is why I fear it is a trick of some kind. Moreover, the messenger that Jacob sent did not say it was a Maorong who brought them."

"Did he say it wasn't?" asked Carlos.

"No," George admitted. He looked around, but the man had long gone. "There is also her further request." He looked keenly at Jim. "It gives me grave pause."

"What is it?"

But still George hesitated. "You would make me tell you, wouldn't you?" he said at last.

"That I can promise," Jim said, and Carlos nodded too.

"You will regret my saying anything," George said with no little bitterness, and looked at Carlos as he said so. "Anna believes it is too late to save the population of the camp where she has been taken. But she thinks it would be possible for us to destroy that tunnel they have made, and that we should, lest the Harvesters cause mischief in the past. There are certain compact and powerful explosives that she thinks might be introduced into the Harvesters' transports as they traverse the tunnel, and that if these were to explode they would destroy their tunnels and the machines that they use to create them. The Maorong tell her that the tunnel has not been used yet, that it has only just been opened, and that some sort of expedition is still being prepared. So we still have time to derange their plans."

"How would these explosives be introduced into the transports?" Carlos asked. "I had the impression from what I was told that these camps and these ships are impregnable."

"That's just it," George said. His smile was tight and mirthless.

"They would have to be smuggled in. Someone would have to carry them on his person, and that person would have to be captured by the Harvesters."

A silence of a very few seconds reigned. It did not need to be interrupted, for everyone at the table knew that Jim would speak, and everyone knew what he would say.

***

If it were not for the dread and anguish of the mission, Carlos would have exulted. He was flying.

It was a heavier-than-air machine of svelte and polished construction of lightweight, gleaming metal and glass. The body was a small cabin holding six plush and comfortable seats. Behind it stretched a long tail, and on either side stretched two wings, and it rested on runners, like those of a sleigh. Propellers, like those on a steamship, were embedded in the wings and tail, and it was these -- George explained to him -- that gave the craft its lift and power of flight.

George had not argued long against Jim, and within an hour had summoned the craft from some nearby location where it and others like it were kept. "We cannot make it invisible," he told them, "but it has characteristics that make it difficult for even the Harvesters to detect. With it we should be able to get close to the camp." The craft -- burdened only by George, the two brothers, Joe, and a pilot -- was soon speeding along over the high plains, and it hardly made any noise as it went.

Carlos would have liked to fly higher, but he understood the reasons for caution, for as they traveled at a velocity far greater than that of any craft he had experience with, their destination loomed larger. It was the great cylinder hanging motionless in the northern sky, the same that had bedeviled Jim and the others during their journey. Carlos had never seen anything so large, and it seemed impossible that it could grow any larger as they approached it, but larger and larger still it grew. Soon he was unable to see its bent, rising walls no matter how he craned his neck, and only its flat, circular bottom could be seen, and this encompassed a great quarter of the sky while they were still an hour from it.

In the very center of this flat bottom, he soon saw, was a great opening. He asked George if this was the entrance to the tunnel. "I don't think so," George said. "Though it's impossible to know. But we have studied these craft at a distance for a very long time, and we believe that is the opening to the tunnel they use to travel from our planet to others. Most of the ship, we believe, is given over devices to power that tunnel. Ever since they arrived, we have seen large craft ascending and descending from that opening. There are other bays, though, through which smaller craft, including their raiding fleets, sally forth."

They had come very close to where the edge of the cylinder loomed directly over the ground beneath, and it was there that the pilot set their craft down. The air where they now disembarked was colder than the air where they had left, for they were some hundreds of miles to the north of where they had started. There was a small bluff near where they sat, and it was onto this bluff that they crept and looked down.

A wide, shallow valley was spread out beneath them. Perhaps six miles off, hanging a thousand feet in the air, was something like a vast platter several miles in diameter. They could only see its bottom, but George told them that this was one of the breeding camps they had heard of, and that on its upper surface were barracks. "There are fenced-in fields below it and around it," he said, gesturing with his hand. "That is where the prisoners exercise and cultivate food for themselves. But there is no escape to be had there, for as you see the ground all about is perfectly open to observation, and they kill any who attempt to flee. The sleeping structures in the floating are also secure against escape, as you can imagine."

"How do they get from above to below?" Jim asked.

"There are craft that transport them. But the craft do not move directly from one to the other. They go first into the ship above." George pointed. "We presume that is another security measure."

They watched in silence for a bit, for even though they had come this far and for a specific purpose, they were all still more than a little reluctant to bring the plan to fruition. Finally George spoke. "You can still change your mind," he told Jim softly.

"I didn't come to sightsee," Jim replied. He belched slightly, for he was carrying a half-dozen gelatin balls in his stomach -- gelatin explosives. They were quite harmless until combined, George told him, and they would have to be combined by hand. They had been easy to swallow, and Jim hoped they would be just as easy to excrete. It was the only way they thought they might get them into the camp past the Harvesters.

Joe was very gruff as he took Jim's hand and wished him farewell. "I'll miss you, old man," Jim told him. "I'm very bad at saying goodbyes, and I didn't even get to tell Father goodbye. I hope you don't mind if I keep this short."

Joe gripped his hand tightly, then released him. "I would have some words for you," he said. "But I do not wish to say more than your brother would say to you."

"I've noticed he's taking it very well," Jim said as he turned to Carlos. "Don't tell me anything foolish," he said to his brother, "such as that you are finally glad to be rid of me."

"Then maybe I'd better not say anything at all," Carlos replied with a lopsided smile. He put out his hand.

Jim took it slowly, and gave Carlos a penetrating and wondering glance. He thought he saw a strange light in his brother's eye, as though he were enjoying a private joke. It killed him, a little, to think that Carlos should be having some kind of laugh at his expense when he was -- or so he believed without telling himself as much -- volunteering for a suicide mission. "I don't suppose you'll tell me what Anna said in her letter to you."

"No, I don't suppose I will," Carlos said. His lips twitched. "You'll see her soon enough, and you can ask her yourself." Now it was his turn to squeeze Jim's hand. "When you see her tell her that I understand, that I thank her, and that I forgive her with all my heart."

Now Jim really did want to know what was in that letter, but he held his peace and turned to George. "I liked you the first time I saw you," he told him. "I've changed my mind about you several times since then, and my opinion has swung pretty violently at that. But I forgive you everything now, for giving me this chance to see Anna again."

"It's a steep price to pay," George told him. Then he surprised all the others by taking out a handkerchief and blowing a nose that had suddenly started to stream. "If I've learned anything about the students at St. James, it's that they have tremendous courage." He wiped his nose, and shook Jim's hand.

"Now, how do I get down into that camp," Jim asked. "I've got a girl waiting for me."

"Just start walking toward it," George said. "They'll see you soon enough."

So that's what Jim did.

The remaining trio watched him walk into the valley with a determined stride. Probably they would have watched until they had seen him surrounded and taken away. But after half a mile Jim was no longer clearly visible against the colors of the prairie. "Well, let's go," Carlos said at last.

"Jim said that you're taking it well, this parting," George said quietly as they returned to their craft.

"Yes, I am," Carlos said before George could continue. "We still have some hours of daylight. If it's possible, I'd like to visit the camp where Sheriff Ghetts is. He might be interested in hearing about what happened to Jim."

"You don't blame him for this, in some roundabout way, do you?" George asked.

"I don't know who I blame," Carlos said. "Unless it's the messenger that brought us those letters from Anna. I would really like to see him…I hope he's still at the camp too."

He said this in a very determined tone, and George apparently took the hint not to argue. He gave the pilot a set of directions, and they soon escaped to safer ground.

***

Carlos found himself chuckling as he studied the camp from atop a small hill. *This is what all the riches of the world can buy you,* he thought. *A chance to live like an Indian.* It was an energetic scene, as children scampered all about, and he actually did feel a pang of jealousy at their innocence.

He and George and Joe quickly closed the distance between the hill where they had landed and the entrance to Jacob's camp. George took the lead, and stopped a tall, strong-looking man to ask some questions. The man pointed to a teepee some dozen yards away, and George nodded. "He says Ghetts is making a nuisance of himself somewhere in the back of the camp, and that the messenger who came through the tunnel is in that teepee. It'll be a man, not a Maorong that much is clear. I hope he can clear things up. I don't mind tell you, Carlos, that I have dreadful premonitions."

"So do I, though I wonder if our premonitions will quite be the same." Carlos pushed ahead of George, and was soon at a quick trot through the camp. When he reached the tent, he paused only to take a very deep breath -- trying to still the beating of his heart -- before lifting the flap and stepping through.

It was much lighter on the inside than he'd anticipated, so his eyes didn't have to adjust to the dark. Almost instantly he was smiling at the man who looked up from the rugs with a smile of his own.

It was Jim. "Don't tell me this isn't a surprise," he said, and his eye twinkled. He looked more careworn and drawn than when he had left them only an hour before, and two hundred miles to the north.

Carlos's smile widened as he took Anna's letter from his coat. "If you'd wanted it to be a surprise, you wouldn't written a postscript in your own hand." He read it in a loud voice. "Don't worry, it will be all right. You'll see when you visit Jacob's camp afterward." He looked up at his brother. "It is all right, isn't it?"

The life seemed liked it washed out of Jim's face. "I wish it was," he said. "And I suppose it is, for me. But for the rest of us, I'm afraid it is actually far, far worse. The aliens detonated a biogenetic bomb, which released an airborne virus that is mass killing humans based on specific genetic markers in your timeline. We need to figure out how to stop it before it happens."

Carlos jaw dropped. "You're not from this timeline are you brother?"

Jim nodded. "We have to move quickly. I can only exist in this timeline for a short period of time. Any longer would cause major butterflies, that would have widespread effects throughout the future."